Testimonials

In *Vows*, Cynthia Linkas has brought back to life a convent school in the mid-twentieth century, a world so far away from us it may as well be science fiction: nuns in habits; a century-old web of obligations and sinful infractions; a deep struggle between faith and reasonableness; and poetry meaning so much its enormous gravitational pull could be a matter of life and death. It not only goes back in historical time but also back to that period of earnest searching that may have been the youth of every one of us, male or female, Catholic or otherwise. The two narrators, a 17-year-old high school student, and nun of 22 about to take her final vows, remind us of the enormous period of growth we all go through during that five year gap, but, as well, both characters, enduring the same torments and ecstasies are fully realized individuals, struggling to be themselves, and—so unusual from the perspective of our era—struggling to subsume themselves into a broader life of sacredness, sacrifice, and meaning. And, of course, in both of them we experience variants of the age-old dialog between the desire of the flesh and need for God. It is a book about driving passions, and young very serious and earnest minds, breaking into little astonishments of poetry in seemingly the most ordinary passages. This is a dramatic story well told with a moving conclusion, and some illuminating truths along the way.

– **Alan Feldman,**
author of *The Golden Coin*; *Immortality* (Massachusetts Book Award);
***A Sail to Great Island* (Felix Pollak Prize in Poetry);**
***The Happy Genius* (Elliston Book Award).**

Although the setting of the novel, a 1960's convent school, is specific and, to this reader, exotic, the concerns are universal – young women's hunger for direction, belonging, and meaning. The characters are so well-drawn that I find myself worrying about how they are doing this many years later. Also: did I mention the humor, the pranks, the girls having fun parts of this wise and wondrous book? Fast-moving, deeply-felt; a remarkable debut.

– **Miriam Weinstein,**
author, *Yiddish: A Nation of Words*,
winner of the National Jewish Book Award

Vows is vivid historical fiction, set in a pre-Vatican II, 1964 convent boarding school, a time and place that no longer exists. Two stormy spiritual seekers, student Janey and novitiate Sister Philippe wrestle with doctrine and discipline as they chart their separate paths amidst the rumblings of a changing Church. Poet Cynthia Linkas knows this world, and rekindles it with grace, humor and riveting tension.

– **Sally Brady,**
author of *A Box of Darkness,*
Instar,
Sweet Memories,
and *A Yankee Christmas*

Vows, by Cynthia Linkas, is a sparkling, entrancing book that draws you into a vanished world as strange and magical as any fantasy realm — a convent school in the 1960s, before Vatican II changed all the rules about a life in orders. Three main characters are caught in this moment of transition: Janey, in her senior year, with her yearning for faith and her opposing wish to test all the limits and find her own path; Philippe, a young nun, Janey's role model, who has taken her vows but struggles to subdue her independence and her deepest desires; and Mere, the mother superior who has lived a life made meaningful by order, discipline, and unwavering belief. The book is full of drama—clashes of personalities, wild teenagers, secret messages, forbidden trysts, deaths and births—and it's vivid, funny, varied, and richly involving. The stakes are high: after Vatican II will Philippe, with her all-or-nothing nature, become 'half a nun,' wearing street clothes and living outside of a convent? Will Janey, like some of her friends at the school, give herself over to the hunger for asceticism and, surprising even herself, take vows? Will Mere, toward the end of her life, be able to navigate a vastly changed world? These are resonant questions: what vows we take, what roads we travel, how we understand our own lives. This is a fabulous read! I loved every minute of it.

– **Betsy Seifter, co-author of *The Inevitable City*, Scott Cowen; *After the Diagnosis, Transcending Chronic Illness*, Julian Seifter, MD and Betsy Seifter, PhD**

Cynthia Linkas' luminous, heartfelt debut novel takes place at Sorrows Academy, an Ignatian convent school run by French-Canadian nuns. The intertwined stories of Janey, a 17-year-old boarding student, and Philippe, a 22-year-old teaching nun, take place during the 1964/65 academic year—also the final year of the momentous Second Vatican Council. Both young women are wrestling with doubt and faith, despair and hope, attempting to reconcile the life of the body and the tangible world with the more austere realm of the mind and the soul. Their arcs will become entangled, and, at times, stretch nearly to a breaking point. Few writers convey so well both the longings and the contradictions of the spiritual life. Linkas has a keen ear for dialogue, and, even more important, a deeply felt understanding of the kinds of conversations that can leave a person forever changed. *Vows* thrums with action and has an unforgettable supporting cast of characters—fellow students and nuns, a stern yet compassionate Mother Superior—each so indelibly herself. Linkas also has an eye for the telling detail: for the heat and weigh of habit cloth, the 'baked bread' smell of freshly mimeographed pages, for modal chants that 'sound like hunger,' for the long sweep of skates on a roller-palace floor, the shuffle of slippers in a cell, and the taste and feel of contraband fried chicken sliding down your throat. What comes through in the end is the undeniable, enduring reality of love, which cannot be counterfeited, either in life or in fiction. I have not read anything quite like Vows. Linkas is a brilliant and caring companion for the journey.

– **Patricia Hanlon,**
author of *Swimming to the Top of the Tide: Finding Life Where Land and Water Meet* (Bellevue Literary Press, 2021)

Vows is about passion, an incredible range of passion — the passion for nature, tradition, friendship, a mentor, a place, a time, and for a lover, and in the guiding conversations with superiors… Vows is lit with passion around the dilemma of trust – well drawn characters trusting one another, the mystery of one's own path and one's own curiosity….. Told in language almost on fire, the interaction, growth, secrets, and intimacy shared among the group of girls, their elders, and mentors reveals through dilemmas of passion what it is to be human, to learn, grow, and make choices.

– **Kelly Cunnane,**
author of *For You are a Kenyan Child*,
winner of PEN New Writer award for nonfiction,
The Maine Lupine Award and The Ezra Jack Keats Award

Cynthia Linkas is a poet at heart. I loved the way she characterized Janey's relationship with her teacher/mentor, Sister Philippe — a woman of authentic, courageous, compassionate faith, compelling in her love for God, her girls and life! VOWS is a four-letter word in our culture. And I'm not talking about spelling. This book invites us to enter a sacred and messy place where real life bumps into faith. It is a school where old and young make choices, learn hard lessons, seek forgiveness, and live out their faith while scrubbing floors, roller skating, asking questions, breaking rules, and learning to love God, themselves, and each other."

– Jan Carlberg,
speaker, storyteller, and author of
The Hungry Heart: Daily Devotions from the Old Testament
and *The Welcome Song, Stories from a Place Called Home*

VOWS

A Novel

Cynthia Linkas

En Route Books and Media, LLC
Saint Louis, MO

⊛ENROUTE
Make the time

En Route Books and Media, LLC

5705 Rhodes Avenue

St. Louis, MO 63109

Contact us at **contactus@enroutebooksandmedia.com**

Cover Credit: Madeline Land, designer; Robert Hanlon, artist

Copyright 2024 Cynthia Linkas

ISBN-13: 979-8-88870-198-0

Library of Congress Control Number: 2024942141

Dedication

This story is dedicated to my sister, Claudia Chadwick Gallant (1945–2013), who shared convent adventures with me. She'd signed up to enter the convent, habit sewn. She never entered. But when she became the Academic Dean of Sewickley Academy, PA, and led that school with indomitable grace and wisdom, she became her own version of our Mother Superior, Mère, after all.

Author's Note

VOWS is a novel set in the Roman Catholic Church (1962-65) before Vatican II changed the Church, at a time when strict rules and vows were the unquestioned way to God.

While I never became a nun, I lived with them as a boarder in one of their hundreds of Academies across America. My French-Canadian nuns entered the convent in those days with true calls to serve God and sometimes the hope of a college education that they would not enjoy any other way. Girls were considered in prep to enter, and my four friends and I were as close as soldiers in war-time.

Schooled under the rule of Ignatius of Loyola—with emphasis on sin, examination of conscience, penance, and asceticism—we were alive from the waist up. Mind and soul were everything.

Perhaps it was my nuns, or the time right before the church burst open. All I know is that when I set out to recall being curbed, chiseled, and disciplined through God's justice, my scenes exploded over and over again, with mercy, God's powerful love—forgiveness sensed and tasted—and abundant light.

Gratitude

For my mentor and brilliant editor, Sally Ryder Brady, "There is no one like her, no one at all."

Elizabeth Hall (1942—2002), for every word.

"Cats," Carol Devine McInnes—for sticking with me through it all for sixty-two years.

My beloved fellow writers: Patricia Hanlon, Betsy Seifter, Miriam Weinstein, Kelly Cunnane, and Michal Brownell for patience and *second sight*. Robert Hanlon, gifted artist, and dear friend. There are no *mots justes* that can adequately thank you.

My editor extraordinaire and friend, Kiki Latimer, for believing in this book.

My talented book designer, Maddy Land.

The Sisters of Saint Anne, Marlborough, MA, who made me a writer.

And for those who, through the years, nurtured VOWS—Margaret Neill, Penny Wingate, Anne Pelikan, George Wingate, Patricia Lorsch, Jeanne Guillemin, Laura Wainwright, Elizabeth Berges, Anne Emerson, Chris Lynch, Glenn and Deborah Morrow for introduction to Enroute Press, Erika Funkhouser, Holly Meade, Nancy Mering, Karen O'Keefe and Martha Kuhlmann for beginnings.

My readers: Jan Carlberg, Patricia Woodlock, Reverend Dean Borgman, Virginia Rogers, Donna Burr, Judy Riggs, Catherine Minnetyan, Sandy Friedrich, Peggy Godin, Stella Goren, Gail Borgman, Jeanne Maurand, Donna Kinney, Candy Bergquist, Susan Webb, Linda Spong, and David Cottingham.

And forever – Celeste Morel Martin, Jesse Mariette, our lovely Haitian friend, Diane Collaro Sarkala, Suzanne Niedzielska, Karen Fitzmeyer Wallace, Denise Picard, Helen Young Oram, Sister Therese Gosselin (Henry of Jesus) and all the precious young women of Saint Anne's. We can never forget.

For family, especially Tom, who has lived with the characters in my head for fifty-five years.

My tender parents, Cecile and Claude who raised me in the Roman Catholic faith. My gentle sister, Cathryn.

Son Christopher, for integrity, for being my rock; daughter Malina, my truth; for our lifelong conversations; daughter-in-law, Danielle, for insight and grace.

And for all who call me Memère—

Thomas John, Louisa "Lulu" Chadwick, Alienna Scarlett, Evangeline Cynthia, Solenne Isabella, and especially granddaughter Sophia Claire, for "seeing" this story with your sensitive heart.

I am inspired by you—always there for me.

Table of Contents

Chapter 1

November, All Saints 1964—Janey

I climbed the ladder to the attic and walked to my trunk, girls all around me. I turned the key, opened the lid and fell to my knees, burying my face in a fresh blouse, washed at home in Ivory Snow. Bats fluttered in the eaves, not dive bombing, so I took my time. The only mirror in the convent was attached to the trunk lid. It showed straight blond hair, high cheekbones, large features, and dark eyes. My best friend, Charlotte Devine, "Cats" said I looked like a deer. I moaned at my face.

Once a week before bed, Cats led us to the attic with a broom and beat the bats away while flashlights cast shadows on the sloping walls. Reaching into the trunk, I pushed aside my folded underwear. *Wuthering Heights* lay at the bottom. I'd already loosened the binding and now ripped out the next chapter and slipped it under my pajama top. Once inside my cell, I would get it into the Latin book; I couldn't wait to get back to Heathcliff.

"I want to write to you," my boyfriend, Michael, had whispered last summer on Horse Neck Beach.

"We can't get letters from boys."

"They open your mail?"

"Yup. One girl got expelled for writing to a boy."

"But that's good, isn't it?"

"NO! I want to graduate. I'm going to college."

"What's wrong with boys?"

"Bad for the soul."

1

"So, the nuns view you as rookies?"

"They do. But I don't."

"What are you doing there?"

And suddenly, I couldn't stop telling him how my parents didn't want me in the public school in our mill town. Academy of the Sorrows of Mary had a good reputation—I'd get into a Catholic college. How my friends and I laughed at the odd nuns—the bell ringer in the tower, her legs flying up with the bell rope, the French teacher, Luce, who'd wanted to be an actress before entering and told us her stories. About the nuns with lovely features peering out of the coif, mysterious and wise; about the processions with statues. Something about the way he'd listened, his ease with the strangeness of my life.

"I'm going to rescue you!"

I laughed.

"I'll climb the wall and whisk you away on my steed!" A mischievous wink.

Done with the attic trunks, we climbed back down the ladder to our dormitory, one huge floor divided into ninety-nine cells each surrounded by white curtains. These were tied back during the day, exposing beds with white spreads and wooden crucifixes on the pillows.

Thursday night was bath night. Now we lined up near the stalls. All week, our morning water in the pitcher and basin was freezing, but tonight, the water would be warm. Our Course Mistress, Sister Lionel, sat ramrod at a table handing out bathing garments. She gave each of us a measured look; she had rough, reddened skin. We were supposed to wear a garment into the water—a one-piece black cotton jumpsuit with long arms and legs and a zipper from pelvis to neck.

There could be no contact with the body in the tub. We were 20th-century seventeen-year-olds, but we lived like 19th-century nuns. According to Lionel, we were seething with lust, and it was her job to cool us off. She ate, slept, and lived with us, helped us examine our consciences, and accompanied us to Confession. We took turns on Friday nights at Adoration, the monstrance, sun-shaped and golden, holding the Blessed Sacrament. The quiet of the chapel at those times held us in awe.

Sr. Lionel had high color and small bird eyes in the white coif. The rest of her was clothed in the habit of the order: long black buttoned dress, wide piece over her chest, huge sleeves, and long black veil pinned to the top of her wimple. The coif extended so far beyond her face she couldn't see left or right, but she saw every-thing anyway.

I loosened the buttons of my uniform and listened to the plink plunk of water, the gurgling of the drains. I undressed, dipped the bathing thing all the way into water, and hung it dripping on a hook. I slipped into the tub naked. Warm water, deep breaths. My friends were doing this, too.

Lionel would never dream of checking the tubs; an occasion of sin for her!

It was a mistake that I was here. I wish I could have gone to my mother's beloved boarding school with the Marie-Claire nuns, but it was closed now. She'd thought Sorrows would be the same. Ha! No blue habits and benevolent nuns for me. Ours was an order from French Québec, a Catholic convent world that hadn't changed in one hundred years.

I glanced at my freckled chest just above the small round breasts. Michael had whispered, "Janey, I want to see you."

I was so lucky to have a boyfriend. By the end of summer vacation, we'd park in a borrowed car by the beach, the oncoming headlights flickering over our faces in the dark. He'd kiss me with his soft lips, and my hungry kiss in response stunned us both.

Now, in the bath, a dry, gritty sound scraped nearby.

Lionel's thick shoes thumped. "Mademoiselle," she said. "What are you doing? Come out here."

I pulled myself up and cracked my door.

Cats came out wrapped in a towel. She was still dry. Her chin jutted, eyes fierce, and she stood there, her firm, naked legs nearly all exposed.

Lionel looked away. "Your garment?"

"I was shaving." The word dropped onto the stone floor.

"Shaving?" Lionel gasped.

"Legs," nodded Cats. "And arms."

"Have you not been apprised?" Lionel kept her eyes down. All of us were peeking through the stall doors at Cats' creamy cleavage.

"We do not beautify the body, Charlotte," said Lionel. "Luke 12:27. 'Consider the lilies, they neither labor nor spin. Yet I tell you not even Solomon in all his splendor was dressed like one of these.'"

Cats stared.

Lionel's lips went white. "Bring me that razor. We will address this at Notes. Now get yourself clean."

I plunged back into my tub.

"Cats, I adore you," I sang to myself, kicking my legs into the air. "Ode to legs—all mine, all strong, they carry me, they hold me up, la la la la."

I entered my cell and pulled the curtains around me; Emilie tapped our code. She pushed a yellow note through the curtain.

"I can't live," in her perfect hand.

She had a sailor boyfriend and a lyric soprano voice, white skin against raven hair, a woman's body. Larry was older than us—they were in another league.

"*Benit soit le Seigneur*," called Lionel, passing by with the evening holy water. I thrust two fingers out through the slit and dipped them into the freezing water, yes, "*Blessed be the Lord.*"

I lay back on top of my spread and waited, listening to the rustling around me.

After a while, I slipped out of my cell to the twelve windows on the far side of the dorm and leaned my face into the cold air, glancing up to the fifth-floor cloister. Once in a while, I'd see a nun up there in her sleeping bonnet.

Across the lake sat the old skating rink, the color of taffy in its windows, a cardboard-looking Roller Palace with turrets and towers etched against a blue-black sky. It was closed to the public now, but sometimes on Saturdays, Mère Supérieure would announce a skating *congée*; preposterous that she allowed it. We'd push off in long glides to rock-and-roll tunes, free for a few hours, released.

We joked that the ancient Catholic geezer who owned the rink let us skate for free, earning his way into heaven.

The next afternoon, Friday. I should have been reading the *Confessions* of Saint Augustine, but no, I leaned out the third-floor lavatory window, hungry for fresh air. In a dusk-blue light, the nuns were pruning the grape arbor, pitching branches over their heads like disembodied tentacles. They were like a swarm of insects attacking the arbor, clipping at pride, curbing friendships. Even from this distance, I knew them by a stance, a jerky motion. I could feel Pacifique's beady eyes, Lionel's head cocked for power.

They say they marry God.

A tall nun emerged from behind the arbor carrying a basket on her head. I had never seen her before; she threaded with grace through the others like an unbroken black line.

The supper bell rang.

I pushed out of the lav, down the stairs, past the Virgin's statue, around the corner, and bumped right into the new nun. Her silver cross stung my cheek. She had laughing eyes, and when I looked down, I saw pine needles in her shoe tips! We gave each other a silent nod.

The bell tolled, and I moved into the line of chanting women and girls, past the shabby elegant parlor, the heavy chapel doors—black-coifed nuns, prayerful, peace-filled as they bowed in their prayerful walks; girls in blue uniforms speaking with their eyes. And rising from the whole, our modal chant sounded like hunger.

Chapter 2

November 1964—Sister Philippe

A loud knock. "Sœur, five minutes!"

I turned over on my narrow bed and stared at the ceiling crack. It was Friday, movie night, everywhere but here.

Would I ever see a movie again?

Had I thought about that when I offered Him everything? No, just the grand things, the pure.

I stretched and yawned.

I was back to where I grew into a Postulant, then a Novice. Mère Supérieure did what she wanted with you—no explanations.

And I would obey. I was made for this life, alone inside my head unraveling ideas, writing them down. I loved a divine being, in me and everywhere around me. It was heady and thrilling to love God.

Except: "My child," Mère would say, "do not chase your thoughts. Formal prayers are food. The saints have given us the way."

I prayed in my own words, my own ideas.

No, Maggie, that was surely the sin of pride.

My wooden walls were bare; a white enamel pitcher and basin sat on a squat stand. My inner and outer habits hung on a wooden peg; the floor, cold beneath my feet.

I dropped my sleep gown on the floor and pulled the under-garments over my head, fastening and shivering, *Benit soit le Seigneur*, praying on each habit piece, *Blessed be the Lord*.

When I wound the wimple around my head and face, it pulled tight against my forehead.

I touched the ache above my nose.

I could control my mind. Even my longing for Andrè, my Skip, filled me with a *known* sorrow. But I never figured on the habit cloth, how it would feel over time: the weight of it, the heat. My sisters here loved the smooth inner garments close against skin—not me. No, I needed to run free, with plain, fresh air through my hair.

At six o'clock Mass, I knelt at the rail, swallowed the Host and all my questions melted away. Jesus held me.

And I was again, solely and forever, His.

On the way from chapel to breakfast, the girls in serge uniforms walked with us, their eyes hooded and sleepy. I glanced out the window over the wall at the Motherhouse. Novices were raking piles of leaves. When I was over there in training, I saw the girls only in chapel. I would hear their laughter over the fence like the tinkling of bells, or their shrieks on the winter hill as they flew through the trees on toboggans.

I'll admit, I'd been jealous of them.

"Sœur Philippe de Marie," blurted through the loudspeaker. I turned toward Mère's office and walked the long hall; I remembered polishing its stone floor as a Novice.

I knocked on the heavy oak door.

Mère sat at her clean desk, hands folded on a blotter. "*So, we come back 'round to where we began.*"

"*And know the place for the first time.*"

"Eliot, none finer." I'd forgotten how her dark eyes could smile. She was handsome, with large features and a long face.

"Why am I here, MaMère?" I tried to keep the anguish out of my voice. "I'm so close to finishing my final paper." I sighed.

"You always did question us. Have you not yet learned the joys of perfect obedience, Sœur?"

"Well, I'm here." Of course I was—what choice did I have? I tried again. "Forgive me, wouldn't you want me to finish my degree? My grades are excellent."

"Of course they are."

I sighed. Again.

Her nostrils flared ever so subtly. "I wish you to attend to our girls."

I gave her a quizzical look. "Girls?"

She drank me in.

"I don't have experience with teenage girls."

"I'd hoped we would not return to your old disdain. I need you here. You'll be assigned, MaChère."

That evening at dusk, the light, cold and silvery, we sang rounds as we pruned the arbor; my sisters in training, Jacinta and Germaine, together for the first time in a year. I clipped tangles of vine and grapes and wrestled them into piles. My sweat felt glorious. My body glowed.

Freckled Jacinta's face in the coif made me whoop with joy. Claire pointed out colors in the sky. "Mauve-blue, teal-pink!" It was incredible to see them again, in black veils now, not our Novice white; I wanted to hear everything about Jacinta's third-grade class at St. John's and Claire's tales of what it has been like to serve here. I wanted to tell them about my studies at Santa Lucia.

Out here in the fresh air, our black veils and skirts mixed with leaves whipped up about us in the wind. Together again!

The supper bell rang.

We dropped the branches.

Ruled by bells, we did not finish, but headed for the door, stashed our tools, retrieved breviaries.

Chilled, hurrying, I headed off, flying down a hall and around a corner and collided with a girl, catching her by her arms!

"Not running in the hall?"

She was dressed in the blue serge jumper, white nylon blouse, red tie.

I stepped back.

Our eyes locked. Hers, brown and the size of quarters, not a French girl at all but British features, large and open, high cheekbones.

The bell tolled.

We fell in line with nuns and girls headed to the refectory—from cloister, school, basement, arbor—black habits and blue jumpers, young, aged and bent, hobbling or pushed in wheelchairs, flushed from work, the chill of dusk about us. Our female voices rose in the longing lines of Angelus, chanting our praise.

I could swim in the beauty of our unison sound my whole life.

It would never be enough.

Chapter 3

Janey

On Monday morning, after a chilly, silent breakfast and some floor polishing, the warning bell rang for English class, and I filed in with the others. Sœur Odilia had assigned a Tennyson paper and I fanned myself with mine as I hurried to my seat. It was cold and damp everywhere in the convent—dorms, refectory, and recreation hall. Only the classrooms were hot, their tightly shut windows lining the wall.

"Dare to be Different" leaped out from a new poster on the wall. "Dare to be Holy," in bold blocky letters.

Up near the ceiling, a new border of book jackets, none of them lives of saints. Literature, classics, poetry. What had gotten into Odilia? Suze raised her eyebrows.

"Excellence, not Excuses," another sign said, in graceful calligraphy.

"What's with old sourpuss?" Cats whispered.

I sat down. They loved to transfer the nuns around, keep them on their toes, obeying.

Opposite the windows, a long blackboard stretched the length of the wall. Up at the front, a desk on a platform, the flag, crucifix, charts. "Do, don't Dread," another sign said.

Suddenly, the classroom door opened hard and slammed against the wall. A tall nun rushed in with an armful of papers and books. I shot a look at Cats. It was her, the new nun from the arbor, the one I nearly knocked over! Jeanne D'Arc bounded up and shut the door. The nun deposited the books onto her desk. A few slid to the floor. Em rushed up to catch them. The nun crossed to the window, drew it open in a smooth movement, and looked out over the arbor, hills and lake. We all stopped rustling papers and watched her.

The room was webbed in stillness.

After a time, she walked slowly to the center of the room and stood there looking at us with the same methodical searching. We were all breathing a little more slowly. She had the coloring of coffee, a shade lighter, and startling eyes of jet, framed by the white of the coif, tied at the chin. Her freshly scrubbed skin glistened.

"Good morning, class," she said. "My name is Sister Philippe."

I got a whiff of the same old classroom chalk and the ever-present Murphy's oil soap. But that was all that was the same.

"I am to be your English teacher," she said. "Please pass your papers to the front of each row; that's right, thank you, class. Now our friend Mr. Tennyson. I take it you were assigned to choose a quotation of his and elucidate it."

A flurry of papers. I kept my eyes on her. Like in the arbor, she didn't move like any nun I'd ever seen.

"Girls, when I indicate you, please tell me your name, then proceed. My dear," she nodded to Celine, "read us the quotation you—hm? What? You didn't read?" She shook her head and looked up and down the rows of fixed desks. I saw them through her eyes—girls in hideous blue serge uniforms, red ties.

I thumbed the pages of my Tennyson.

"Please," Sister Philippe indicated Suze.

"My name is Suzanne. *'For so the whole round earth,'*" she read, "*'is in every way, bound by gold chains about the feet of God.'*"

"Ugh," I whispered.

"You have a comment on the poet's image?" Sister Philippe said, looking straight at me.

"Janelle," I said. "Gold chains around the feet of God is so... heavy."

"I know what that means," Suze rushed in. "In Hebrews, the writer tells us that God made all the world by His Heir, the Son, who is the brightness of His glory, and the image of His substance and He upholds all the world and all things in it by the word of His power."

"Excellent, Suzanne, a compelling source for Tennyson's image. But surely you haven't been given leave to read Hebrews on your own, without doctrinal interpretation?"

We shook our heads no.

She touched the tips of her fingers together thoughtfully. "Girls," she said, "raise your hand if you have a quotation you are excited to share with us."

No hands went up.

"Who did the assignment?"

All hands went up.

"Hmm," said Sister Philippe. "Girls, put away the Tennyson."

She crossed the room and threw open the window. We will do something special in honor of my first day," she exclaimed. "The time to begin is now!"

I felt a breeze, fresh air.

Rushing, Sister Philippe passed out copies of a poem she'd mimeographed on the old machine in the library. I covered my face with it. The purple-lettered copies smelled like fresh baked bread. I loved their smooth gloss. Papers rustled and day girls buzzed about their plans for after school, but even they sat stunned when Sister Philippe began to read in a musical line of sound:

"*Glory be to God for dappled things,*
For skies of couple-color as a brinded cow"

"Who wrote this?" asked Jeanne D'Arc, hand in the air.

"What is your name? You're interrupting," said Sister Philippe.

I looked up and swallowed hard.

"*For rose-moles all in stipple upon trout that swim,*" she continued.

I could see the trout, the brinded cow.

"Girls," Sister Philippe said, "Gerard Manley Hopkins has broken all the rules. What do you think he is doing in these lines?"

"I don't know, but I can see pictures," Suze mumbled.

"He is naming," nodded Sister Philippe, "invoking the reality of the thing, he is calling it forth."

She read on:

"*Fresh-fire coal chestnut-falls; finches' wings;*
Landscape plotted and pieced—fold, fallow, and plough;
And all trades, their gear and tackle and trim."

Finches' wings, rose-moles, chestnut-falls. And this poem was about God? The same old God? How? I glanced at Suze whose lips were parted and at Cats who looked back at me, bemused.

"We will memorize the poem," the nun was saying, "Hopkins takes effort of seeing, girls, he sees things differently from the rest of us."

Her eyes snapped in the coiffed face.

"Sometimes his meanings are obscured," she continued, "and need interpretation, which bothers some readers. But with Hopkins, all our efforts will explode into meaning the more we delve to understand. Listen, now.

All things counter, original, spare, strange;
Whatever is fickle, freckled (who knows how?)"

"'All things counter,'" I repeated the words.

Jeanne D'Arc's hand shot up. "I don't understand this, Sister," she whined. "I don't get fickle, freckled."

"Good for you," said Sister Philippe. "You did well to understand the rest."

"I didn't say—"

"Never mind that now. Let us tear into some of these words. You there, Emilie, what is 'counter'?" She paced up and down the aisles, calling out the words, her body like a great diving porpoise of energy.

"Means 'against,' opposite to expected," said Em.

"Excellent. Now, 'fallow'?"

Cats took up her dictionary. "Unplanted," she said, pointing at the page.

"'Stipple'?" asked Sister Philippe.

"I know without looking," said Suze. "It means 'small dots.'"

The nun's cross swayed, the round chocolate beads of her rosary clicked. She looked at me. "What do you think he means by 'spare-strange,' Janelle? Look at the contexts, girls."

"I don't know," I said, "but he's using words that remind us of other words and all together give us a sense of nature—like we were standing under the tree and feeling it ourselves."

"Example." Philippe rubbed her hands together.

"Like when he says 'whatever is spare-strange, fickle, freckled,' I get the feeling of a bird's nest with tiny eggs, or, or, a calf's nose," I bit my lip, "and shells with amazing designs, and gray rocks that have tiny bits of color close-up, you know, but they're actually plain gray from far off."

"Okay, this is not for me," mumbled Cats.

Sister Philippe shot her a look. "Class," she said, taking each of us into her glance, "quite often, God is opposite to what we expect. Our poet, Hopkins, grasps this. And you will not understand him in one day. We will memorize 'Pied Beauty,' and believe me, it will dawn, it will come. Hopkins performed a creative violence. He is an original. In his own words about the ideal poet, he, himself, is the 'species in nature that can never recur.'

"Here, listen," she said.

"With swift, slow; sweet, sour, adazzle, dim;
He fathers-forth, whose beauty is past change:
Praise him.

We laughed out loud. The bell rang.

I folded the poem carefully, my throat parched. I felt the words still. "Fresh fire-coals, fathers forth."

Sister Philippe filled the desk drawer with the papers, smiling, bantering with girls. I thought, how old could she be, 22, 23?

Suze beamed; Em's face was flushed; I stood from foot to foot near the desk. *Whose beauty is past change.* The same God we'd been praying to.

When all my friends had filed out, I said, "Sister, can I borrow everything you have by Gerard Manley Hopkins?"

She frowned. "I'm afraid not," she said.

"Oh," I stumbled.

"I'll work through the material with you." She looked me over. "You have to realize that not everyone agrees with my teaching of Hopkins. He's terribly original—"

"I'm in love with him," I blurted. "I want to learn everything there is to know about him."

Sister Philippe's face broke into a smile.

Chapter 4

Saturday, November 6—Philippe

That first class, I'd prepared their Tennyson, but lost my head in a fit of excitement for Hopkins, a poet I'd been studying on my own. Oh dear. I'd had them all in my thrall and yes, I'd discovered that I love teaching.

At silent breakfast, I heard Mère sweep into the girls' dining room and call out "*Congée*! Roller Palace, *mes filles*! Enough of silence and hard work!"

I could hear every word through the wall. I'd never been inside the Roller Palace; novices didn't go there; but we could see the palace on its hill across the lake with its lights and turrets. What a strange recreation for a convent full of girls. But it showed that we loved them, didn't it? We'd never have children of our own, but these girls were truly ours, their hearts and souls formed by us—nothing could be more important.

"And," Mère continued, "Sœurs Philippe and Liese will accompany you."

I took a sharp breath. Now I was going *everywhere* with them. Ha, I wanted to love them, but from a distance. Well, that distance was over!

After finishing my cleaning—dusting the banisters and stairwells—I went to find Mère.

She was expecting me and didn't even look up. "Sœur, we are delighted that you're teaching our Seniors."

What? She wasn't angry about Hopkins? "I thought I'd teach after I got my degree."

"No, MaSœur. Now."

"But can you tell me why?"

"Not yet, my dear." She lifted her eyes. "Think of it—you'll discover so much about yourself."

I waited for the correction. "I already know I enjoy teaching."

She frowned. "But you've no experience."

"I love the poets. I want young minds to expand with them as I have."

Mère stared at me. "Are you speaking of Gerard Manley Hopkins words, Sœur? Changing us?"

I stayed very still.

"Ideas," I said.

"Well, that is all very well. Your *poets and ideas* are exactly what brought you back here. Stick to the lesson plans, Sœur. Today you will accompany our girls to the Roller Palace. You will get to know them. And on Monday morning, once again, you will kindly teach—Tennyson."

I could see her mind working behind the lined forehead and tight cloth.

Nodding, I turned to leave.

"Please sit down, my child, I have something to tell you."

Her expression changed to pleading. I shivered.

"It's Sœur Germaine."

I slowly sat down, heart rushing.

"She's not well. I think you and Sister Jacinta should know. You can be of help to her."

I sat back in the chair. "What's wrong?"

"It came on fast," Mère winced. "She's very ill."

I closed my eyes. "I don't understand."

"She has lupus."

"Lupus? What is that?"

"She was hiding it from us. It's an auto-immune disease."

"Oh, Claire."

"The doctors at our hospital can't help her."

I lowered my forehead into my hands. Sister Germaine, my Claire, running through the garden, sledding through the orchard. I looked at Mère and saw grief in her softened eyes.

I left her quietly, and gently closed the heavy oak door.

Germaine had asked Jacinta and me to meet her in the basement, she had something to show us. Confused, scared, I hurried there. I almost ran down the stairs.

Germaine stood before a narrow door, Sister Jacinta, beside her.

"Mère just told me." My voice shook.

Jacinta touched my shoulder.

Germaine gave a shrug. "Caught a cold, carried it around." Her dark eyes peered at us, her smooth skin with its sheen of sweat.

"Why didn't you tell someone?" My words came out like a cry.

"Couldn't stop."

"Stop what?" I felt faint.

She whispered. "I'm showing you." She turned the key, pushed the door open and entered a small room. My vision adjusted to the dark as she reached for a lamp.

"I've worked here since you both left, right after our first vows."

All around the cramped cellar room were canvases, paintings of such deep color, I stood very still. Scenes from the Gospels; Nathaniel in the tree; the raising of Lazarus; the prodigal son; the convent hill and lake; edgy portraits of children and animals; ordinary creatures.

"You gave up your art for God! You made art after all?"

"Just look," she said.

The room was damp with dull walls and no windows. But everywhere was color and light in the paintings. Germaine found a brighter lamp and leaned it toward the mosaic of a city, about four-foot square.

Bits of color were embedded in stone, unusual and intense. Close up, its hundreds of tiny uneven tiles created texture, grain. The farther we stepped away from the grain, the more powerfully the images emerged. Studded buildings, an enormous intricate wall across the middle, angel standing guard, and many-colored gates. Near the mosaic was tacked up, on yellow paper in a round wide hand, scripture verses from the Apocalypse, Chapter 21. Sister Germaine read in a soft voice:

"And I saw the Holy City of Jerusalem," her voice strained with feeling, "coming down out of heaven from God, and the city shone. And all about a great high wall, twelve gates and twelve angels. And its wall was built of jasper, while the city itself was of pure gold, bright as clear glass; jewels of every kind, the first being jasper, the second turquoise, the third, chalcedony."

I gazed at Sister Germaine and suddenly saw her—skin and bones in the habit that hid everything, her flush was not healthy. But there was something new in her tone; was it wonder?

She was a consummate artist. We thought she'd given it up for God.

There was a list in her rounded hand. I read out loud in astonishment:

jasper—red, brown quartz, ancient times green
turquoise—mix of blue/green
chalcedony—milky-grayish
emerald—rare green, clear, deep
sardonyx—kind of onyx, brown, red
chrysolite—olive green
beryl—blue or rose, opaque
topaz—transparent yellow
jacinth—reddish brown
chrysoprase—apple green
amethyst—violet

Our eyes went back and forth, searching each color in the mosaic. "How could we not know about this?" I held onto a table nearby. "You created every color in the passage."

Sister Germaine's eyelids fluttered, a wan smile. She breathed a choke and coughed.

"There's where I fired the tiles," she said, pointing to a small kiln, "and I mixed the glazes here." She swept her hand over a long table. Jacinta's eyes were round.

I was leveled. And Mère had allowed it, encouraged it, bought her materials.

"But we thought—"

"Mère arranged it—here is where I've lived, thanks be to God. I have known wondrous amounts of grace. I've made my art."

Her grainy voice broke my heart.

We stepped away from the city, its walls, its angels with their onyx eyes.

We moved to Sister Germaine, one on either side of her and held her in our arms. She leaned her head. We were forbidden to touch each other.

Today that rule was irrelevant.

I had one hour before the outing and went out to walk in the orchard. The air was fresh and cold. I'd been turned upside down.

Germaine, ill, her art, *oh my Lord*.

Art supplies from Mère?! My own strange talk with Mère.

What did she mean, my ideas and poems brought me back here?

For me, being the tenth child in my family, there were no poems, no art. We had nothing. One of our Aunts would make us dresses out of old draperies. There was only striving. My sister Dolores sat with me when I was afraid to go to sleep and told me stories. The day I was born, Dodie said, her arm around my shoulders, the older children went into the room where Maman lay against the pillows, Papa close beside her. They'd stood before our parents, arms crossed. Roger, their leader said: "We took a vote.

We have enough kids. The new baby can go to Mrs. Marcotte who wants one and never gets any."

"Her name is Margaret," whispered Maman, her own life ebbing away, me, the healthy baby girl in her arms.

At my mother's wake in the parlor of our small house, my sister Gillie, a year and a half, and three-year-old twins John and Ovide crawled on her in the casket, bawling and trying to wake her up. I was sleeping in the bassinet nearby. Our father stood the entire time just outside the door, Dodie said, retelling the story over the years. Papa could not look at his dead wife or take the babies away.

What could be sadder than a baby crying for its Maman who will never wake up?

The bell clanged in the courtyard. Boarders lined up and headed to the front gate. My stomach churned. Would Germaine get well? Would she come back? *Dear Jesus, please send your healing power to Sister Germaine.*

Liese had joined the boarders' line. The small stooped French teacher with her tiny-lined face looked as though a small puff of breeze could knock her over. I'd heard she taught the girls the old Canadian folk songs. What a treasure.

I reached them just as they started down the hill, snaking in a line two by two in navy serge uniforms, white collars, red ties, and flesh leggings. Liese led the way; I brought up the rear alone, sometimes swallowed in my veil in the wind. It was a battle to keep my eyes on them.

A boy flew past us. "The nuts are looooooose," he called and then bounced up onto the path, waving as he went.

Janelle and Charlotte, the one they called Cats, walked just ahead of me, and I caught her saying in a muffled voice: "He's driving toward us right now, cig out the window."

Oh, why was Mère doing this to me? I did not know what to do with these girls. Liese was the one to choose—she was getting forgetful. And every other sister was supposed to be at the Chapter of Faults for the latest critiques. But at least today, I would at long last see the inside of the Roller Palace!

We started up the hill on the path that rounded the lake. Gray clouds tinged with lavender moved behind the Roller Palace. It had been a beacon through Postulancy and Novitiate. We'd joked that its entrance across from the convent's was a direct line to sin.

I smiled to myself and allowed one quick memory, not a good idea, but there I was at another roller rink, me skating backwards, Skip holding my hand, shuffling and placing one foot over the other around the corners—*no, Maggie, quit that.*

As we rounded the edge of the lake, I glanced back through November's brown and yellow leaves at the austere brick convent—five floors, three wings, chain-link fence, high walls. A precocious child could have drawn both buildings and rubbed her hands together with pride when she placed them across the lake from each other.

We walked for about fifteen minutes. Up close to the palace, the peeling pink paint and light blue trim was a shock. Above the porch, the rusted sign's Rs were missing: "OLLE PALACE," it read.

There were poked-out lights, a creaky porch, and boards missing from the steps. Liese waited on the crumbling porch, two girls hanging from the columns. They parted to let me through. The old geezer met us in a tattered flannel shirt and fatigues. "Sister," he cooed, bowing, smooshing his cigarette with the toe of his shoe, showing respect for the church.

"Thank—"

"No need, no need," he waved us in.

There was an embarrassment of dust on every surface, benches, floors, bar around the rink, cubicle for music, even in the air, dust motes in a silver sweep, and over all the records and moldy skates. But on went the skates anyway, not to miss a second of our time. Liese was forgetting herself, her color high; she was bent on skating, and I'd better get some on my feet, too. I had to stay in control. Mère would probably arrive here at any moment and check on how well I managed the girls.

Charlotte's long hair swung as she leaned over her skates, whispering to Janey, the inquisitive one, who looked like an English girl in this French place—slender, with a long nose, huge eyes and expressive mouth. Three small pretty girls skated around in a circle, singing a pop song. The music came up bleating. "Dee-Dee Sharp!" they cried.

I looked around quickly, what do I do?

The girls pushed onto the expanse of the wood floor and picked up speed, shouting and skating. My heart soared out there with them. Well, what did we expect them to skate to, the Blue Danube?

Liese's open face was full of frenzied happiness. The old geezer waved from his cubicle, grinning, a new cigarette in his other hand. My limbs were loosening—I was feeling the music.

I wanted to skate by and steal the geezer's cigarette, I could taste it!

Cruel assignment. Mère knew it, too.

I leaned against the cubicle and watched the skaters. The air stirred with their spirit. The old man had set his ancient popcorn popper going and the smell—well, we might all pass out.

There was as much salt as you wanted over there, riches of salt. Butter was out. But I could see the butters of past times in the walls of the yellowed popper along with all the skating afternoons of my life—so many little girls grown, and the boys, with their smells of grass, wood smoke, spearmint, basketball leather.

I willed my legs to be still. Janey disappeared into the ladies' room with Charlotte. I started toward them; they came right back out. Would those fearless boys come?

The girls joined a group skating to a corner, hiked up their skirts at the waist. Out came the lipstick, passed from one to the next and whipped on as they flew by, and how was I supposed to curb them here, forget it, surely Mère was aware of all this, or she'd have kept them home.

They hadn't chosen a nun's life yet. Some of them might, but they hadn't been disciplined or walked the steps that would make it possible to give all this up.

"Come on Baby, let me see you shake a tail feather!"

"Do Tones!" They danced and skated.

I shook my head, no at the old man.

He leered. His body swayed from side to side as he walked to the jukebox, leading with his shoulders like an ape. The song was axed.

The next was worse. Haley and the Comets, and the old man shimmied. He must have invited us so he could play the old songs. But now I was skating back to my spot, one long glide after another, shaking off the tightness, feeling the motion, weaving in and out, keeping it under control. I stood off to the side again. The old man grinned and did a toe-heel-toe. I noticed Janey's two more trips into the ladies' room. Liese leaned against the opposite wall, eyes twinkling in her lined face. I prayed the boys would not come, for the girls' sake and mine.

Music blared; popcorn bounced. I pushed off with my right skate and the long glide released my whole breath, my questions; the unease and the relief of it frightened me. The girls' speed passed into me like electricity. Rounding the corner, Emilie flipped around and skated backwards, my favorite dance in the world— girls jumped out of her way. I let out all my breath, and there was Skip in a memory so real, his reddish-blond hair and blue eyes, his wide shoulders and strong legs—dancing me, shuffling, driving, and speeding the floor. This WAS a test, but I didn't fail. I felt lifted just remembering—and *watching* this joy.

That night after lights out, I knelt beside my bed, grateful. The girls had gone back with long faces, so be it. The Roller Palace was the most curious gift. They must feel both relieved tonight and confused coming back here. Girls had skated over there for eons.

Years ago, before the palace closed, we'd even borrowed skates for them to fly up and down our shining convent halls.

Suddenly, hot and sweating, I stood up and went to the window. Our cloister was on the fifth floor, one up from where the boarders slept. The windows were open, sometimes even in winter. I let the air cool my face.

I'd watched the Roller Palace out the window of the Motherhouse all through Novitiate.

Today, I'd gone inside.

The stars were pinpoints of light that felt like nourishment. *"Dearest Savior, please heal our Sister, please. She has so much to give, but you already know that. Please don't let her die, forgive my sins. Make me be like a circling bird around your glory. Make me a good nun."*

A wave of cold panic swept over me. Was she dying?

The bad Catholic's leer floated before me in the dark.

The girls' hair had blown wild today, their faces flushed; was I supposed to stop them? Curb them?

"There's body and there's sin." Père would scowl in his homily. "And they go together."

I was only seven years old when this dawned on me for the first time.

I'm new at confessing; we're preparing for the greatest moment of our lives, First Communion. The nuns march us to the church class by class and line us up to confess to priests on folding chairs

all along the communion rail; no dark confessionals for young be-
ginners.

I stand in line, trembling. I've been seeing Jesus naked. That is
my sin.

Not the baby boy, Jesus, no, the grown man-God standing
there, his penis hanging, every time I pray. And it isn't like I never
got to see penises. My brothers pee in front of me all the time while
I sit on one side of the toilet seat. No, this is what the nuns warned
us about—this is the devil making Jesus naked all the time.

It takes forever for my turn.

I kneel close to the Monsignor's ear, red, veiny, filled with odd
tufts of white hair. He turns to pray the greeting. His breath smells
like bad potatoes.

"Oh, my God, I am heartily sorry for having offended thee," I
recite, feeling faint.

"I accuse myself of having...of having seen..." My mouth falls
open like a plea. The old priest sighs, our noses touch. "Yes?" he
growls.

"I've been seeing Jesus naked."

"What?" he says out loud.

The priest ahead of him turns around and stares at us.

"I see Jesus naked," I whisper. I look up at the dome ceiling.
There are serpents and whirlwinds up there. There is woe in the
whole church.

"Where?" he asks.

I don't know what to say. I see him and that's all.

"How many times?" The old priest falls back into his chair.

"A lot of times." I start to cry.

Monsignor stares at my tears. He stands up and looks around for the nearest nun.

All the children stop to watch.

"Say three Hail Marys, my child," he says.

What will Hail Marys do? I'm going to hell.

Chapter 5

Monday, November 6, 1964—Janey

Michael! I held an envelope.

He hadn't come to the palace, but mailed it to my day-hop friend, Denise. I hid in the bathroom stall and opened a single page, a poem. Suze came in. "Janey, Lionel's looking for you."

Memorize and flush it. But I stashed it into my front, no bra, my little infraction!

I was late and rushed into the dining room. We were being read to from the Foundress's book. Mère Marie-Anne. Lionel pursed her lips and read: "Our sword is discipline."

I scraped my chair and sat down at table. Her eyes were on the book; I reached into my blouse. The onion skin paper rustled as I slipped it under the table inside my shelf.

Keeping my eye on Lionel, I opened it.

> Hey kid
> Love's a wish, a smile like yours,
> Happiness over bound
> Live and flowing like your hair
> Fair and clean so sound
> Leaping, joyous, healthy-made,
> Like when you're around.

"Our sword is obedience," read Lionel.

> Love's a tale like your eyes,
> So gay, profound, and deep,
> Bright and bursting with desire

As blinking stars do weep.

Lionel read in a commanding voice, "Discipline undergirds all our actions—."

Never hurting, deeply searching,

To find, to know, to keep.

Cats passed me the pitcher, frowned, and then grinned.

Lionel's voice deepened: "I grind myself to powder if, so doing, I accomplish your will, oh, Lord."

Monday morning, at six a.m. Mass, the bell jingled for Communion, and I tried to stay kneeling, my face buried in my hands. Had I sinned? If you didn't know, then you hadn't. Good. I jumped up and followed. Lionel would question me if I stayed in the pew. I carried my questions and doubts to the rail. Could I still be His if I lived my life outside this holy place?

Chapter 6

November 16—Philippe

Choir practice. First time since coming back. I followed Sisters Jacinta, Julie, and Thérèse up the creaky, winding staircase to the front row near the rail. From up here in the loft, the old wooden chapel shone with its hanging yellow lanterns and painted Stations of the Cross. The ever-silent Saint Joseph stood decorated on one side altar and the blue caped Virgin Mary on the other, forever separated by the Annunciation. That was my wrongheaded view, but I felt for Joseph.

The English class had taken me by surprise. The girls were so deadened and resigned to Tennyson. I'd memorized "Pied Beauty." And then just before class, I made copies. I knew I was on thin ice, but I'd been immersed in him when Mère had stopped my studies and couldn't let him go. How they'd stirred awake and come out of their shells like turtles! I could feel new life crackling. Hopkins had been excommunicated; what did I think would come of this? but, oh, what a class!

Choir consisted of professed nuns and girls, audition only. Jacinta and I had auditioned yesterday for Sister Robert, the conductor. I could not believe I'd made it in. She needed three female parts for the anthems—soprano, alto, and baritone—and had plenty of voices to choose from.

Germaine, white and small, slipped in beside us with flashing eyes and shiny lips. She couldn't sing anymore but had come to be with us. Ten nuns up here in all. And now came the girls, clomping

34

up the stairs, not having learned to walk demurely, to have custody of the eyes. We couldn't wait to be a part of the harmony. Jacinta and I were altos. I breathed out all of my air, then pulled it back in; warm space, scents of incense and candle wax permeating everything, missals and music books, prie-dieus, arched ceilings. Incense could dry singers out but quieted everything within for worship.

We gathered around Sœur Robert, a stocky, light-filled nun. We never got this close to one another. I could smell the naptha soap used to clean our wool habits, our plain skin without creams, something lemony and sweet—from the girls.

After some vocalizations and stretches during which Jacinta and I elbowed each other playfully, Sr. Robert told us in a raspy voice to take up the Vittoria. She had the nickname "frog" because she'd had a long laryngitis and couldn't demonstrate the musical line. But it was affectionate—everyone wanted to sing with her. She jumped up onto her box, conducting with a swift stick, like a magnetic pull on our voices. I relaxed and sang the alto line. The Tomas Luis de Vittoria anthem, written in 1585, looked forward in my mind to the great composers, especially Brahms.

Sr. Robert was rigorous with the music, distracted in everything else. Lifting her stick, she slapped a head: "The note is A sharp, Jeanne!" "I need your eyes, you." "Give it here, more."

Our voices rose up from the circle of women and over the empty pews, over Michael, the Archangel and Saint Anne. The long lines wove in questions that resolved in perfect, tender chords.

I was fixated on Sr. Robert. Now here was a nun who absolutely loved her vocation! She'd studied choral music before and after entering, especially anthems set for female voices. She always beamed as though she had a cheerful secret.

The choir loft was warm, its wood dark and creaking. The other nuns' mouths forming vowels, so soft; the girls, focused and intent. "Blend, Janelle!" said Robert. "No such thing as a star here," she winked at Emilie's full soprano. "Sit out the next piece. You will see that you're not as important to the sound as you think."

After choir, we had recreation and continued to sing rounds, *"Fish and chips and vinegar, One bottle cap two bottle caps,"* walking to the basketball court.

"Sister, I'll miss your defense on the court," I told Germaine.

She turned her wide-open smile on me. "Can't play anymore— but I'm fortunate to still be working."

We stood under the basketball hoop. Germaine held her frontispiece to her chest, gasping for breath, laughing at herself, her color high.

She sat on the bench and watched. I dribbled the ball around Sister Lucie. Our skirts and veils flew around our heads, confusing our plays. Lucie streamed from behind and I wove in to steal the ball. I was good even in a habit, my brothers had made sure of that, testing me constantly out in the street in my skirts and skinned knees. I scored and Jacinta won the ball. Five foot three but never mowed down. Laughter pealed; we were always in tune, our team of five.

Germaine was slower than usual walking back up the hill. Jacinta and I held her by the arms on either side. "Where are you these days on taking final vows?" she asked us.

"I'm there," said Jacinta. "I haven't had many backwards glances in the convent, seems it's where I need to be. The routine, the chants, the prayer, the Eucharist of course, the retreats and teaching out in the parish school—all of it."

"Mère has been astounding about my art," said Germaine. "I never dreamed. I must show you again. I'm the most fortunate artist in the universe. I get my meals, sheets washed—no one questions my vocation."

"No one knows!" I laughed.

"And you?" They both said to me at once. "The restless one."

"I have puzzling doubts. I get so lonely."

"But you have Christ! And you have us!" said Jacinta.

"I want to write, study, and climb those mountains. I've had to leave my work."

Germaine frowned, then looked at me with warmth.

We shared a light supper in our refectory next door to the boarders'. Both had long tables, cream-colored oil cloth, set with the same color plates. As we passed the girls' table, I saw their hungry eyes trained on platters of celery as they stood behind their chairs waiting to pray.

As I sat in my place, I realized that the girls on the other side of the wall were quieter than usual. A lot was expected of them; cleaning duties, prayer and fasting just like us; hard studies and long study halls after school and not much time off. I'd never thought about them before. They weren't Postulants.

But they weren't normal teenagers either.

After supper, Mère required me to stay in the dining room for a planning meeting; girls would be out for recreation with the cleaning sisters as monitors.

First, she lined out events of the semester toward Senior graduation on June 1st. "Sœurs," said Mère, "now to the matter up for discussion. We are considering letting the girls have a Senior prom."

Lionel wrinkled her nose. "Surely not."

"Do they even know how to have a prom?" asked Sœur Richard.

"Day girls will have to plan it," Mère said. "They've been pushing for years."

"Why encourage them in that?" asked Sœur Giselle.

"We have to," Mère interrupted. "A committee can work with the other Catholic schools nearby. It's 1964. We must let them be a part of their generation, the culture."

"Or we'll lose them," I said. Jacinta had told me that the Academie was losing students.

They all looked at me. It was Mère's turn to sigh.

"But how do we have a prom here?" asked Sœur Paul.

"I'll believe it when I see it," said Fiacre.

A prom won't do it, I thought to myself, it's too late to save this school.

As if she'd heard, Mère turned to me. "Regardless if we survive as an educational enterprise or not," she said, "we must change and we must change now. I don't like it any more than you do. But Mère Generale let us know that a fresh wind is blowing from the top down."

"I can't picture our girls," groaned Liese.

"They can leave from home," I said. "The girls from far away can stay with ones nearby. They can't be expected to dress and be escorted to a prom from here."

Mère's eyebrows met together.

"That's a great suggestion, Sister Philippe," said Sister Paul. "They could come here with their dates on the way to the prom. We could have a receiving line."

"We'd have parent chaperones," Mère beamed, "and we wouldn't attend, but at least we'd be a part of their special night."

I pictured the boyfriends with slicked-back hair shaking the nuns' hands and answering their questions. I accidentally let out a short laugh. Mère scowled in my direction.

In just one week, Germaine couldn't stand near her bed without vomiting. She'd fallen completely ill. We knew she'd been pushing herself for a long time. We all hoped it was a spell, that she'd come back. I spent that night sitting beside her bed, talking softly. She slept.

Other nuns chanted and prayed around her. It was six a.m. when I headed to Mère's office, pulling open her heavy door. "She's in pain. I can see it in her forehead." I felt it on my own.

"No," Mère said. "Sister Margaret is relieving her pain, she's a trained nurse."

"How can this be happening?" I crossed to the window and looked out over the lake. I folded my arms.

"Calm yourself, Sœur. She never belonged to us."

I turned around and Mère's eyes were full of feeling. "She wasn't strong like you. We discovered during Novitiate that she had lupus. There's nothing they can do for it. And she hated attention. She spent long hours working."

"And here I was thinking she was a seamstress." She was not only leaving the world, she'd had work that I never knew about.

"You still have so little faith in us, Sœur," said Mère with sorrow. "Look around you at what our order accomplishes. Hospitals, a college, grammar and prep schools."

"What does that have to do with her?"

Mère remained patient. She slowly opened a drawer. "Did you think we would let our own genius disappear?" She sat up straighter, her eyes glistened. "It's time for us to acknowledge Sœur Germaine who has deepened the beauty and holiness of our chapel and many churches."

I gazed at her. "You're going to celebrate her now? Now that she's fading away?"

Mère drew back, shaking her head. "Sister did not want recognition while she lived."

"But she suffered in Novitiate giving up her art, accepting it was God's will."

"It wasn't," said Mère.

"What do you mean?"

"She offered up her art to God—and got it back one hundred-fold; that is His way."

I let out all my breath.

"She took us down there, Sister Jacinta and me. We were stunned, both of us. But why didn't she tell me?" A wave of betrayal. The way she'd point out colors and patterns on walks through the arbor; it all made sense now.

"Being hidden freed her. I'm sorry it hurts you, my child. She claimed she couldn't create any other way."

Mère tilted her head and glanced toward the door; I gently made my escape.

Walking the long hall, I felt elation, then shrinking. Germaine. Her anonymity, her secret life.

The totality of my loss.

I had to see her art again—had to study it.

My shoes clicked against the stone floor. I reached the door leading to the cellar. We'd always been forbidden to go down there. My heart pounded in my chest. There was a flashlight on a shelf at the top of the stairs. Through boiler and storage rooms, along the dirt floors, helmet bugs scooted for cover. The rock walls were slick and wet. I stopped before a narrow door, plunged the key into the lock. Fumbling, grimacing, I shoved it open.

Darkness and smells hit my nostrils: oil paint, chalk, strong glue, and an underlying pungency of burnt coal. And stillness; a strong sense of her, even though I'd never known her this way. Was it possible that she would live, pull through, be a miracle healing?

I lit a lamp and stepped in, then stood transfixed.

Again, I was overwhelmed with her pieces crowded along the walls, egg tempera colors so vibrant and alive they might leap off the canvas; and each more original than the next—St. Anne with the child Mary in bold strokes and cubes, their capes taking up most of the canvas, and their white, innocent faces like Renaissance

Madonnas. There were still-lifes in oil and one would think we ate like royalty here—the oranges, apples, and pitchers of milk, the amber honey jar, the gorgeous fabric of the tablecloth; but it was the large mosaics that once again leveled me. Those small tiles of color fired in the kiln, brought together in images that swirled before me, within me, and exploded.

The face of Jesus. One would imagine something stiff in mosaic, instead, because He was beyond the man with the brown hair in religious art, he was warm-hearted, divine—streaked, saturated in color and light.

I pictured my friend, young and open, then Sister Germaine, laboring to finish, coughing.

I sat down in a chair and stared. I heard the buzz of the heating system, the clanks and whoosh of forced hot air. I don't know how much time passed. Then someone was shouting my name from upstairs. "Sœur Philippe!"

I backed out, keeping my eyes on the riches of color, my heart breaking. One last deep breath of the colors, *her eternal breath will forever be in this work.*

I hurried up the stairs; the chapel bell sounded a bong. It stopped me mid-step, then bonged again, tolling now in an even rhythm.

No, Germaine, so fast.

In a tiny moment, all your breath gone.

Chapter 7

November 17–18, 1964—Janey

We were in study hall. The sound of a gong made us jump. Lionel stood at her desk at the front; she strode from the room. I took advantage and pulled out Pied Beauty, the purple copied poem, even the smell of it was comforting. The bell continued its loud toll. Cats shook her head.

"Death," she mouthed from across the aisle.

"Who knew a nun was dying?" I asked aloud.

I pictured the bell ringer nun in the tower. It had to be her, the oldest nun I knew. She'd pull the rope all the way to the floor, then cling to it as it flew up, black shoes kicking.

The bell continued, slowly, evenly. "Who died?" whispered Em.

It could be anyone. Our convent housed the whole gamut from Postulant, Novice, working sisters, and the ancient retired, their faces as dry and crinkled as tissue paper. I tried to recall the most fragile, an even older one who had to be pushed up to the refectory table in her wheelchair, her skin a pale green.

Nuns never seemed to sleep or bathe; they could be as loving as angels; as mean as fairy-tale witches.

I did not like the idea of a dead nun.

I exchanged a nervous glance with Suze, who'd stiffened; to her, revealing her feelings was like unbuttoning your blouse.

The door cracked open.

43

I shoved Hopkins into my desk. Sœur Lionel came in chanting the Requiem. She swept past the statue of the Sacred Heart and down the aisles, shoving a holy water sponge into our faces. She stood at the front of the classroom. "Mes filles," she said, "this afternoon, you will eat your collation and spend recreation in silence. For three nights, we will keep watch with our dead, departed sister." And then, she marched out. No mention of a name.

"But who died?" said Cats.

We sat there shivering with each loud bong.

Then in danced Sœur Liese, her face flushed from running, her small berry eyes glittering. She looked like a little wood mouse.

"Mes filles," she said, "our sister has met her God at the gates of Paradise." She gestured upwards. "This is all joy," she clapped her hands, "and for the rest of the day, we rejoice by breaking our silence. Happy recreation!"

We stared.

"Bien," she laughed, "stand up! Parlez!"

No one moved. We adored Liese, but she was a little off. Some said she'd been planning to be an actress before going into the convent, that her beau had committed suicide when she went in.

Liese stood there, her feet wide apart, round red spots appearing on her cheeks like two apples. "Talk!" she said. "*Ad Dei Gloriam*," taking herself out of the room with a lilt in her step.

Jeanne D'Arc stood up. "What did Lionel mean, keep watch?"

"They'll lay her out in the parlor," said Suze.

"No!" said Emilie.

"Don't talk," said Boissy, the resident snitch.

"Liese said to talk!" said Cats.

We were out of our seats now, feverish with the thought of a wake, of who had died, all talking at once.

"Let's make plans," said Cats, gathering us around her. "How about getting some food out of this?"

"You're kidding, right," I said.

"They'll all be occupied. Perfect time for a raid!" Cats exclaimed.

"Who'd want to eat what we find?" Emilie made a face.

Lionel appeared at the doorway. "Talking?" she shouted.

She jutted her chin, cheeks blanched.

A spider flung itself off the corner eave, skydiving, tethered by a single, silk thread.

Finally, Jeanne pushed her red hair out of her eyes "Sœur Liese told us to break the silence out of joy—"

"How dare you?! Jeanne D'Arc LaFrance," Lionel said. "You will retire to my office."

"But Sœur..."

Lionel glowered. "Talk on the day of a death?"

Jeanne D'Arc backed out, keeping her pleading, muted face before the rest of us.

"Proceed," said Lionel at the door. "Your silence will continue until after the funeral, three days from today."

"Does anyone know who died?"

The next morning, on the way to class, Denise came running to me and slipped another thin envelope into my pocket. I threw my arms around her. "You are the best."

In Latin class, we were bursting to talk. I was dying to open my letter from Michael and hid the envelope in my book. I kept my eye on Sœur Fiacre. We had a whole system of note passing, even in the best of times.

Fiacre turned to the blackboard; I unfolded a note from Denise. "You make him sound so handsome. But it'll cost you. I need a paper for English class."

Suddenly, I could feel my cheek against Michael's leather jacket, flying along in his car.

For a second, I could see him—bony forehead, soft, full lips. The way he said certain words, thick and abrupt. Meanwhile, Sœur Fiacre was lecturing about Cicero. Cats passed me some jelly beans fuzzy from her pocket. Suze had to go to the bathroom. I was up to my tenth sneeze.

"D'accord," shouted Fiacre. She lunged for some paper, a shiny blue strip and began to scribble.

Suze rolled her eyes.

Fiacre flew at us, waving the paper: "Janelle, Charlotte, Suzanne!"

"Your names are going into the coffin! The COFFIN," she yelled, jumping up. "You are undisciplined and unruly. It is for God to judge you now!"

I bit my lip to keep from laughing. God checked coffins for special messages? We sat and stared. Spit clung to the corners of Fiacre's mouth.

The bell rang.

We spilled out into the hall, arms around each other, who needed to talk? Fiacre had gone too far. The punishment was looney and it gave us a wild relief!

We headed for collation, passing the company parlor where two freshman girls were combing the fringe of the oriental rug, one of Lionel's favorite penances.

With no nun in sight, I turned into the lav and sat on the toilet lid. Opening the thin paper, my fingers trembled.

"*Hey Kid,*" it said,

"*I'm just sitting here on the window sill—kinda looking out, watching the emotionless night. I'm all alone—my roommate has gone home. As I sit here against this shadowy window, looking at the radiant lights beaming and reflecting impersonally in the muddy river, I'm thinking. About love, and friendship, and the million little extras that keep people together. It's really lonesome here, and I'm thinking of you. And it's because I know that looking out a window at the peacefulness of night with cars and the river and the stars and the breeze—these are things that I have only been able to share with you. You have just so much to offer a guy—not just outward appearance to attract everyone, but you've got what holds the world together inside—feelings, understandings. These are things I've always missed with other girls. I know how easy it would be to fall in love with someone like you. And in fact, I can't deny that I've had, since the day we met, feelings that I've not known before. As I look at the stars, and the lights on the water, I feel a feeling that I knew once as a tear rolled down your pretty cheek, and I realized that your tears and your heart were a part of me.*"

I held the paper lightly in my hands. I couldn't flush it, would have to risk getting it to my trunk. I wiped my eyes with the back of my sleeve.

The next morning at Mass, we lifted our voices—the girls from Haiti, Jesse and Elaine, and Em with her dark hair and fair skin. All our mouths open to perfect "o's", our faces full of hope. The chant wound itself around me. As a little girl, I'd adored the scents and colors of the Mass, the vestments, the candles, the singing in our big old neighborhood church with its statues, a larger-than-life Jesus on his cross with the truest deep red blood pouring from his side, the wiry blue of Mary's cape and the stars in her long hair. The church was my earliest brush with beauty in our mill town, Mills Falls. But this morning, all I could think about was the beauty of Michael's words.

At breakfast, Sœur Liese read La Vie de Saint Philip Neri, a comedian for God.

Philip Neri was punch-drunk with joy—acrobat extraordinaire. She came to the part about his autopsy, fixed her bird eyes on the page as she read: "And they found his heart swollen to the size of a watermelon. Such was his love for God…"

"Such was his heart condition," whispered Cats as we filed out. She passed me a note: "I told you Liese was going senile." I ripped up the note, swallowed the piece that said senile, and dumped the rest into the trash.

At seventeen, we were treated like twelve. But we obeyed because the punishment was losing your Excellence pin worn on the shoulder of the uniform. There were many punishments but only one we cared about—we'd forfeit our home weekend. The nuns kept us in line.

There was no one around—I ran up the stairs for my cleaning job. Suze followed and opened the closet door. We were throwing the rags into a pail when she elbowed me.

Midway down the hall, six nuns stood at attention by the front door, opening soundlessly, from the outside. Four men, dressed in black coats and hats seemed to blow in; the day was stormy with high winds. They stepped inside carrying a pine box with a thick black cloth over it, their gloved hands firm against the base. They paused, balancing the box between them artfully.

They removed their hats. Sœur Portress fussed around them.

During the confusion, in walked a white cat. Suze covered her mouth. We'd seen the cat skulking around the kitchen door and named him Casper the Friendly Ghost! He lifted his front paw daintily and disappeared around the corner. The men straightened the heavy cloth. Then like soldiers, they carried the coffin into the company parlor.

So it was true. The dead nun was here. "That's creepy," said Suze's note. "Gross," said Cats' note. "I want out of here," I wrote back. And if it weren't enough that the corpse was under our roof, Lionel announced at collation that we boarders had been assigned, "two by two, to keep watch all night with our dearly departed sister," for whom we still had no name.

We were no strangers to keeping watch in the night. The first Friday of every month, woken by Lionel, we'd tiptoe down to chapel in our pajamas. Truly, we all looked forward to it.

During adoration of the Blessed Sacrament, the monstrance couldn't be left alone, a round and brilliant sun with rays of gold surrounding the small circular window that contained the host. We'd kneel sleepily in the pew, gaze at the rich gold—doze and pray. The quiet filled me, there was no peace like it in the world.

But keeping watch with a dead body?

Even the most blasè of us were creeped out.

At two a.m., Emilie and I met in the hall for our turn to keep watch. There were tension lines under her eyes, I was shaking. Neither of us looked sleepy even at this hour.

We entered the parlor. I looked up at the white ceiling. Our nuns never talked about our bodies—periods didn't exist; we weren't supposed to get headaches or cramps. Tears were frowned on. Nuns revered the mind, worshiped the soul, ignored the body. But we were all going to have to deal with a body now.

Em took my hand. We approached on a long, dusty blue rug. The pine box lay raised on a hall table, the body sunken into it, impossible to see yet. Two candles in mighty stands stood at either end. Two nuns with fixed gazes sat motionless beside them. Their faces were ruddy, and their stubby, thick fingers held rosary beads. From an oil portrait just above the box, Sœur Foundress Marie Anne peered down. We'd been told she'd slept in her own coffin for penance.

We knelt before the coffin on the *prie dieu*. There was nowhere to look but in.

The dead nun was deep inside in a white cotton sheet. She was no one I knew. She had the whitest of hands, wrapped round with her heavy black rosary, her fingernails smooth. She was as flat as a boy. A scent of melting wax and some other pungent odor hung heavy in the air.

The wakes I'd been to all my life for relatives held the distractions of scents, flowers, silken pillows—there was none of that here.

The lower half of the body was hidden in a black coverlet. Had they taken off her shoes?

Yes. They were poor, they would need them for someone else. I stared as long as I could at the coverlet, but then curiosity led my gaze to her face.

I startled.

The skin was satiny smooth. The face, chiseled, chin firm and supple, as young as me. Coiffed in its three inches of stiff white, the face was whiter still, a touch of rose on her cheek. The lashes lay on her bluish lids like delicate spiders' webs, so long and black, I kept checking to be sure I'd seen them. Dark hairs stuck out of her coif at the temple—one, two. I had an urge to push them in for her with the silver crucifix that hung over her chest, a habit they all had. The line of her lips had been touched a pale pink. Her look of containment, of mockery, her full lips turned up a bit.

In my middle, I felt a squeeze of shuddering grief.

I'd never seen her before. What kind of nun? Gardener? Seamstress? Her name? There was a faint hint of muddy color embedded in the lines of her fingertips and under the sliver of nail. Sweet thing, she was so young, so alone. We shouldn't be upset with her for dying; we should stay with her in the night, she needed us.

Where were her parents?

I stole a glance at Em. Her eyes were closed. My knees hurt against the hard wood; time passed, minute by minute.

The nun's graceful nostrils were stiff as carved stone.

Wait, they moved.

I shook my head. My mind lunged.

PRAY.

From ever dying alone, away from anyone who truly loves me

God, spare me.

from dying where no one even knows my name

God, spare me.

from ever being a nun at all

God, spare me.

to make me realize that the only thing she ever did to me was die

God, spare me.

from thinking that raiding the kitchen will make this better

God, spare me.

Someone poked me in the back.

I'm spared! Jeanne D'Arc and Cats.

Oh, thank you God!

A few minutes later, I was curled up in my bed, under the blankets. I kept seeing her pink lips, maybe the only lipstick she'd ever worn; poor thing, dead so young.

We took turns for three days and nights. By the last night of the wake, we knew her name, Sister Germaine, and I thought I'd seen her small face in chapel.

At two a.m. we met by the stalls in the second-floor ladies' room. "When did she get sick?" "What killed her?" "Could we catch it?"

"OK," whispered Cats, "we have to move. One of us checks the parlor to see which nuns are there. Then we head for the kitchen."

We tiptoed down the stairs, one behind the other to the first floor, and hid behind a door.

"You, you're the smallest," Cats said, pointing to Jeanne D'Arc.

"Not on your life," said Jeanne.

"Look we can't all go," said Cats, "we need to know where Lionel is."

Jeanne D'Arc frowned.

"Okay, go back to bed."

She disappeared into the dark hall.

When she returned, she whispered, "Six nuns with the casket, Lionel's there."

"How about Mère?" Cats asked.

"No. Hermenegild, Cyril, Aloysius. I didn't know the others."

"Oh God," said Em.

"Sh," said Cats. "At least we know where Lionel is. Come on, one at a time. Janey, you be last."

Cats went around the corner, then the others, one by one keeping close. They were all into the kitchen when I heard a swish of footsteps. I flattened against the wall.

Six shadows breezed down the murky stairway, fully coiffed ghosts, skimming the polished stone. They disappeared for a minute so that I thought I might have dreamed them. But no, there they were in the band of light, entering the company parlor.

I bolted and pushed into the kitchen, panting, "Six new nuns into the wake. Lionel's on the move."

"Who?" choked Cats. She pulled a green can down from the shelf and pried open the lid.

"How should I know, it's black out there. They were like ghosts."

"Oooo," said Suze, shoving raisins into her mouth. I plunged my hand into the can. "Wait," Cats held my arm. "Not too many. They count 'em," she grinned.

The kitchen was large with high ceilings, stainless steel sinks, tall wooden cupboards, long closet doors, stone floors. It was amazingly warm. All the smells, the steam and bustling nuns were silent now and asleep. I looked at my friends' hungry eyes. As much as I craved a normal teenage life, I wouldn't know what to do with it now. The thrill of transgression muted any other feelings, the delicious freedom of stealing raisins in the middle of the night, and I hated raisins!

We munched, against the stainless-steel sideboard, Cats, Em, Suze, Jeanne, and me.

Em wandered to the pantry and opened the door. "Here, here," she said, "corn meal, bran buds, wheat flour."

"See?" I said, "horse food."

We all turned toward a sound coming from outside. A soft, high-pitched hoot.

"Get me out," said Jeanne D'Arc, heading for the door.

"Oh, no you don't, we'll get caught," said Cats, grabbing her arm.

The sound got louder. "Casper!" Suze pushed the thick old door, and it gave way with a rush of icy air. In walked the white cat. I dropped down to him. He swept my hand with both sides of his nose and then all our hands, stepping from side to side. He began a deep rumble-purring, his green eyes watchful. I held back respectfully as I picked him up, but he nestled against me.

"Someone must feed him here," said Cats, amused.

"The scullery nun?" said Suze. "Can you imagine?" The scullery nun was grumpy, but then, I would be too if my job was dishes.

"He comes in here on his own?" Jeanne D'Arc petted his head.

"Don't forget he can get out," said Em.

The cat leaped out of my arms and headed for the fridge, mewling. "He's going to wake them up," said Suze.

The thought of some nun feeding the cat in secret warmed my heart. I got him some milk.

Then we passed around the jug, gulping thirstily.

But Cats pushed into another cupboard. "Don't they hide sweets?" she grumbled. "Ugh, flour, oatmeal, nothing but horse-hay. Um, wait a minute."

She appeared with a large, squat jar of honey and placed it on the counter.

For a moment, we all gazed at the thick gold, glinting in the faint light. Then she unscrewed the lid and dipped a finger in. "Well, what do you know?" she said with glee, sucking on the tip of her index finger.

We gathered around, dipping into the rich, amber liquid, placing it shyly on our tongues.

"The nuns' nectar," exclaimed Suze, her voice deep and warm.

For a second, the drop of honey sat on my tongue. Unaccustomed to delight, taste buds, sluggish, I closed my mouth. The sharp sting of sweetness spread up the back of my throat and into my ears.

"This is the night the Lord hath made," Cats sang.

"This is the land of milk and honey," Em sang, doing a cha-cha. She and Suze cha-cha'd around the kitchen, dipping and singing as they went. Jeanne D'Arc plunged in too deep, then it dribbled down her arm.

"I'm drunk, I can't stop." Em licked her fingers.

I teased myself by darting my tongue in and out of the little pool in my hand. Bits of my hair got into it by mistake. I licked these strands too. Then somehow it escaped to my wrist, the hairs on my arm. Cats twirled around the jar like a nymph.

The door opened.

We gasped.

A nun stood in the doorway.

For an instant, I dismissed the gravity. Casper's hearty lapping was the only sound. I followed the strong lines of Sister Philippe's face and felt stabbed with admiration. I remembered in an instant the comfort of Hopkins. Her eyes were steely, yet full of tears. Her skin, a flushed high color, feverish, mournful. Then I looked around the kitchen and saw what she was seeing.

Drops and dribbles, long shiny, transparent designs of honey— all over the floor and stainless-steel surfaces. Cats' huge sticky glob at the tip of her chin. Jeanne D'Arc's upper lip. I rolled my tongue over the roof and sides of my mouth. We stood on sticky feet and watched Casper with envy. He looked at Philippe, unabashed. Then he walked to the door, sated and content, shaking his backside.

Philippe's eyes followed the cat. Still, she said nothing.

We all stood there.

Then Jeanne opened the door for Casper as if he were the chief offense. He sauntered out.

When Philippe still didn't speak, we all began to move at once. Em screwed the lid back on the honey jar and picked it up. Honey rolled down its side and in accusing drops onto the floor.

We stopped to watch the honey. The jar had been nearly full. There was barely half left.

Cats took the jar to the sink and ran water over it. The night hung suspended from her rinsing. I wet several washcloths and handed them out solemnly. And we began to wipe down.

Now here was something we knew! I was reminded of the great, white chalk souls the grade school nuns liked to draw for us on the blackboard and the sins they'd make with pencil erasers dipped in their spit, small dots for venial, huge balls for mortal sins. Then when the soul was riddled with sins, they'd take it to confession with a sweep of soft white chalk over the whole expanse.

We rinsed and wiped. Counters, sinks, floor, ourselves.

Philippe still said not a word, but with sorrowful eyes, willed our compulsion for wiping up the sweetness. It took a long time. My front and hair damp, I wiped the shining counter one last time.

Then Philippe opened the door and walked out.

We followed her as surely as if she'd commanded us.

At the last second, Cats went back and took the honey jar.

Chapter 8

November 19—Philippe

I should send them to bed and report them. But into my soul came Germaine's vibrant still life, with its amber honey jar and shining droplets of gold rolling down its sides.

Tonight, the girls found her honey.

I led them up the stairs to the parlor, turned on a lamp and sat down in a visitor's chair, my chest tight, heart thumping; Germaine's body, broken.

You are with Him now, with Him...oh my dear Germaine. What is it like to be with our Beloved?

I looked up. The girls were perched on the edges of their seats, rubbing the rug with their socks. I scanned their faces. Cats tried to hide the honey jar under the chair, but it was useless.

Now she held it in her lap; we had even more of a theft.

"It was the death, Sister," she blurted.

"That made you steal?"

"There's been so much silence," said Jeanne. "We've never raided the kitchen before, never even thought of it."

"So now, it's Sister Germaine's fault?" I asked, raising one eyebrow.

They looked bereft at that, Janey especially. There were dark circles under her eyes. We stared at each other. The mantel clock struck four a.m.

"We were talking in Latin class and Sœur Fiarcre got angry," said Janey.

"She wrote down our names on a piece of paper and put them in the casket," Jeanne whined.

"What?" I looked away to hide my surprise.

"To punish us," said Cats.

"To scare us," said Suze.

"I've never heard of such a thing," I said. "Did it work?"

They nodded. "Truly creepy," said Em.

I didn't condone such foolishness, nor could I side with the girls. "It was just a threat to make you behave," I offered.

"No, I saw the paper in the casket," said Jeanne.

"What would be the point of placing the names of sinners in a casket?" I straightened my veil.

They looked at me.

Then we smiled, tentative, shy, but beginning to trust. What could I say?

"The older sisters, you know—they have their ways. Still, that's no excuse for what you girls did."

They were so keyed up. I guessed no one had told them about Germaine, the real person who died. Oh, Claire, how could you die? And there's nowhere for my grief. Just now, I wanted so much to pour it out with the girls—to dance around the honey; to steal and lick it and let it run. I wanted to claim life in all its messiness right along with them!

Suddenly, I had a sense of her surrounding me, not the nun, Germaine, but a delicate girl named Claire Gagnon standing on the convent steps, suitcase in hand, her dark abundant hair falling to her shoulders, like mine—in fact, we could have been blood sisters. She'd given a full-on smile when the Portress introduced us. "We're going to be great friends," she'd whispered, and I smiled at that in the place where *great friendships* were taboo. Oh, these girls had no idea. I would so love to tell them about her.

"Sister," said Janey.

I startled. I'd been far away.

They sat patiently watching me.

"Go to bed," I told them.

Janey shook her head, a gesture of hopelessness. They wanted to know if I'd turn them in.

I let out all my breath. "Bring me the jar," I told Cats.

She brought it to me.

"Unscrew the lid, please, would you, dear?"

She gave a skeptical glance. I looked into the golden liquid and dipped my finger halfway in. I brought sweet honey to my lips. "Mmm," I tasted, "No wonder you were dancing!"

Chapter 9

Monday, November 21—Janey

Requiem in pace, dona eis requiem. There could be no burial on a Sunday. Monday in the early morning, we filed out of the chapel behind Sister Germaine's family, the pairs of nuns, then boarders, two by two. We proceeded to the grave, girls in blue uniforms, nuns in their everyday black. Thank God tonight our parents were coming to pick us up, that is, if Philippe hadn't turned us in. I had never craved my home more.

And yet once home, a strange desire would sometimes hover over me, craving quiet and the hush of prayer. That wasn't supposed to happen, and it confused me.

Cats walked beside me. "I'm sorry."

"It got to be too much," I whispered back.

"Philippe will tell, or she isn't much of a nun."

"Mmm," I said. "There's hope she won't."

"I got us into this mess. I can't believe we might spend Thanksgiving here."

"Sh. Give me some credit. We all ate the honey. Even Philippe."

"Mark my words, she'll turn us in."

Mère walked past us, sprucing girls' ties and straightening white collars. She wanted us to represent the school well with outsiders present. A few of us would be attending collation with Sœur Germaine's family. The rest would go back to class after the burial.

62

Later that day, most girls would be picked up for Thanksgiving break.

The line started to move. Ahead, the coffin was held up on the shoulders of eight men, four of them her brothers and father.

The nuns' graveyard was down at the base of the apple orchard and around to the side of the property. A deep hole had been opened among other scattered gravestones in the blessed ground, some old and askew. They lowered the coffin directly down inside the shaft by placing one end in first, then gently easing the other into place. Some of the men picked up shovels and poured the black earth in. I watched from the third tier of mourners, close enough for me. There were around forty nuns, ten members of Germaine's family including three small nieces and nephews, the whole school of girls.

We packed into the tight space after her poor mother, father, and brothers. Nuns came forward to take a turn at the shovel. Philippe took hers with stunned round eyes. She never stopped to acknowledge us as though we were an illusion. We could hear the quiet hum of traffic from the road beyond the chain link fence; a sniff and a sob here and there; the dull slapping sound of the dirt against wood and then dirt against dirt. No one prayed or sang, and the silence was cacophony.

Finally, Father Girard pulled up his breviary from a pocket in his robes. "O Lord Jesus Christ, King of Glory," he prayed, "deliver the soul of the faithful departed, Sœur Germaine de Jesu, from the pains of hell and the bottomless pit; deliver her from the lion's mouth, that hell swallow her not up, that she fall not into darkness, but let the holy standard-bearer, Michael bring her into that holy light which You promised of old to Abraham and to his seed; we beseech You, O Lord, that Your mercy, which we implore may benefit the soul of Sœur Germaine and that by your goodness, she may obtain eternal companionship with Him in whom she hoped."

Our strong Catholic prayer. You needed courage to hear it.

We made our way up the hill then, and the five of us found each other and walked quietly. The others were buoyant with freedom and chattered for the first time in days.

We went to Philippe's classroom where she passed out quizzes that took up the whole time. Her eyes were red-rimmed and when she finally used her voice to give us instructions, it was low and husky. I calculated that she was the same age as Sister Germaine; they might have been in Novitiate together.

At recreation, we stood together under the trees. Had Philippe told? And who was the dead nun, really? We'd attended the wake, the funeral and the burial and still knew nothing about her. I sat back on our wide wooden swing, there were two suspended from the trees. These were coveted—and today the long glide through the breeze felt like new life. Em joined in on the other and we sang out as we often did, *Swing Low, Sweet Chariot.*

A Junior student came running toward us. Mère wanted all five of us in her office. "Now," she nodded.

I hated her smug little grin.

Suze pulled in her lips; Cats said, "Well come on, let's get it over with." We jumped off the swings into the leaves. And Jeanne stepped on the Junior's foot as we brushed past her.

In the office, Sister Philippe sat in a straight-backed chair next to Mère at her desk, her hands folded calmly on the large brown blotter. Her fountain pen sat at the ready in its metal holder.

"Mes chère filles, you enjoyed our finest nectar. And left very little for us."

Of course, Philippe had told.

A frisson of fear ran up my spine. I folded my arms; Cats' chin jutted out in defiance. I touched her elbow. We had to be careful, or we'd never get out of here again.

"Sœur Philippe tells me you were pushed to the brink by recent events." Mère's eyebrows went up.

We all nodded. Where was she going with this?

Philippe sat ramrod, not moving. But her eyes on us were kind.

"You have stolen what was not yours. Reparations must be made. I fail to see what stealing food has to do with waking a servant who has gone to her God."

No one spoke.

"What worries me the most about what you did was not so much the desire for fun amid sorrow—but that you have been disrespectful. Our Sister was no one to you, expendable."

"We didn't think that," blurted Jeanne.

"Your actions prove that you did," said Mère sadly. "You wanted release, you got it. Sister was never even real to you, nor was our mourning. That was selfish and thoughtless."

Cats lowered her head.

I took a breath. "Mère, really we were told nothing about her."

"Be that as it may, you now will learn. Sœur Philippe has convinced me that she has a consequence for you that befits the crime of, well, your honey fête! Mère glanced downward, covering her mouth with her hand.

She'd had her own raids in her day! We looked at each other.

"We've arranged your rides for tomorrow morning," said Mère. "You'll forfeit going home tonight because we need you to help Sister with a project, one that will prove instructive. Now, see to your packing," she said, indicating the door. "And consider yourselves fortunate that your teacher was thinking on her feet today. This twenty-four-hour punishment is not what I had in mind but will be efficacious enough for your souls."

Leaning out the study hall window, we watched cars come and go. Though we were lucky to be going home at all, I mourned the loss of even one night. The first night home on a holiday was my favorite—bursting into the kitchen and dancing to my sister Gloria's forty-fives; Maman, mashing the potatoes in our thick crockery bowl, an apron over her house dress, her lovely, tired warmth. Dad poured his beer and twirled Maman around in a close cheek to cheek; my grandmother's happy face, full of lines and smiles; the kitchen smells of cherry pipe tobacco; toast and tea.

When everyone who was being picked up had gone and we'd eaten supper, the girls who lived too far away settled in the course, knitting, and playing games. We sat around one of the tables and waited. "At least you're not giving up all your dates," said Cats.

"Larry will be furious," said Emilie. "He has such a temper." She shook her head fondly.

"I'm not sure we like him," said Cats.

"Cats!" I said. "He's waiting for her, isn't he?"

Philippe appeared in the doorway, and I leaped up. The others looked rueful, worried, but excited too. Like the night in the kitchen, we followed her without a word, down the hall, around the corner. She turned back to be sure we were with her and blew through pursed lips as though exhaling. My God, she used to smoke?

She stopped in front of the cellar door. I'd always wanted to go down there but that was one rule we hadn't gotten up the nerve to break.

We felt a cold gust of bitter, moldy air. She shined the flashlight. We followed her, Suze, Jeanne D'Arc letting out a soft moan, Cats, Em and me. The rock walls were slick. Philippe wasn't carrying any cleaning implements. Cats whispered, "It's a dungeon down here."

We came to a door. Sister plunged her hand deep into her pocket, pulled out a key, fumbled with the lock and shoved it open.

The darkness and damp smells wafted over us; I felt myself shrinking, paint and turpentine.

Philippe disappeared inside.

We stayed crowded at the door.

This already felt like a punishment. I was shaking, the others looked gray. Philippe lit the lamps and suddenly the room bloomed with more light. There was color everywhere—all kinds, big and small canvases all along the walls. Philippe waved her hand to us to come in.

As shapes emerged, we saw, in one corner, a small black coal stove, in another, an oak drafting table, square on thick legs. All around, barrels of shiny, colored tiles, oranges, reds, greens, blues, yellows, and small pieces of colored glass glistening in the pale light.

Philippe cleared her throat. "Girls," she said in a calm, even voice, "this is where Sister Germaine worked."

"She painted?" said Cats.

"She made mosaics?" said Suze.

"I didn't know a nun could be an artist," I said.

"Don't they have to give that up?" said Jeanne.

I thought of all the ways we'd been so wrong in the last three days. We moved slowly around the room. I stared at an oil painting of a strong Jesus and his rough apostles.

"Gosh, she was the real thing," said Cats.

Here and there, tubes of oil paint, a bin of chalks, another of pencils, a wall rack for tools, a kiln. Our sounds of surprise echoed from the rock walls and wooden racks.

"See?" said Philippe in a low voice, shaking her head. "You didn't realize how special she was."

Time passed; I couldn't tell how much. And we girls exchanged surreptitious glances. Far from a punishment, this was a gift. And we tasted again, *sweet honey, God's mercy.*

Finally, Cats cleared her throat. "How could an artist of her caliber work in this bad light?"

"How long did she work down here?" I asked, gazing around the room.

"And us, clueless upstairs," said Suze.

The young face in its coif in the coffin wafted before me—a brilliant artist we'd jokingly called the dead nun. We hadn't known a thing about her, and we'd wasted little sorrow. She'd labored in this cramped room, covered in black, colorless herself, and out of bits of colored stone, the great city had not been so much captured as released. It was then I understood.

It was enough to feel shame, seeing her immense talent, discovered by all of us too late. She'd been such a warrior. She'd fought for her gifts, God's gifts, and found a way to express them through the understanding of Mère. And now a gift had been given to us as well.

"Girls," Philippe startled me. "Your job is to wrap the pieces to be moved tomorrow. Here are the materials. It might take us a while. And I shouldn't have to encourage complete care; go slowly and work together. I'll show you exactly what to do. And as we work, I'll tell you about Sister Germaine."

Philippe had arranged some brown paper wrapping and twine on one of the tables. She oversaw each transfer of canvas or mosaic to the table and the balancing and wrapping of it. We worked in teams. It was slow going, and there were many canvases.

"Where will they ship these?" asked Cats, tightening the twine around my finger on the top of one small piece.

"Saint Gregory's, Chicago. Saint Anselm's, New York. Saint Margaret's, Manville, Massachusetts," Philippe answered. "Other places too."

"Did Mère sell them?" asked Emilie.

"Gosh, I hope so," said Cats.

Philippe pushed her hair up under her coif with the end of her crucifix. "Mère has been selling them as they were completed for some time."

"It's important," I said. "She's an original and these must be seen!"

Philippe held down the paper while Cats wound the string on a canvas. "Our order will now be able to build a new school," she said. The corner of her eyes glistened.

Jeanne had wandered to a dark corner of the room. "Hey, come over here," she called.

She'd found a large bin and had begun to pull sketches toward her one at a time. I approached and saw lilies pass by, an olive branch, an eagle. We gathered around Jeanne. A serpent, keys, fish, a cross, a crown, a dove; symbols so familiar to us in our convent life. Then the sketches became less religious—bowls of fruit, vases of flowers, studies of the human body, wait, what?

Philippe joined us at the bin; her lips parted.

"Let me see," said Cats.

"I guess her early studies were not destroyed," Philippe spoke softly to herself. "My goodness, she studied, trained, apprenticed— she developed as an artist. It's astounding." She pooled the lamp light on them.

I watched her furrowed brow. How much was she going to let us see?

"It's okay, Sister," said Cats, "she would have needed to keep all her studies for reference, don't you think?"

"Yes," nodded Philippe.

"You're surprised they let her, right?" I asked.

She gave me a quick look. But, interested, she continued to peruse the studies.

"Oh my lord!" said Jeanne, her face turning red. A male nude leafed by, then a female, varied nude poses, one after another. I'd never seen actual pictures of a penis; it was hairier than I'd expected, smaller. It looked no more unnerving than an elbow. But there was something else that drew me. There was movement in these limbs. The forms, breasts, bellies were lovely, alive among the symbols of faith and the still-lifes. "Oh, look," one, or the other of us, kept exclaiming.

Her bodies were beautiful, the very body she herself had willingly covered in black and given to God.

Watching the sketches as they leafed by, I realized that Jesus had intended this body—made just like this, precisely like this. I gazed at the woman's round, full breasts, the man's muscular legs.

I took in the brilliance of colors all around the room, every bit of line and pattern; all of their meaning, and then, at Philippe's astonishing generosity towards us.

She was standing in lamplight, surrounded by darkness and shadows, looking wistfully at the sketches. She had the kind of face that depended, for its stabbing beauty, on bones.

We were all held in this moment.

Chapter 10

November 22—Philippe

The next morning, after the girls left, I went to the cellar alone. The darkness and smell of mold made me grip the railing and, head spinning, I fell backwards onto the step in sorrow. Mère had assured me that finishing the wrapping would help me to grieve. Mère had encouraged Germaine in this damp, unhealthy cellar. Why didn't she find a place for her upstairs with better light? *Unless she was hiding her.*

Of course she was hiding her. There were many reasons she would hide her; she couldn't do this for everyone; there must be many who would enjoy making art, but Germaine was a true artist, and contributing enormously to the Churches. Materials were expensive; but sales of the canvases took care of that. I sat there sweating, forcing the days backwards to when I was writing papers and yearning to see Germaine again, how I would count the days.

And her work, her glorious work. It explained why I was so drawn to her from the beginning—that she was in the world to make truth visible. And I was in the world to be a scholar and get at that truth another way.

I never made it to the cellar, but dragged myself up to my classroom, honey colored with the sunset streaming in. Lesson plans piled up untouched on my desk. I would have to turn on the lamp but no. I sifted through the ungraded essays, not seeing them.

Later, poised on the edge of my bed, the clock said 11:10. This convent was a well-oiled machine whose parts broke and were replaced without notice. The routine crushed me right now.

I pulled my small box out from under the bed, made of cedar, six by eight inches worth of personal possessions allowed after First Vows. I drew it to my nose and sniffed the cedar; the outside. In it was my own rosary—shiny white, each bead a tiny pearl egg. I fingered them and whispered the Gloria on the silvery medal in the middle. Next, I lifted the pink silk sachet to my lips, filled with Papa's roses. Incredible that the scent could still be strong. Mère had to approve these items, of course. No photos, but I did have a letter opener with a pearl handle. It felt light and smooth in my hand. Our letters came to us opened, so it was a keepsake. Tears sprang to just inside my eyelids and held there. I suppose I could ask my family to send me photos after final vows, but I think they'd make me too lonely.

The box was my sister Dodie's gift at my Clothing Ceremony, my only keepsake, lined in brown shiny fabric. At our celebratory tea, she'd whispered to me that she'd slipped my letter from Skip into the lining. I pictured her devilish smile cutting a secret space in the lining. With the letter opener, I slipped a thin paper out.

I should have gotten rid of it by now. What did it mean that I hadn't?

I unfolded the onion skin single page—slanted handwriting, plain, strong words.

Dear Maggie,

When you left, I didn't believe you would stay and prayed you wouldn't. I knew it was something you had to do, I didn't understand completely why, but in our final days together, I saw a confidence in you and a solidity that was only good. You know who you are. I wish that knowing could have made you mine.

I do genuinely respect your God, though I don't relish having him as a rival. It could be cool, if it didn't mean that I've lost you forever. I thought you would grow and discover that you do need to be with me after all. Couldn't you have us both somehow? As the months pass, I guess this is less and less a possibility.

But think of me, darling, and the simple joys of our world. It's not too late and I'm still waiting for you.

Love, Skip

The words blurred as I finished and quickly slipped the sheet into its hiding place. The lining, flush with the cover, was tacked at both ends. I lowered my face into my hands. Oh, my love.

What am I doing? Shouldn't I let him go? Shouldn't I want to?

The answer was no.

But if no, doesn't that mean I cannot remain a nun, should not take final vows?

I was still a woman with desires and needs; God had told the earliest people to offer their *first fruits*, not the rejects. I thought of my offering to Him as my *first fruits*—of a desirable woman, giving herself fully. But even as I loved Jesus so hard, my body remained tethered to the earth. Why did I break out all the time, hungry for freedom? Why hadn't I let Skip go?

I pushed the lining again with the letter opener. There was one more thin sheet of paper in there, a confession in my own hand. I should destroy that one now too. I slipped the box back under my bed and turned off the lamp.

After Sunday Mass, with most of the girls away, we headed for the basketball court.

Jacinta and I stretched and then ran laps. We were two teams of nuns playing by girls' rules—limited dribbling curtailing the freedom to break away with the ball. But we managed to sweat anyway and whoop and fight one another for it. Jacinta was in top form. Fiarcre on the other team shouldn't be able to play like that at her age, but she did with her thick limbs. We had on our colors—green team 1, red team 2—bibs over the front of our habits. Honestly, we should wear athletic shoes, our ankles twisted all the time in our nun-shoes, but nothing stopped us.

I was on the green team, ahead 6–2. My team had worked out a few plays. Passing the ball so often we spun the heads of team 2. I zoomed in and scored, shouting YES! Our faces, red and slick with sweat, made every trouble melt away. Our plays were working like a fine-tuned clock: why did this feel like a most important moment, in touch with myself, body and soul, for the first time in days? I didn't miss Germaine here with that stabbing ache. Here, I wanted Jacinta, Lucie, even Fiarcre.

Fiarcre. Did she really bury the girls' names in Germaine's casket? We chugged paper cups of water, standing by the fence, a rush and ebb of traffic below on the highway. Our team had won. It mattered to me, and it shouldn't. To Jacinta too, and it used to matter to Germaine. I looked at all of them catching breaths, drinking water.

"Sœur," I nodded to Fiarcre. "Walk with me."

She looked flustered but joined me climbing up the hill. "Did you really put students' names in Sister's casket?" I asked.

She narrowed her eyes. "Why?"

"Were you punishing them?"

She glowered. "We have to corral our girls. Mon Dieu, they all need to be taken down a peg."

"But your action was absurd, Sœur. It didn't achieve the desired result."

"Says who? And why not? The result will work on them now and forever. They'll think twice before they throw their weight around again."

"I doubt it. They didn't take it seriously."

"Maybe not, but that old method will work its magic, Sister, tried and true," she spit the words. "You'll learn."

"Magic?"

"Of course. You're still far too worldly if you can't grasp this. The line between life and death is thin."

"I don't follow you."

"The dead are all around us, watching us, helping us. Where is your faith, Sœur? We have no idea how these actions work their truth. We simply believe that they do."

I noticed a few hairs on her chin. Now that was something she hadn't bargained for. No tweezers here, the poor thing couldn't even pull them out. Dear Lord.

We reached the door to the course. I looked back at the grounds. The fall had been colder than usual, and the dry shrubs and grass sparkled with a tinge of frost, turning everything into a promise of the white mounds and shadows to come. *God's hand in everything.*

How awestruck Germaine had been by the world. "I will praise God's creation every second of my life," she'd say.

I reached my classroom and sat at the desk. The quizzes still sat in a pile, before me, my red pen. Next weekend, I would be in choir for the Clothing Ceremony—a new set of Postulants would take the veil. I'd only seen the ceremony from the inside when it was me, Germaine, Jacinta and the others. I could still hear the strong voice of the sponsor calling out our new names. "Germaine de Jesu." Beside me, she'd fallen on her face to prostrate herself before the altar. "Philippe de Marie."

I'd joined her on the cold marble floor.

Chapter 11

November 22, Thanksgiving—Janey

Dad drove holding the steering wheel lightly, taking my hand that rested on the car seat beside him. I watched the tall firs like soldiers in formation all the way down the convent drive, their tops bowed over in the wind. My father and I never needed to make conversation. His patience and calm were traits I craved. He was a perfectly proportioned small athlete, wide shoulders and strong arms. "How've you been, love?"

"Starving." I winced.

"Your mother's thawing the turkey. And she made ragout for tonight!"

I threw open the window and breathed the air. "How's the new garage coming along?"

"I could use your help." He gave a teasing glance.

He saw my lips part. "Just kidding, sweetheart."

"And Michael," I said.

"He called. He'll be over. He's a good lad, that one."

"I can't believe he still wants to date me when I'm stuck in a prison."

"You're a pretty special young lady," said Dad. "So how come they made you stay the night?"

I told him everything. He gave a distasteful frown at the wake, laughed with glee when he heard we had raided the kitchen, licked his lips over the honey. He tried to lecture me about patience, obedience to rules and getting out soon. But I was already comforted.

I watched the blur of trees out the window. I'd lost a day, but there were three more; tomorrow, Thanksgiving, then Friday for the lighting of the Boston Common, Saturday to Sunday afternoon when he'd drive me back – a lot of driving, but it was worth it to him, he said. It meant our time together, conversation and silence.

At home Mama would wash my clothes; I'd fill up on her good food, play cards with my little sister, Gloria; tease my funny dear little grandmother, Memère; sleep in my own bed. Michael, maybe every evening. I was never sure he'd still be there, couldn't imagine what it was like for him to hold onto me. But right now, I pushed that thought aside.

As Dad turned the car off the highway into our town, he asked about the young nun who died. "We read a detailed obit about her in the paper. Her art has gone all the way to the Vatican! And we didn't know a thing about her."

"I know, Dad. Our job last night was to wrap the remaining paintings to be shipped. No one knew until now."

"Why keep her a secret?"

"I guess she wanted it that way," I shrugged.

"Now she's immune to the sin of pride." He gave a soft laugh.

I watched the familiar houses slip by out the car window and heard, "*Love's a wish, a smile like yours, that your heart could be mine...*"

Suddenly I could see Michael, clear as day in front of me. Six foot three, football player with wide shoulders, deep set eyes, long-ish black hair. If I closed my eyes, I could almost remember the woodsmoke in his flannel shirts, his minty kisses.

Our car turned up our street lined with huge oak trees, their old roots breaking up the sidewalks. It pulled to the curb in front of our tenement between the two oaks with fat branches that reached out to us like hugging arms.

I walked through the kitchen door. There was our wooden table, cracked and smooth, the bumpy linoleum floor with red diamonds, wallpaper of the anemic fruits. The curve of the banana, the oval apple, the whole floor a bit slanted. Out the back windows, Dad's garden ending at a high stone wall, against which his climbing roses grew in the summer months. I caught a whiff of morning toast and vanilla pipe tobacco. "Maman, I'm home!"

"Janelle," she called from the cellar. "Throw me down the stairs—the key, eh?"

I smiled. Maman's French phrases, translated.

The key to her canned goods closet hung by the door. I tossed it down to her. Turning into the living room I realized that our baby grand piano swallowed all the space; Memère was sitting in her favorite stuffed chair. I lifted her by her hands and wrapped her in my arms. Her thin, now white braids wound around her small head and made me sigh. I'd thrown my books and bag on the couch. The bedroom I shared with Gloria and Memère was off to the right, my parents' small bedroom next to it.

Maman came up carrying laundry. She put it down. "I thought this day would never come," she said. "Bien, let me look at you."

She held me by the shoulders. "Come on, I've made you ragout." She looked around at my stuff piled on the couch. Hands on her hips, "I want you to dump all your stuff, *mon chou*, and make all the messes you want!"

Gloria came in, kissed my cheek and flew to the record player to start a 45: "Who put the bop in the bop sh bop sh bop?" We did the frog around the living room.

The cornices over the windows were lined with ceramic statues and school pictures. Dad had built them, and he'd made the cabinet across the room that housed the new television. Inside those dark doors you could imagine anything—Boris Karloff, Gunsmoke. "How long are you home for?" Gloria danced around me. "How many times did you lose your Excellence Pin?"

Eleven years old, she had long straight brown hair that she swept up in a ponytail. The kettle whistled. The faucet whooshed. Memère clapped to the music.

I went into the bedroom and took off my uniform, pulling on a top and pants. Maybe I should put on a bra? I sat very still on the edge of the bed. For the first few hours home, I always wandered around lost. I let down my guard and would catch a cold. My craving for the hush, the long, dark halls had invaded my bones.

Maman called us to dinner—Gloria, Memère, Mom, Dad and me around our wooden table. Hardened bread dough filled the table's cracks like a series of veins. Maman rushed around, her dark hair thick in waves, treating me like a royal guest.

"Janey, tell," her favorite opener. "I spoke with Mrs. Devine and she says, well I think they got in trouble with Head Honcho. And with that new teacher, the lovely one. And I says, it's not a surprise, is it? They're just tired of it all. I just hope it wasn't too too bad, Janey, because you're almost out now."

I was about to tell them about Fiarcre and the names in the casket and about Sister Germaine's art when I heard Michael's GTO pull in the drive. And then in a beat, he was filling the doorway.

His dark hair fell into his laughing eyes. I could tell he'd been lifting weights. His arms bulged in his long-sleeved shirt. I stood up and went to him. "Oh, come in," I took his fingers in mine.

"Hi," I said and led him to the table. I was aware of my flurry of excitement. His face, lit from inside with pleasure, he sniffed when he couldn't contain it.

He shook Dad's hand, kissed Maman, hugged Gloria and Memère, then sprawled in a kitchen chair, his feet stretched out across the floor taking up all the tiny space. "You'll join us, young man." Maman disappeared into the pantry. She had her cupboards there, with papers and envelopes for bill paying, dishes and glasses and platters, calendars and lists.

She called to us as she prepared his plate. "Michael, how're your classes?"

"I'm pulling a 3.5," he called.

I gave a whistle.

We had a feast; Michael told stories about his frat brothers and I, about poor young Sr. Germaine. Still Maman was prudently not asking about the kitchen raid. She bustled around us, slicing hunks of apple pie and slipping cheese on the heaping plates. Michael and I both ate like escaped convicts, smiling, gulping and complimenting the food, then without talking about it, we stood up.

I hugged my parents. Michael held the door. We stepped into a light rain and drove out just as the streetlights came on. He reached and touched my hair, settled back in the seat with one hand on the wheel.

"I'm out!" I rolled down the window and drizzle whipped in.

"Boss hair, Kid—told you to grow it, I love the new hair."

We drove onto the highway. "Thank you!" I yelled into the blowing night, "HELLO WORLD, HELLO TO YOU, HELLO!" I threw back my head. I pinned back my bangs with bobby pins. One fell out immediately and he started a stash for me in his pocket.

He flicked a switch. The radio boomed on, and we swayed, shouting "my boyfriend's back and there's gonna be trouble, hey la, hey la..." We forgot to ask each other where we were going. It didn't matter. The new highway had been built in tiers and curves, sometimes four roads twisting to their destinations, one on top of the other. The lights of these snake-roads flashed in the slick wet of the streets, red and yellow streaks and dots, flickering and turning.

We hummed and bounced, "Let's twist again! like we did last summer."

The car purred; wet night air poured in the windows. "Rabbit's foot!" I shouted and swung it, hanging from the mirror, had sent it to him in a letter. "My letters are getting out!! Denises, I hug you," I sang.

"Where d'you want to go?" he called out above the drums. We were dripping, both of us, and we rolled up the windows.

"Again, I want to do it again," I sang, and he pulled a U-turn and went back the way we'd come. And so we did it again in the cold night rain. He pulled me to him across the seat, one arm holding me while he steered with the other hand. My heart flew with the car. It was almost worth being so confined at school to feel this freedom.

He pulled the car into our favorite parking space that overlooked the beach.

The darkness was like an inky mouth with tiny white teeth of light, miles offshore.

I studied his full lips in the dark, smelled his earthy scent. He dug in his pocket and pulled out a bobby pin, fastened the bangs out of my eyes.

"No offense, Janey, but I think you'd make a lousy nun."

How was he so sure?

The muscle in his cheek quivered. He searched my face, his eyes pleading, not with need, but desire. Suddenly the reedy chant wound its longing in my head. I brushed the sound aside and then the artist nun, dead so young, and the incense at Mass, and did we have a choice?

Wasn't it all seductive?

He leaned in and kissed me, a tender question.

I pulled away a little.

"What?" he whispered.

"It's just, there was a scary priest brought in and he told us our bodies could, would, lead us to sin."

"Says who?" He slipped his hand inside my blouse, finding the bare skin of my breast.

"Hey!" he laughed, impressed. "Free as a bird."

I laughed too. "I don't wear it there, forgot to put it on. It's my little rebellion they'll never find out."

"About your body..." he whispered. He pulled me closer, moving his hand like a gentle question. And I was inside this skin. There was sin but this was not it.

We kissed until we couldn't breathe. I could never be afraid of him, even with all the warnings. I wouldn't see him for months. I squeezed my toes in my shoe tips trying to get control over my feelings.

I pulled away.

He was tender even then and did not press. He took shuddering breaths, holding on to me, loose-limbed.

"I want you home," he said, gently.

"Michael..."

"I think about you all the time," he said. "Do you think about me?"

"All the time. Just not in chapel! My life there is so bizarre."

I watched the froth of waves catch the cold moonlight along the shore.

"Janey, look at me," he said, in a tired husky voice. He held me away. "You don't want to become a nun, do you?"

I let my breath all the way out. I hungered for God. But I didn't hear Him calling me to be a nun. I loved the stained-glass windows, the geometric pools of light, the silence, the Mystery.

"When I'm there, it's hard to know what's real," I said.

He kissed me, his feelings all poured out, his arms holding me close.

"Me," he said. "I'm what's real."

Chapter 12

November 25, The Clothing Ceremony—Philippe

Mother Superior processed down the center aisle of the Sorrows' chapel. She carried a silver cross, her face and the wisps of hair that escaped her coif, white as snow. A bride followed her in a gown of lace tulle that outlined her curves and through a starry veil, her black hair shone, long, loose and free. Another bride streamed down the aisle, tipsy in high heels, and another, weaving, six in all, graceful in their bridal finery -- tulle or satin -- beaded, seed-pearled, long veils as wispy and fragile as spiders' webs. From up in the choir loft, I closed my eyes and remembered my own gown, sewn by Dodie for First Vows, a slender fitting silk with high neck and regal train.

Sœur Robert lifted her hand. We were five nuns and our full-bodied chant spun over the heads of visitors below. I risked a look with Jacinta, her soft gaze. The brides faced the altar side by side, their backs to the congregation. The Bishop regarded them while his acolytes removed his golden mitre. He lifted the aspergium and blessed the brides with Holy Water. Two priests flanked him and others milled about swinging incense, or standing at attention by the tall burning candles. Mère stood sentinel from the side altar, her elegant features wide open in joy.

Our chant eased to a long note of conclusion.

The Bishop intoned, "Qu'est-ce que vous voulez? What do you seek?"

The brides fell to their knees, their sponsor nuns fussing with the gowns as they went down.

A murmur rippled through the congregation. My throat tightened.

"I seek grace and the habit of *Les Sœurs de Douleurs de Marie*," the women said in a unison French, lilting and musical. "I seek to renounce the world and all its snares; to follow Christ, to study His Holy word; and to take the vows: obéissance, de chasteté, de pauvreté – obedience, chastity, poverty."

Incense stung my eyes; it rose into the choir loft in burnt, pungent clouds.

The Bishop slipped a gold ring on each bride's fourth finger. The *All- seeing- Eye of God* with its curly eyelashes stared from a painting above the altar. I glanced down at my ring.

A light fell through the stained glass windows in blocks of pale color over the brides, the families in the pews, the three altars with their lilies and feathery greens.

A thick pile of black habits had been placed before the Statue of Mary altar. With deliberate gait, the Bishop moved to the pile and sprinkled it with holy water. The habits had been sewn by sponsors who came forward now to usher the brides through the side door.

My hand went to my coif. It was time for the cutting of their hair. A lump in my throat, I remembered standing in white under garments, our downy tufts falling to the floor; Claire's and my jet black, Jeanette's blond, Jacinta's carrot red– thick, soft piles around our feet. Our breasts were bound with long flat cloths, inner white garments pulled over heads, black habits, coifs cinched tight. *Couldn't you have us both somehow?* whispers Skip.

I float away.

I'm in a scorching hot field with two sisters. We keep silence while the rushing river sings. We pitch hay into a wagon. Noon. We kneel and sing Nones, our lone voice in the field. We walk to the shade of the woods carrying satchels, hungry, hot. Crusts of bread and cheese. We lie on the river bank, a pine needle carpet, breviaries untouched. Burning hot.

Slowly, I unbutton my habit. I remove my work boots, stockings. Casually, my sisters follow. We release the pins of veils, pull off the frontispiece, unwind the wimple, remove the coif, then pull the habit up and over our heads – then inner tunic, peeling, unwrapping. We expose our skin, remove undergarments until we stand – breasts, bellies, mounds of soft hair... red-gold and dark brown, faded tans of bygone summers, strong young limbs.

I enter the pool, slip all the way under, cool clear water over my skin, teeth and tongue. My beloved God is in everything. Pure water and smooth stone--

"WHEN YOU WERE YOUNG," called the Bishop. I startled.

"You could go where you wished, but now you will be led where you do not wish to go." Jesus' words to Peter.

The new novices had returned to the altar. The Bishop held a thatch of ropes over his arm and proceeded to tie one around the first nun's waist. Called a cincture. My eyes tightened. He pulled the rope around a thick waist, surrounded a tiny one, down the line.

"Name this nun," the Bishop said.

"Sœur Edouard du Sacré Coeur," said the sponsor, pinning the white veil to her novice's wimple. The novice fell on her face before the altar. Again, "Appelez cette réligieuse!" The second nun's sponsor said her new name and she fell. Like bowling pins, they each fell in turn, one by one.

Now we chanted: *Requiem aeternam, dona eis Requiem* while they were covered, waist down, in the palls that would shield them in death.

Brides of Christ, dying to self, offered, set apart from the world.

I held my wet cheeks. The chanting stopped.

A smoky silence ascended, heavy with cloying lilies, an effusion of smells.

The holy men bowed and recessed. The people stood in the lingering incense.

The altar boys extinguished the candles, the sanctuary candle burned on in its flaming presence.

Blocks of honey colored light streamed through the stained glass. Nuns filed out of the loft, everyone out of the chapel. The Novices stayed still, and I with them.

The line of new nuns remained, prostrated before the altar, legs straight out, foreheads, noses, flat against the stone, new nun-shoes peeking out from under the palls. I joined them in my heart, arms outstretched in the form of a cross, majestic black birds flying in formation on their journey to God.

Chapter 13

November 26, Feast of Christ the King—Janey

On Sunday afternoon, Dad drove me back to school. We'd had a luscious Thanksgiving with family all around and I'd gone out with Michael a lot. Dad would worry if he knew Michael and I parked at Horse Neck Beach. I turned eighteen, though, in June. I leaned my forehead on the cold window. The colors of trees and shrubs merged in a liquid line that washed along my thoughts. Michael with his hair swept back by the wind, the highway twisting its curves and tiers. I rolled down the window to remember more. His lips, my immediacy, the stirrings of my body's mystery, *deep down things*. The vibrations of the old guitar Michael lugged around everywhere; the songs he was writing. *It was all honey.*

"Cold, love," Dad shivered.

"Sorry," I said, cranking the window back up.

We passed a brown-green field; there was no snow yet this season. I thought of Philippe by her classroom window, gazing out at the orchard, collecting strength.

"*Landscape plotted and pieced*," I said aloud to the fields—"*fold, fallow and plough.*"

"What?" Dad smiled, his eyes never leaving the road.

"My favorite poet."

His gray eyes stared straight ahead. "Say more."

I watched the shine of his head, his pensive frown. "Gerard Manley Hopkins!

And for all this, Nature is never spent. There lives the dearest freshness deep down things..."

"Wonderful," he said, as he turned the car into the drive toward the statue of the Virgin.

As we rounded the immense figure of Mary, I noticed a folded piece of paper stuck between her two stone fingers, way up as high as the fir trees.

"Dad, look," I pointed up.

He peered up then eased the car to the curb at the front.

We walked toward the statue, hand in hand. "It's a special intention," I said.

"A what?"

"A written request to God."

"Isn't that nice. Who reads them?" he asked.

"God," I said, and we laughed.

"He'll have to send an angel flying up there to get it."

"Well, somebody's angel climbed up and put it there."

We continued to stare at the folded note in the waning light.

"That's the Virgin I'm climbing on a ladder to crown on the first of May, Mary's day. They'll all sing, *Mother at thy feet is kneeling*, and I'll go up the ladder."

The Virgin had a great marble head, and a long thin nose.

Dad shielded his eyes. "Have you ever written God a note?"

"No, the nuns write them."

"If you did, what would you ask for?"

I could hear worry.

"A clear message about what to be," I said. "Like the nuns get. Like a call."

"Hmmm," he said. "But is their call always so clear?"

We headed for the convent steps. He put his arm around me. "God has His ways, Janey. He's guiding you, don't fuss so much."

He turned back to the statue and shielded his eyes from the sun. "They actually make you climb a ladder and stick a crown up there? In front of everyone?" He shook his head in affection.

"It's an honor."

He hugged me. "They'd better have a strong, safe ladder. Will they let us come?"

"We can ask."

I waved and watched him walk to the car, his strong wiry legs in his Sunday slacks.

Dad's family was Baptist. He'd converted to Catholicism for Maman and thought of the nuns as benevolent angels in charge of my bright future. He missed me and preferred I be in high school at home, but he let Maman decide. Maman was a faithful, stalwart Roman Catholic.

As I was growing up with the nuns, Dad often told me that God was everywhere and in everything. His own parents were extremely religious, their life lived around their Baptist church community.

Dad never talked much but instead gave us his gorgeous tenor voice. It was what I missed most about home; *Danny Boy, Where'er You Walk, When the Roses Bloom*. His slim, fit body, quick moves contained thoughts and words like the bits of gems he worked into the rings he made as a jeweler, welding them together into things of beauty by the light he wore around his head, fusing them and bending their shapes. There were trays in his jewelry shop that clinked with these fine, filigree pieces and thick, heavy school rings with cloudy stones.

Once everyone had returned, after a light supper, we gathered in the course. Sunday evenings were Showtime! We had pianists to accompany and willing singers and actors. Our skits were legendary, and the nuns let our creativity fly as far as they could. Tonight, some of us had practiced a scene from the new musical, *Oliver*. When it came time for me to sing the solo *Where is Love?* I knelt on one knee and sang it with all my heart. I'd been asking many questions this year; this question belonged to us all. It became the theme song we all sang together, and no skit-night happened without it from then on.

Then, Notes with Lionel. She lined out the events of the spring semester toward our graduation on June 1st. Roller Palace, a play to prepare. The Seventy Fifth Anniversary of the school, called Conventum, on April 15th; Perpetual Vows for the Seniors along with the May Day crowning of the Virgin; and the very first Academie Senior prom. Lionel explained what had been decided by the faculty.

Why plan so soon? I thought. But the nuns were nothing if not planners. The day girls had found a venue—The Holiday Inn. Couples would come to the convent to introduce their dates to the nuns in a receiving line.

No.

Michael in a receiving line with nuns? How would I do that?

I was not going to the prom.

Chapter 14

December 8, Immaculate Conception—Philippe

On the feast of the Immaculate Conception of Mary, a Tuesday, I slashed the film of ice on top of my pitcher of water with my toothbrush. In the frigid air, the prostrated new Novices flew like black larks in my mind; Germaine, Jacinta and me, side by side before the altar. Germaine and her musical laughter.

I splashed icy water on my face and washed with the brown cloth, shivering. What would Skip think if he knew? My gentle Skip with his patience. I mustn't take final vows in this state. I'd written down what Mère would want me to confess if she knew—that time at the Motherhouse. But I had not confessed to Père. Because God knows I didn't commit a sin by that river. We were burning up, working hard, being human.

Then there was Skip. I had not let him go.

Immaculate Conception Mass. The boarders in their blue uniforms ahead, nuns together behind them. I knelt writhing in my habit, itchy and tense. Germaine, dead; my master's degree on hold.

Final Vows to be taken soon. I'd been in the convent now for four years. My vows felt cracked. I bowed my head over folded fingers, not in my old Novice pew of course, but this chapel was known; the space enveloped and began to calm me.

"Lord dear Jesus, I beg you to bless and keep Germaine. She believed with all her soul. Help me to become the nun she was."

Disbelief that she was dead still shot through my veins, *the dearest freshness deep down things.*

I'd been gone from here, but the celebrant was the same stocky, gray-haired priest.

Communion filled me with the tangible Holy Presence, beyond my conscious mind. We chanted the same unison prayers and responses. Our voices threaded the space with power and tenderness. Full tone and long lines gave visceral, physical proof that our whole was more than a single voice.

That evening, I was more able to focus, correcting papers in the pool of light at my desk, the rest of the classroom in shadow. I gave myself to the task. At least I was hitting my stride with the teaching and most of all, the girls. We'd formed a bond, another transgression to sort out before vows. They so wanted real poetry, full of beauty and spirit. And I was giving it to them.

"Excuse me, Sœur." Janey stood in the doorway. That pin-straight dark blond hair.

I continued marking the test. My coif pinched my chin as I leaned over it.

"Sœur."

I studied her slim waist, long neck. She reminded me of a llama.

She walked into the room toward her own desk. "May I ask you a question?"

My red pen darted in and out of the words. When I looked up, I saw that she was blushing.

"I, um, I'm having a problem with the Trinity."

"Yes, Janey. We all have problems with the Trinity." I sighed my perpetual sigh.

"Mine is with the second Person."

"Jesus? But He's the easiest."

She shrugged.

"Do you have permission to be here?" I asked.

"Sort of."

"Yes, well?"

"I told Sœur that I forgot my book."

"And did you?"

"To be honest, no," she plunged. "I have to give a talk and Sœur is insisting it be on the Trinity." She moved from foot to foot with her words. "It's so abstract I can't get anywhere with it, and I need to know more about the Christ Hopkins talks about in his poems. Like, '*he sings in thousands of eyes and men's faces.*'" She placed her hands on the edge of my desk.

I glanced down at the test paper. My corrections were like the tracks of a tiny, bleeding bird.

"The Trinity is doctrine, Janey, fact. Three Persons, one God. Seems a thorny subject for a class."

"Sodality. I'm Prefect. I'm supposed to run the meetings."

"I never had a chance to be in Sodality," I mused.

"We take Perpetual Vows in the spring."

"Forever vows? Really?" I knew nothing about these girls. That they took lifetime vows, so that even if they didn't enter the convent— "Wait, you all take them?"

"It's frowned on if you don't."

"Hmmm."

"I don't understand the Trinity at all." She raked her bangs with her fingers.

"Well," I said, "the persons of the Trinity exist and do their work without your understanding. Your job is to believe."

Her eyes sparked. "Do I have to believe everything the Church says about God?"

"Yes. That is obedience."

"But the Trinity is so abstract. It's just out there, it has nothing to do with me."

"No," I said, "you're wrong. The Trinity is about love and that has everything to do with you. It's the Father loving the Son in a whole universe of stars and planets and life forms, culminating in you and me. And the Son loving the Father in all of His creative genius."

"That's fine if you're a nun," she shrugged.

"NO. The love between the Father and the Son is so personal that the Love *is* a Person, the Holy Ghost. And we're all called to love." I stood up. "In relationships just like that—giving and receiving and full of hope."

Janey's eyes were on me; she was listening.

"God made you out of *Himself*," I continued. "So you know all about creating and enjoying. What remains is for you to find your true self. And that has everything to do with God."

"Maybe for you." She lifted her chin.

"For all of us."

I turned to my bookshelf. "Here, Father Hopkins' sermons. The one on page 13 will help."

"Oh," she said, "thank you."

She took the book and headed for the door. Then she turned back. "Jesus is not in sermons. He's not in the doctrines." Her brown eyes widened. "They're just a bunch of words and rules. I need for Him to be real. I need for Him to make a difference in my life."

I sat back down. "I know."

Janey came toward me. "But I thought..."

"Do you think I *have* God?" I said quietly, "Do you think I always feel Him?"

"I thought nuns did."

"No."

"But."

"Janey, no. None of us knows, completely with the intellect, for sure."

Janey's lips parted. "If we were sure, we wouldn't need faith."

"Correct. But it's not blind faith. It's faith supported by, well...*the dearest freshness deep down things.*"

Chapter 15

December, Christmas 1964—Janey

We sat in study hall, Lionel at the back of the room. I knocked the wooden gavel, a hollow sound against the block. There were my friends—forty in all, eyes on me. I had run for class President last spring during our class elections, but that honor had gone to Suze.

Sodality went to the candidate who came in second, me. The nun who had been moderator at the time was Luce, crazy and warm—but she'd been replaced by Lionel. Just my luck.

"Janey," Lionel called from the back row, "read us the Seniors' Perpetual Vows."

I looked at her stiff mouth. This was a student-run club, but she'd taken over the meetings to preach, just like at Notes. At least she'd let me off the Trinity talk. That would take place after Christmas. Today, she was giving me ten minutes to discuss the Perpetual vows Seniors would take in the spring.

"Over at St. Patrick's, Sodalists get to sort clothing and blankets to send to soldiers in Vietnam," Emilie had told me. "There's a Sodality conference this year in New York too."

Naturally, the Academie chapter had never been allowed to do these worldly things.

"I'm going to argue for us to do at least ONE real service," I told my friends when they elected me. And that was not going well at all.

"Today," I said, "we'll discuss what it means to make a vow."

My voice sounded strong. I knew the vows were supposed to help us to be more intense Catholics. But we needed something else from them if we were to make them at all.

"We each have one life to spend, like an allowance," I said. "We decide for ourselves how to spend it, and no one can do it for us."

"You're using a monetary image?" Lionel called in her scratchy voice, "for a life of devotion?"

"It just came to me."

Lionel thrust out her lower lip.

I cleared my throat. "Please, Sister," I said. "It's important that we first look at what it means to make a lifetime vow."

Cats' eyes bulged. Suze smiled.

"We intend to promise," I rushed on. "As soldiers of Christ, we want to be ready when we face the moral wrongs of the world."

"You mean evil, why don't you say evil?" demanded Lionel.

"We want to give ourselves to others. Prayer is our sword and doctrine, our compass. But I believe it would help us to read some great contemporary minds next semester. Say, perhaps, Dag Hammarskjold's great work, *Markings*?"

Lionel jumped up. "Janey, read the duties as written: Daily Mass," she emphasized each syllable, "recitation of the Rosary, daily examination of conscience —"

"I will," I said, chin in hands. "But —"

"I command you to read us the Sodalists' Perpetual Vows or I will take over this meeting!"

"Please, Sister, "Mass every day for the rest of our lives? We can't promise that, a lifetime vow is grave. We're not in a position to make that vow."

"That is enough. This meeting is adjourned."

"Here we go," muttered Cats.

"But Sister," I argued, "is it not my job to chair this meeting? Let us just reflect for today. If we're not careful, we'll follow each other into the vows like sheep."

By now she was standing at my desk, our faces were close.

"The Sodality of Our Lady (*Congregationes seu sodalitates B. Mariæ*) is a Roman Catholic Marian Society founded in 1563 by a young Belgian Jesuit, Jean Leunis. Have you not studied this, Janelle? Deeply devoted to The Blessed Virgin, he wished to establish for young boys, a lay group that would promise a life of piety."

"See? Just for the boys!" I said.

She waved me off. "Later on, Sodalities would be established for particular groups in society." She spit the list. "Priests, Noblemen and Women, Merchants, Laborers, Clerks, the Married, the Unmarried and the Soldiers." She nodded emphatically. "There, now you know the dignity of the society you wish to degrade."

She took my elbow and guided me out the door. Cats wrinkled her forehead.

"Sister, a vow is holy," I protested. "We're young. What if we break it?"

"And what if our Sodalists go out into the world without their vows? They will be lost!"

"But that's not what I mean, Sister," I turned in the doorway. "I want to live for Christ. I just can't promise until I know myself better. I don't want to make an empty vow. I've been asked to be a leader and I'm telling you, none of the other girls are ready either."

"You're speaking for other girls' souls? You think you know everything."

"I just told you; I don't know ANYTHING. People all follow one another and don't think for themselves. And that's exactly what's wrong with the Church!"

"Blasphemy!"

We'd reached Mère's office and stood facing each other. Mère lifted her head from her papers.

"She's a heretic!" Red-faced Lionel thrust a finger at me.

Mère gave me a hard look.

Lionel rushed on while Mère stood up, her arms folded under her frontispiece.

"Janelle claims that our Seniors are not in a position to make Perpetual vows! And other blasphemous ideas."

"Now, now, Sœur." She was sober yet interested. "Leave us, Sœur Lionel."

"Well, I must explain—" she sputtered.

Mère stared at the door. Lionel stormed out.

"That is enough, Janey." Mère's spirit leapt with her words. "You are headstrong, but your ideas are often heartfelt. You must find a way to work with Sœur. And your Excellence is in the balance." She nodded at my shoulder.

"I know." I stared at my shoes, relieved that she wasn't taking my pin.

"You will table all discussion of vows for now. I want you to speak on your moderator's choice of topic after Christmas. The Trinity. I want a paper from you on forgiveness. Do the best you can, ma fille. I admire your willingness to lead, but you must do it in the right way."

I was going home for Christmas on time. Whew!

That afternoon, boarders had recreation in the orchard, freezing, holding scarves around our necks and pulling our hats down to our eyebrows. Emilie's color was high as she lined out what she and Larry had planned for break. Cats wanted me to come to the farm for a few days.

But I couldn't make any plans until I saw Michael.

Suze threw her arm around my shoulders. "I want to talk to you," she whispered. "I've been thinking."

I nodded. "Spill, Suze." Thinking was complicated in here.

"No time now," she smiled. "But I want to tell you soon."

Now I wondered about Suze, always steady and sure. We were all tired and quiet moving under the grape arbor, then apple trees. "Remember Freshman Year when they didn't let us leave the convent until Christmas morning?" said Jeanne.

"Yeah, my parents were furious!" said Cats.

"I'd decided not to come back after break," said Suze.

We'd all felt that way. The rules were too hard, the nuns, too strict.

"Yet here we are four years later!" Cats threw a ball, we ran through the arbor, chasing and trying to stay warm.

Now for the Seniors' last time it was the night of Christmas Eve! In bed by nine, our bags packed.

My toes tingled with excitement.

In the middle of the night, I sat up in bed. A silvery singing wafted from far away, unearthly beauty, close harmony. And though I knew it would come, I thought I was dreaming.

Then slippers swished in the cells around me, the curtains rustled. I threw mine open, other sleepy girls did the same. Suze's hair was a mess of curls; Em's framed her face like a dark halo. We exchanged knowing looks. And the haunting singing came closer. This was something we shared that no one else in the world could imagine.

Angels stood at the wide door of the dorm. Emanating from their creamy robes and filigree wings, an aura of light glowed. To my wonder, warmth seemed to come from their candles and presence and the radiators hissed with it. We stood together in the dorm without shivering.

"*Il est née le Divin Enfant*," they sang, "*Christ is born, awake and sing*," advancing toward our cells. As the angels passed, they handed each of us a candle, spreading the light and the song. Helpless as always, we fell in procession through the dorm, gathering everyone.

My eyes moist, I exchanged a loving glance with Suze, even skeptical Cats joined in.

We processed two by two, Angels we have heard on high: "*Les anges dans nos campagnes*," into the forbidden wing to rouse the sleeping nuns; we proceeded down the stairs into the long school hall and entered the chapel, trimmed and adorned with every kind of natural glory, from flowers to greens, mosses, berries, pine cones, oils—incense, ribbon and long sheaves of wheat. Only the crib was a poor thatch, the wooden figures rough-hewn. As our ritual went, after weeks of an empty manger, a carved baby had appeared in the hay. Wasn't this just what liturgy meant? The rituals again and again until you craved them for solace and for assurance that God was not just in your imagination.

Mon Père intoned the Mass, dressed in white alb, the long garment tied with a cincture, a rich white chasuble, the liturgical cape, and a golden stole. Philippe's classroom poster floated before me, "Dare to be Holy."

Dare? But this was a nimbus of holiness, one in which novices pretended to be angels so that we could be astonished all over again by Jesus' birth. Did we have a choice?

The fall semester filed before me—Hopkins' poems, edge of our seats in English class.

Holiness? I saw the hint of mockery or was it holy confidence? in young Sister Gemaine's white face—hidden in a cellar, making art; our wild dance around the honey jar and Philippe's love for us that night. Mercy. Patience. Nectar.

The angels were the Novices in white veils we'd watched over the fence. "*Messiah is here on earth*," they sang, "everything from now will be reflected in the light of this birth." How could each new crop of Novices always have wondrous voices, all blending as shimmering lines of longing?

The Mass unfolded.

At the Creed, we fell all at once to our knees. "*And was made flesh*."

The choir of angels sang Bach, "*Et incarnatus est.*" I was caught by it all over again.

We all were.

Then, off to the refectory, transformed by greens and the nuns' best gold rimmed china where we were served by angels. Once again, a creamy, lemony soup, a heavenly taste. My friends' hair shone, a line of glistening hair in the warm light.

Yes, Freshman year, we had wanted to stay home and never come back. But we had all come back after Christmas. We always came back.

This Christmas holiday 1964, our family had parties and music. Gloria and I decorated the house with greens and cards, the crèche and the tree. We always had a party set up with chairs for the neighbors, to sing the carols in harmony and solo on instruments for each other. We attended my father's Christmas concert at the Cathedral in Providence. The day before, I'd gone with him to rehearsal and once again experienced the drafty church, all dark except for the lights in the nave where the choir rehearsed. Dad, in his pure tenor, intoned the psalms. He would reach out through all that dark emptiness and touch me with his sound.

Back to school in the New Year! January 1965. This was the year we'd graduate. There were stirrings about an encyclical that Pope John the 23rd had written to make major changes in the Church. Maman had heard about it, but I had my doubts. What kind of changes? And our church was monolithic, never changing and, at least for our part, the Academie rules and rituals were the same as ever.

Our days back at school were cold and slushy, no pure white snow. Em had come back to school more in love with Larry, unable to focus on anything but their plan to marry in June. She was less and less excited about her Juilliard audition in March. We all tried to talk to her about it. And my hopes of seeing a lot of Michael had been dashed over Christmas because of his forestry internship. He'd given me as much time as he could, but not enough!

I tried to picture myself outside these walls—in the fresh, normal air of college with outfits to buy, a license which I had yet to get, dates. I'd feel like a Martian.

On a random Wednesday in the beginning of February, Philippe asked us again to clear our desks. She looked rested and sparkled somehow as though she'd been out running a race.

"Now," she said, and passed out another purple-copied poem of Gerard Manley Hopkins.

Firedint, stanches, disseveral, foundering—another language altogether.

Philippe read the words, "*Shivelights and shadow tackle in lace, lance.*" The tone enveloped me, then the line:

"*I am all at once what Christ is.*"

I drew in a sharp breath. Philippe looked up.

"*I am all at once what Christ is, since he was what I am.*"

She walked toward us. I could see green flecks in her brown eyes.

"*And this Jack, joke,*" she pointed to herself, "*poor potsherd, patch, matchwood, immortal diamond,*" placing her hand on Jeanne D'Arc's head,

"*Is immortal diamond.*"

The bell rang.

How did Hopkins do it? I'd been craving this image of Christ. It was perfect. If God had such a destiny for us after we died, he must also expect huge things of us now.

I stayed behind.

"Sister," I said.

Philippe looked up, smile lines visible in the sunlight coming in the windows.

"I am what Christ is?"

She blinked. "I am filled with the stuff of Christ," she said, picking up a stack of papers, "I think with His mind. His life is my life. He rose from the dead and I will rise with him. Were you asleep?"

"I was bowled over."

She nodded. "Yes, yes, so am I."

"And He was what I am?"

Philippe closed her eyes. "Saint Paul says—'He counted oneness with God not a thing to be grasped but emptied himself and took on the form of a servant.'"

"Sister, please stop quoting things." I held my forehead. "If Christ is ME, I am —"

"Slow down," Philippe said. "God is not something we feel."

"Do you ever feel?"

Philippe flashed me a look.

"So, it's all in the mind?" I asked softly.

"No," said Philippe.

"In the imagination?"

"There is use in all of this for the imagination."

She leafed through a pile of papers and picked up a sheet. "Here, take this for all your chewing."

Onion-skin typing paper, red lines all around the edges. There was a three-stanza poem typed out in the middle.

"INCARNATION," it read at the top.

"Hopkins?" I asked.

"Me."

"You?"

Philippe's tense face broke into a smile. "You don't think much of us nuns, do you, Janey?"

Her amusement washed over me.

I folded the sheet carefully and when I was out in the hall, pushed it into my secret pocket.

There, Philippe's poem kept company with Michael's.

In mid-February, the day came when I had a chance to make Sodality more relevant.

Denise's Mom came to see me in the parlor. She'd spoken to the United Church of Christ about their free art program for needy children and how to get us involved. I couldn't wait to explain to Mère. In the meantime, I would give my talk on the Trinity, but even that was possible now. Since the meeting fell on the feast day of Saint Helena of the True Cross, we processed from the lower court two by two in uniforms and white gloves, singing the doxology, nuns bringing up the rear. Four girls held the wooden palate upon which sat the Saint Helena statue.

Convent processions! They were so much a part of our liturgy with their colored ribbons and candles and a special cookies collation. When we reached the back door, we stopped in a circle to pray. Saint Helena was dressed in a white robe, about four feet high, and between her second and third fingers someone had stashed two thick folded notes. Cats nodded at them; her eyes disappeared into slits.

I itched to know what they said.

It was time for the Sodality meeting. I stood at the front desk in our recreation room, holding my hand-written sheets, taking in the forty faces. Em crossed to me, her warm smile reassuring, dark shadows under her eyes.

"Come see me at the window tonight," I whispered. She stood in the front row.

Lionel sat at the back, notebook in hand.

I said the prescribed prayer and they answered, "Amen"—the twins, Benjamine and Virginie and the three Irish girls behind them. I asked everyone to sit down and took a deep breath.

"My topic today is the doctrine of the Trinity. I want to focus on the second Person."

Lionel nodded her approval.

"Let's consider what the second Person of the Trinity might have looked like," I said, gingerly. "I think we need a picture, our own image of Jesus, at least I do. We need something different from the paintings and statues."

I saw encouraging smiles.

"How can we pray to an idea?" I said, a little stronger. I exchanged a glance with Suze whose reaction was good. "I want to give you some of my thoughts on this, and then I'd like to hear yours."

"Excuse me, Miss Chadderton," Lionel called. "Did you say you were planning to talk about Jesus' looks?"

"Yes, the way he might have looked," I nodded.

I felt a knot of anger pushing out of me and placed my written talk on the desk.

"We follow Him," I said, "we're His soldiers." I threw that in for Lionel. "But how can we follow an abstract idea? Okay, picture this young man walking by the Red Sea." I lifted my arms, "He's tanned, muscular, shortish in height. We wouldn't think of him as handsome exactly. But his body is quick, strong. He never seems to light anywhere. He has curly dark red hair, dark skin. His feet in the open sandals are dusty." I leaned over to indicate my own feet. "Picture the toenails crusty with mud."

Lionel crinkled her eyes.

"He reaches up to pick a fig," Gosh, this was feeling good, I was full to the brim with ideas. "He has long fingers, dirt under his fingernails; he's a rough carpenter."

A throat cleared at the back of the room.

"He pushes aside the brush with his powerful shoulders."

What was I doing?

"He stops to watch a bird flying in the gray sky— his eyes are pools, the color of the sky."

"Stop this at once!" Lionel slammed the desk.

I paused. "I found part of the description."

"Where?"

"In a sermon." I folded my arms. "But I wrote some of it too."

"Bring me that sermon. Where did you get it?"

"I changed it a little," I said.

"To suit yourself," said Lionel. "You will close this discussion about the physical good looks of Jesus Christ at once!"

I felt a small thrill. Cats' eyes snapped.

I said in a quiet voice, "Some of those ideas happen to belong to a great poet."

Lionel jumped up from her seat. "This meeting is adjourned."

"Sœur, with due respect," I said, "This is a lay organization."

"Who do you think you are, Janey Chadderton, the POPE?"

She strode to the front of the room and took my elbow. "You are all dismissed, Sodalists!" she cried. "And you, Janelle, Mère will see to you in her office. I have lost patience with you," she said, "and more's the pity."

But Mère did not call me to her office. We went on with special collation for the feast day. Nor did she call me in the next day. I jumped every time the loudspeaker came on. I didn't think there was a single description of Jesus in the Bible. Well, the Isaiah passage: *He had no beauty or majesty to attract us to him. Nothing in his appearance that we should desire him. He was despised and rejected by men, a man of sorrows...*

What Jesus really looked like was left to our imagination because they didn't have photographs back then. So why shouldn't we try?

Lionel made insulting remarks to me like: "Watch yourself, ma fille." And she poked my back with her stick in refectory.

I was losing heart. Michael and I had seen each other only twice over Christmas.

Everything seemed slow and difficult. Our only bright light was English class with Sister Philippe.

At bedtime, the white bedspreads with their crucifixes up and down the aisles looked like a graveyard. The windows were ripped open, pouring frigid air into the room.

"You know a lot about love..." Philippe had said. What could she mean in a place like this?

I needed some orange juice. Something green to eat. Our diet was all starch and tonight, I'd been embarrassed when we all dove for the celery.

I'd told Philippe not quite the truth that I'd never felt God. In fact, I felt Him while talking with her. While reading Hopkins. For Hopkins, God was in everyone and everything.

In Philippe's poem!

I didn't understand it, but the words lodged in me...*distance is the lover's terror, God is boned in flesh...*

I rummaged under my pillow for my PJs. The church taught that the way to God was fixed from years of tradition and rule. But I wanted something else—like taste, like conversation, a sensation of when God was there, a known, wordless Presence.

Like that time in first grade when I made my First Communion.

We are seven, we line up outside on the Church steps, everyone in white dresses and veils. Maman let me have a Toni home permanent, my first curls. My partner is my best friend, Buster, dressed in a borrowed white suit, slicked hair, shiny nose. I love him. He's my own special little husband for the procession in the white dress. And I've been chosen to be the lovely reader because I'm the loudest and the best. Standing on the steps as the organ music begins, my mouth goes dry.

I'm about to swallow the Creator of all the heavens and earth for the first time with a sin on my soul. The sin of pride. Pride at being the best, most lovely reader. There's nowhere to turn.

I can't receive Him. I bolt out of the line.

"I'm not ready," I cry, and fling my arms around the nun.

At first, she's patient, reminding me about my perfect answers in the Catechism test, my good confession. But I refuse to get in line, spilling tears into the nun's habit and now they're wetting the front of my white dress. My veil tilts to the side; one bobby pin sticks straight up into the air. I need a priest all over again for a brand-new confession. And since that's not possible, there is no hope.

They locate Maman. "Sweetheart," she tries to comfort, "where do you get these ideas?"

But, no, I won't get back into the line. Sister Rachel-Marie said that the devil might try to make you sin right before you eat the Host, the wafer, the Flesh of God. And she's right. I've been caught. If I swallow it now, I'll die forever.

She picks another child to do the reading. I'll be the tallest in the First Communion line next year. I'll wait all that time to have God inside me.

But all I feel is peace. God has come into me anyway—not in a wafer, not swallowed, just there. Inside me.

Chapter 16

February, Winter Break 1965—Philippe

Jacinta stopped me in the hall to tell me what she'd heard. Janey had described Jesus at the Sodality meeting, something about toes crusted with dirt. She frowned with worry, and I saw myself handing Janey the Hopkins sermons. "I have to go," I said.

I hurried to Mère's office feeling foolish and impulsive. When I rounded the corner, Sister Lionel was just leaving. Furious and white-faced, she pushed past me. Mère leaned back in her chair, arms folded under her frontispiece. Janey stood before her; head hung. I stayed in the doorway, neither in nor out.

"Mère, may I speak with you," I asked. Neither of them acknowledged me.

Mère nodded at Janey's shoulder where her Excellence Pin shone in the lamp light. "I've had enough now."

The pin would not open. Janey tried again with buttery fingers, then dropped it into Mère's outstretched hand.

"Sœur Philippe, I will call for you later," Mère dismissed us. But later never came for the rest of that week.

On Friday afternoon, the students left for winter break, all except for a few that lived far away. Losing the Excellence pin meant that Janey would have to stay. Suze's parents were on a trip abroad, so she stayed as well. They watched everyone leave from the front porch. I watched too, standing at my classroom window, sorry I had ever let Janey talk to me.

Where was my judgment lately? Cats was waving goodbye out her father's car. Em drove off with her family, her long black hair flying out the open window.

Good, she would get a rest now. She'd been looking exhausted. I sensed it was more serious than the usual girl dramas. Or at least, that's what Jacinta thought.

There were only a handful of girls left: Elise and Suze who lived in Georgia, lovely long-limbed Jesse and Elaine from Haiti. Cats called out the car window that she'd call Michael as soon as she got home. The boy they'd been waiting for at the Roller Palace. He'd be dashed.

Janey sat alone on the top step. Her straight hair glinted in the waning light. She looked over her shoulder then pulled out a sheet of paper. Even from this distance, I could see it was my typing paper with the red lines at the edges. I pulled away from the window and went to my desk. I had a copy of my poem and read what she was reading.

"God's presence is *absence* felt in flesh, God's presence is *union* felt in God," and the line, "*distance* is the lover's terror." I'd tried for strict sonnet form but inside the form were wild notions—how could a human being feel in God? And who was the lover?

All of a sudden, Janey was at the door.

"I get it now." She hurried toward me. "God became human so we could really know him. We have to be that close, or we can't love—because then it would be abstract and I don't think love can be that —admiration, I think but not love."

I held her off with open palms. "I'm not sure we should think about God that way."

"But Sister, with respect, *you* do." Her spirit leapt in the look she gave me. "God took a body. He let us know Him. That's what touches us."

"Wait a minute now—"

"No, hear me out," talking with her hands. "He doesn't hate bodies! I think the saints got it wrong. Saint Rosa who starved herself was crazy. Hopkins writes about nature and bodies filled with spirit."

I pressed my fingers to my eyes. "Janey, you quoted one of Hopkins' sermons in Sodality?"

"Paraphrased."

"What did you think would happen?"

"I tried to picture Jesus through my own imagination. A few of Hopkins' images leaked in."

"Janey, you're going too far. Our bodies can deceive us."

"That's not what Hopkins says! 'I am all at once what Christ is—*immortal diamond*!'"

"But in another place, he says: 'man's spirit will be flesh bound.'"

She stopped pacing and threw up her arms. "I love what he does with words."

"Yes, so do I."

I gathered my papers and stood up. "Janey, the Incarnation, the Resurrection are mysteries. You will never figure them out."

"But I can't discard my mind!"

"No, you cannot and ought not. But Christ says, 'follow me.' We don't know what that is going to look like, but we must be ready to do it."

"Well, I have to know what it's going to look like. It's not Theresa of the Roses who was thrilled when she coughed up blood. That can't be God's will."

"What is it you can't believe? That God wants us to hurt our bodies to be closer to Him?"

"Does he?"

I frowned. "No, but suffering is part of every life in one way or another. That, we don't get away from. Jesus bled and died, Janey, that's how far he was willing to go into our humanness. He conquered death."

"But we still do die!"

I nodded. "Yes, we follow Him into death. Baptized into his death, remember?"

"Sister Philippe. Does He LOVE us or not? Did He save us or not?"

The next morning, Mère left the Academie to attend a three-day conference at the Motherhouse. With the girls away, I was relieved to have her gone as well. I would work hard to prepare all my English classes for the semester. There was a knock on my door. Sister Portress plowed in. "You have a visitor, Sœur Philippe. Your brother. He insists he must see you in person about a grave family matter."

I caught my breath. "Which brother, Sœur? I have seven—"

"He said his name was John. Ordinarily Mère would see to it, but this falls to me. He says it's urgent."

John worked in construction. He always had a ruddy tan and the roughest hands. I warmed at the thought of him but felt a wave of apprehension. John was Skip's best friend. Something was very wrong.

"John is not an alarmist," I told the Portress. "If he said it was imperative that he see me, it must be serious."

The old Portress, whose name was Sister Marc, insisted it was highly irregular, but gave her permission.

I went downstairs to the visitor's parlor; John stood up and opened his arms. His height stunned as always, his dark wiry hair combed down in respect. I forgot who I was and ran to him, stopping just short of a hug. "Is it Papa?"

"Yes, Papa," he said in a strong voice. "He's fine," he whispered to me. Then, "He fell ill two days ago. And you look ill."

"I'm quite well."

"Baloney," he shook me by the shoulders. It stung to be touched, even by these rough brotherly hands.

We sat in opposite corners of the horsehair sofa. "Papa has been delirious. He said it was a premonition and couldn't get you out of his mind. He insisted I come here." John eyed Sœur Marc who was standing sentinel at the door, listening. "I thought it strange. But now that I see you—"

"No, no, I'm getting used to teaching, that's all."

He nodded toward Sister Marc. "Sister, do you think we could walk on the grounds? Papa—it'll take time to explain."

Really it could have gone either way. Had Mère been there, we never would have gotten out of the parlor. But Sister Marc was old and slow and liked my brother. She called for a Sister to accompany us.

We walked toward the back door. I put on my cape. John took my elbow. "We should wait for Sister," I told him.

"We will," he said as he shepherded me. "Papa did have a dream about you but it's not why I'm here." He guided me toward the path along the rectory. When we were out of earshot of any nun, he said: "Skip is waiting in the grotto."

I flung myself back. "John!"

"I'm sorry, Maggie, there was no other way. I promised him I'd try."

I stared at the mix of wet, grassy mud at my black shoes. I felt trapped, anger pulsed in my ears.

"Please, hear me out," said John, "Skip hasn't seen you since you entered, and he remembers you the way you were. He can't get on with his life. You're strong, you'll release him. Do you see? He's about to get engaged."

"A huge risk. How can it work?"

"He knew Mère would be out at the meeting—his aunt, the nun, is in Shrewsbury too."

I stared at my brother and his worldly air.

"He needs to see you, Maggie. If you ever loved him, you'll do this for him."

I winced.

"I told him you aren't coming back. I talked to him straight after I saw you at your clothing—your heart in it 100%."

"But he doesn't believe you."

"Then it'll help you both. Sounds like you need to see him too."

Sœur Jacinta ran toward us. "What's going on? Is it your father?"

I closed my eyes. Of all the nuns Portress could have chosen, she'd sent my friend. I asked John to explain it to her, then plowed ahead on the path. "I will see him for five minutes. Five, do you hear?"

I did not look back, knowing I was safe with Jacinta.

The grotto was surrounded by old plush evergreen shrubs up to and shadowing the cave in the rock where the Virgin stood. She was beloved, carved in stone, a graceful mouth with full lips, deep set eyes, elegant nose, not one of the severe Marys. We all cherished the grotto. I turned around, headed back, and bumped into John. "I can't do this."

"We'll guard the entrance and whistle if someone comes. We cased it out. He can hide if need be. The shrubs are thick, plenty of places."

"My God," said Jacinta.

"Look, Pitou (his baby name for me), you promised that if Skip ever truly needed you, you would find a way. Come on, honey, you're supposed to be the most loving of all of us."

Hearing this, my thoughts floated, spooling out like fine thread, unraveling. Skip and his passion—I knew what passion was—I had my own, in here and out there.

In a low voice, I told them to keep watch. Jacinta nodded, eyes like saucers. But this impossible meeting had fallen together. Wasn't it God's will?

I entered through the one opening in the stand of shrubs. Everything I'd sacrificed and worked so hard for rose up like a vision.

There he was with his close-cropped red-blond hair, feet plant-
ed, hands behind his back, eyes so blue, holding mine, the lines
around them intense even as the rest of him smiled.

I walked straight into his arms.

"Maggie." His husky voice.

I sank into his embrace, pulse beating in my temples.

We breathed, I panicked, could not move.

He read my mind, opened his arms and stepped back. "You
don't look well, what I can see of you."

"No, I am, I am."

We drank each other in. I cleared my throat.

"Thank you for meeting me," he said. "I don't know what I im-
agined, it was not this," indicating the habit.

I straightened my wimple and frowned.

"The costume, just like your strong will —"

"It's not a costume."

"What then? It's medieval."

My forehead burned. I placed my cool fingers where pain was
flickering. "Why Skip? John said—"

"You moved on. I can't."

"I went toward something. Not away from you."

"Oh, it was away."

I sighed hard.

"Maggie. I have to make a life now. But not without seeing you
one last time."

I placed my fingers on his lips. But he held them and went on.
"God hasn't whispered his will in my ear."

His lip curled, hurt, or derision?

I backed away, punched, had never seen him like that. "It's been three years," I said.

"And isn't that worth considering? Aren't I as faithful as your God?"

"I told John," and started toward the gate. "I can't do this."

"Thought you were so in love with God, it was safe to see me? Are you failing your test?"

"What do you want?" I wheeled around in anguish to face him.

He lowered his eyes. The air was saturated, still.

"Look, you haven't taken final vows. If there's a chance you're coming home, I don't want anyone else. I love you and it never gets clearer for me. In the night, when I can't sleep, I feel you. I don't sense you're at peace."

I walked toward him. *Of course he would know.*

"I have been having doubts." I let my eyes meet his. "I'm not sure I will take final vows. Mère's not sure I should."

"But you wanted this so much. What kind of fool would not want you? You're such an asset to them."

"I thought you wanted me to come home?"

"But not like that! I know you," his color deepened. "If this is your destiny, I want it for you."

He blinked once and pulled me to him. "Oh God, Maggie. Why does this not get easier?"

I heard a bird twitter not far away.

"I miss your hair," he pleaded.

Our lips met, carefully. It was I who kissed him back with a hunger that swept through me. To my shock, I wanted this, wanted it full and deep, my chest stirred with want. My coif slipped, my habit bunched, my heart pounded. "I'm still me," I whispered into his lips.

"Yes. Maggie, yes."

I pushed him with all my will and ran through the gate.

Chapter 17

Janey

My penance during my lost break was to wash the great entrance hall floor. Suze was helping me when Joey came to find us. "Janelle, Suzanne, you must deliver an envelope to Père."

I grabbed Suze's hand. What luck! A walk, some fresh air.

We went to the course to pick up my purse with its cigarette and matches hidden in the strap.

We retrieved the manila envelope from the Portress. She waved her thanks.

Père lived in a yellow house down the curved path that went past the hidden grotto of Our Lady then out a gate and across the street. We started out through the arbor and rounded the apple trees. We picked a bunch of frozen mint to chew for later. Suze's soft voice slurred through the blade of grass she sucked on. She liked the boy she'd asked to the prom; he might want to become a priest. He had wavy hair. He pulled her close when they danced. He was eating all his meals at her house now when she was home. They were deep wet kissing every chance they got. "It's his way of testing his vocation," she said. "He'll discover God's will. And hey, so will I!"

"By kissing?" I kicked a stone in the path and watched her creamy-tan, cat eyes, the wiry curls. "I feel physical and weak," she said.

We were passing by the grotto, a snug little thicket. "But maybe your feelings are as much God's will as his—" A man's voice floated up, "your hair—"

We ducked down behind shrubs.

"Maggie," his voice, thick.

A breeze stirred the bush.

"It's Philippe," I whispered.

We pulled out from under, on fire. "Let's get out of here."

Père answered the door and took the parcel. Back in through the gate and around the arbor, behind a huge tree, I lit the cigarette. Suze pushed her glasses up on her nose. She placed the cig between her lips and drew in, when she exhaled, "What do you think of that?" through smoke. "Holy Moley!"

"Maybe it was her brother?"

Suze drew in a doubtful sigh and passed the cigarette. We stood close together, smoke rising, breathing in the delicious rebellion and passing it back and forth with the seriousness of a convent ritual. Afterwards on the way back, we chewed the mint. And worry for Philippe swept through the freedom.

On the third morning of the break, we awoke to a lush snowstorm; had craved one all winter. Snow blanketed the entire body of the yard, the orchard, grape arbor, and sloping hill in graceful white drifts, the lazy double flakes sticking to our dorm windows. The snow's deep silence, its mystery, like early morning Mass.

And then it was time for Mass. Then during breakfast, the snow still fell in clusters out the refectory windows. We few girls were eating in the nuns' refectory. I scanned the black bobbing heads down the rows of their dining table; the monitor nun, Sister Agatha was slowly making her rounds with a stick, poking into the backs of slouchers, both nuns and girls. We were supposed to sit ramrod straight at table, left hand poised by the plate, right hand managing the fork. I felt the damn stick in my back.

She was poking everyone. A sadist monitor. Suze thrust her hand toward me, palm down, the silent sign for bread. I passed the basket, stopped it in mid-air as Mère Superieure streamed toward our table. What now?

She stood erect at the head; arms extended. "Today," she announced, "to celebrate the feast of Saint Barbara, oui, today we will toboggan. Mandatory tobogganing!" She laughed with good cheer.

I pointed to myself, eyebrows up.

"Oui, Janelle, a congée from penance!" She smiled at me.

Really? My rebelling would still have to be paid, but so what? Snow play, yippee!

After breakfast, five girls each pulled on hats, mittens, and two pairs of leggings. We borrowed boots from the nuns' entering closet and put together garish, unmatched woolens. With no boys around, who cared how we looked.

When we were bundled, Suze pushed open the door to the courtyard. The flakes had stopped falling, the air heavy with moisture. Fruit tree branches bowed almost to the ground. I called out into the quiet, white world. *"When I see birches bend to left and right,"* and Elise called, *"I like to think some boy's been swinging them...."* Her wiry hair was covered in a knit cap down around her eyes. Two toboggans were pushed up against the lower wall. They were of deep brown wood, their cracked and worn leather cushions hollowed in their centers. We needed only one, lifted it over our heads, Suze and Nanette on one end, Elise, Julie and me holding up the other. We headed for the hill. The snow poured into my ill-fitting boots; it had to be two feet deep. I shook with cold; we would not last out here fifteen minutes. The arbor vitae we passed had been sliced in two by drifts, brown scraggly insides exposed. We stopped to shake the branches free, muscling loads of snow to the ground.

Something glittery fell with the snow. Suze dove under and pulled it out by its chain.

"Jeanne D'Arc, we love you." She laughed, throwing the chain to me. "She prayed us this snow!"

"What?" said Elise.

"She hangs her medal on the arbor to get the weather she wants."

"But for a sunny day," said Nanette.

"God got mixed up!"

Just then the courtyard door opened again, and we watched, mouths agape. Three nuns stepped out, bundled in black wool capes over their habits. Sisters Philippe, Jean and Jacinta, galoshes making deep prints in the snow, dresses trailing behind. Philippe looked different to me, brand new. They grabbed the ends of a to-boggan, thrust it high up over their heads, and ran toward the or-chard, calling: "Come on cold molasses. How much time do you think we have?"

We just stared. We'd heard that the nuns tobogganed during our vacations but had never seen it.

Instantly, on the far side of the orchard, the three nuns jumped on and took their first hill, inching slowly, wind blowing them into a black and white cloud.

"We'll have to pack it down," Sister Jacinta called, laughing.

The five of us climbed onto our toboggan, leaving one girl at the top of the hill—we would take turns. We slid down the run next to theirs, snow blowing us too—delicious icy taste! The paths were narrow between the apple trees, ending in the lower court at the chain link fence.

We bailed short of the fence just in case. Beyond it, the hill became a cliff to the street below.

Philippe ran to get a shovel. She grunted and dug and mounded the snow at the top of the nuns' run into a jump.

We sledded down the runs; the snow was packing down. Eyes sparkled with cold. We borrowed the shovel and packed up a jump of our own. There was snow inside my brown scarf; up my sleeves; my hands in the thin mittens, a raw pink. "Let's go in," Nanette called in the wind.

But we kept on—all morning we steered the toboggans between the orchard trees—four girls on one, three nuns on the other, spraying the snow, throwing ourselves off before the fence.

Wet to my underwear, I tumbled and turned, called out directions, laughing and rolling into the snow. The nuns were hilarious too with their lovely ringing voices, taking their own runs. After a while, I forgot how cold I was, and all about my Excellence pin, Michael, the lost weekend. The snow was hard packed now and the speed, picking up. Philippe's cheeks glowed as she ran, hopped on, bent the toboggan to her will. She loved to push off and ride at the back of the nuns.

And I was doing the same—riding at the back with the girls. Around noon, "All right," Philippe called, "a race! We three sisters against your best team of girls. Ha! We'll make use of our well packed runs...may the fastest win!"

We exchanged quick looks. Philippe jumped from foot to foot, her brown eyes glinting and intense.

"But Sœur," said Suze, sending me a worried look. "Let's go in now. It's getting icy." Philippe's coif was askew, her color high. Always sharp and alive to everything, she suddenly seemed to notice nothing and turned to huddle with her nuns. Jacinta found a rope in the shed for a finish line and placed it at the bottom of the hill.

We organized our team of four—our weights and positions on the toboggan. Philippe's team of three nuns did the same.

Sister Joey had just joined us with the message to come in soon. She called out the start.

We all jumped on at the same time and whipped down the runs. The girls team edged over the line first.

"Ta da! Ha! You see, the supple bones of youth, Sister. Sorry to say," called Suze.

"Rematch!" said Philippe into the wind. "It wasn't fair. We are only three."

"Time to go in, MaSœur," said the gentle Joey.

"Just one more race," she argued, "the right weight for this snow. I need one more body. Janey."

My stomach lurched. I saw Philippe's crackling eyes, so caught up. Had she forgotten herself? Who would remind her who she was?

"Right here," she said to me. I gave her a questioning look, but she only laughed. Her spirit seemed to leap in her. "Now you push off," she said, "we want your weight in the back for that turn."

So again, Joey called, "Ready, set, GO."

I pushed with all my might, jumped on and then froze, my legs straight out to the sides. Apple trees sped past; it was all a blur. "Grab me with your feet," she shouted, but I could not bring myself to throw my arms and legs around her cape. My limbs froze in the wet snow clothes, I shivered and leaned—somehow, we negotiated the turn and bailed in time.

But still again the girls won, and now Philippe's sparks flew, her voice resonant in the icy wind, "One more time, one more time. And we will take this run here—this one."

"No, Sister," called Suze. "That one's all ice now."

"We'll take our chances; use the ice. Skill, Sisters, these matters take skill." Jacinta jumped up and down to stay warm. Sister Jean glanced nervously at the courtyard door. Philippe fumed, her voice rising with the heady goal of winning, not a silly game anymore. "We had these limbs hanging out everywhere, didn't we, Sisters? For heaven's sake, Janey you could have broken everything."

"I'm sorry, I—"

"Never mind that now. I will take the back. You ride just inside this time. And keep yourself in, in." Philippe, the same whatever she did—her passion for Christ, her press toward truth. "*I am all at once what Christ is, as he was what I am*—" In this icy wind, for an instant, I knew what it meant.

Christ was in Philippe as she was in him. And He didn't make her less human or elusive like God, but more human and full of life.

"Get this over with," Joey called. "Get set, GO."

Philippe pushed off with a YEEHAH! and swallowed me in arms and legs. Snow and the bark of trees, it was fast now, white, brown blur, warm speed wind tickling cheeks, I clung to her long legs round my waist, hugged her soggy boots.

Trees sped past—the turn in the run was coming. "ONE, TWO, THREE," she shouted, and the nuns and I leaned to the right. Shriek...crack, the front rotated too far, snow spray, Philippe's arms around me, pulling. Then sting, cold, black.

I sat up, dazed. The toboggan, cracked into an apple tree, tipped upside down. Philippe sat up next to me, white with snow. She leaned over as if to brush the flakes from my eyes, but stopped and looked me over carefully instead. Her own habit and headpiece were completely askew but she seemed unaware. There was snow inside her wimple, under the veil, in the collar, in her eyes and nose. Sister Jacinta stood up and shook herself all over like a little squirrel that had fallen from a tree. There was a Sister completely missing.

We stood up at once and together, lifted the toboggan. Sister Jean filled a curiously small hole in the snowdrift. The icy breeze played in ripples on her black veil, her head and face, down—arms and legs drawn in—a ball of nun.

We pulled her carefully out of the hole. She moaned, her one leg unmoving, as we rolled her onto her side on the now broken toboggan. Her tears ran free, something you never saw in a nun. Philippe was already running up the hill.

Chapter 18

Philippe

Mère had returned from her Chapter meeting and that night, after Vespers, I knelt before the community. My sisters sat in a circle, their black shoes side by side. They were waiting for me to speak.

"I let the excitement of the moment rule me," I confessed.

"Sœur Jean is badly hurt," Mère stated, in a firm but gentle voice.

"Will she be all right?" I asked.

"Apparently, God willing, yes."

"I'm truly sorry."

"You have taken vows, Sœur Philippe. You can toboggan, we all toboggan, but this?"

"I'm sorry."

"I know you are. It will become for you, for all of us, the lesson of the necessity that we must hold the reins, MaSœur. As penance, you will forfeit your teaching."

I raised my head in surprise. The nuns murmured.

"Maybe for the best," Mère said in a faint voice.

Hmm, I'd failed to control my passion for Hopkins too.

I took in Mère's airy flush and the lines around her eyes.

I stayed in the cloister. The alone time felt less like a punishment than a boon. I tried to keep from diving into my work because I would mourn giving it up again. And then I did anyway, loving the first sips of organization of passages I needed. But I felt responsible for Sister Jean. The only time I left my room during the day was to visit her in the cloister. The break had been clean, her leg was in a cast; she'd be all right in time. She was so understanding it made me want to weep; we spoke tenderly. "We should have gone in at the first sign of ice," I mourned.

She placed a finger to my lips, but it was true, I'd fallen into joy.

I touched my lips and felt him, the faint taste of his cigarette. What had I done? What would we do?

I could have walked out of the grotto with him, over the wall, and never looked back.

Mère would know, I could not meet her eyes. I'd exploded my feelings for Skip out on that hill. I felt his fingers in mine, the pain in his eyes, the current between us. And then abruptly, I smeared my eyes with both hands. This was solving exactly nothing.

The week went by. I was at my desk outlining chapter six when Mère called for me.

"You will be the new course mistress of girls," she told me. "Starting today."

"Course mistress?"

"The Sister who lives with them," she said, "organizes, eats, sleeps with them, monitors study hall, well, you will learn."

"But who will teach them?"

"That is none of your affair. Your first task will be to help them plan for Conventum, April 1st, Academie's 75th. Among other festivities, our boarders will present a play for the 'old girls' that we will ask you to oversee."

I frowned. "MaMère, there is something you need to know." My back straightened. "I'm having grave doubts."

Mère slipped her crucifix under her coif in a sweep. She was listening. She sat down and motioned for me to do likewise. I stayed silent until she nodded.

"I cherish my vows, but I seem to do nothing but sin through folly and stupidity; I let Him down. He's given me talent, intelligence, a good nature—and yet, sometimes, I feel that I'm the worst thing ever born."

We both waited. The quiet surrounded us.

Mère stirred, "My dear child. All that God creates is good! Alone we are good for stupid things, but with Him we scale heights."

Scale heights. That is all I ever wanted to do.

"You have intellect," Mère said, "and you have great passions. You know that the intellect without the heart is cold, but now you are learning that the passions without the intellect can be quite dangerous."

I nodded. "I met my former love in the grotto, MaMère. My brother tricked me and led me there."

"I know," she said.

I blinked. "You do?"

Her gaze was steady and loving. Loving?

"You were tempted. I understand, child. Do not allow it to upset you. Temptations are given to strengthen us. Which great saint was not tempted?"

"But Andrè and I embraced."

Mère's eyebrows moved up ever so subtly. But her head tilted again gently to one side, her eyes meeting mine.

"I discovered that I'm still drawn to him, and it stings." I closed my eyes to this.

When I looked up, Mère lifted an encouraging hand.

"I want to serve Christ; my promises are true. Shouldn't He protect me from these feelings?"

"We're human!" she said. "Carnal pleasures offer delight, so why wouldn't the devil make use of them?"

"NO! It's not like that! I still love the man. Love him..."

Mère gave me a look of discernment. "My dear, remain at peace and keep busy. As you give yourself to His work, these doubts may well fade. I believe you will come back to Him, and you won't do it alone—He will be there with his grace."

"MaMère, no. My doubts are beyond that, graver. I need your guidance, your wisdom. What should I do about my Final Vows?"

She sat in silence.

Then she said, "I gave up marriage and children to offer my life to God—I cannot but encourage you to do the same, if God indeed calls you. The rewards are one-hundred-fold—poverty, chastity, and obedience. We are blessed beyond measure, but not without a cross. Please, mind the word chastity. We give up marriage." She bowed her head and I listened to the silence.

Finally, she stood up. I was dismissed. But not without a look I thought I would never see. Was it, could it be, affection?

That evening in chapel, I knelt in my new place trying to focus my mind. The boarders, all back now, sat ahead of me with bowed heads, but they were fidgety, sneaking glances my way. Well, this was a challenge for me, but I hoped, good for them—anything would be an improvement over Lionel. Now that was a catty thought, more to confess.

I bowed my head, incense, Holy Rituals, and chants brought everything back—that moment at the rail when I heard Jesus call me. When I offered my whole life, prostrated before the altar, offering, offering. Even in the face of change and confusion, I must serve His truth.

Now I trusted myself to the chant, adjusted my eyes, scanned the kneeling girls in rows.

The back of Jeanne D'Arc's red hair; Cats' solid back; Janey's pale face partially hidden in her hands.

Ave Maria gratia plena

Oh my Lord, I'm their mother. Hail Mary, full of grace.

Outside with them at recreation; planning their weekend activities; and disciplining them with notes. Was this Mère's punishment or another gift like the grace of beholding Germaine's paintings? The convent's low stations were scullery, cook, cleaning, but I didn't know course mistress was one of them. Could it have to do with the body, caring for girls' physical needs instead of their minds?

Sancta Maria Mater Dei

The Church and the body—it was good, the Church said, for sweat and toil, for building a home, a house of prayer. The body could do evil, the Church said, occasion of sin—separation from God.

"I love your body…" Skip had murmured.

miserere nobis, amen amen

How was it that his whispers, his touch never went away?

We filed out of chapel after Compline, the girls two by two. They craned around to be sure I was truly there. Janey placed a hand on Cats' shoulder.

Up the five flights of stairs and into the icy dorm in silence, white beds in ordered rows with a wooden crucifix on each pillow; white curtains, illusions of privacy, all tied back. The girls stood still and stared as I entered Lionel's old chamber across from the cells.

The curtains swished around the cell frames; the girls came out again in the requisite PJs, cotton, white, styled for men. No night-gowns here, occasions for sin, suitable only for the marriage bed. They lined up at the sinks to fill their pitchers with cold water. I sat and waited in my room, door open, not sure what I was supposed to do. How many more transitions would there be? I would make my ablutions after they went to sleep. They were splashing cold wa-ter on their faces now inside the curtains. Mère had given me charts that outlined their rules and rituals. It was time to pass out the holy water and then turn off the lights.

I walked toward their cells, thrust the holy water sponge into the slits between the curtains.

"*Benit sois le Seigneur.*" Down the rows, girls were happy to see me, it lifted my spirits. Some sat on the bed, others lay between the sheets and sat up to receive the blessing. Some knelt.

Emilie dipped her fingers into the freezing water. She lay back, her arms in the form of a cross over her chest. They'd been given the rules of novices! If she died in the night, she'd meet God in the correct posture.

I thrust the water into Janey's cell. She took a bit in her fingertips, crossed herself, then lay back freely placing her arms behind her head, elbows stretched out over the pillow.

"Bad for the heart, the way you're planning to sleep."

She shrugged. She looked impish and young.

I closed her curtain and went on.

Anger licked at my soul like a flame. I returned to my room.

The flame grew hotter—at Mère, but wonderingly, not just Mère; at Skip, at my indecision. And yes, anger at the immense silence of God.

I pressed myself against the solid wooden door and slid to the floor. Hot tears stung my eyes and scalded my cheeks.

All week, I walked through the various tasks of a course mistress. Mère had imported an older nun from the college out in Paxton. She was a fine English professor, and that hurt more.

During the hours the girls were in classes, I worked from Mère's plans—skit writing for Conventum; a trip to the Roller Palace; Friday notes on their faults. Still, there were moments of love for them—our daily Eucharist—as we knelt together at the rail, my heart held each one.

Whenever they were out of class, I was with them—at meals, in study hall, recreation. There was no time for the "life of the mind." But something new and rather astonishing was happening; I laughed more, ran more outside, sweated more, and slept soundly.

On Friday afternoon, I split the girls into five groups of eight. We'd been given tasks in preparation for Conventum. Some girls joined Sœur Fiacre in the refectory where they would practice serving tea in white gloves; others to the visitors' parlor to clean and organize the chairs; still others to the auditorium for a thorough cleaning of the stage.

I stayed with the group in the library to oversee the organization of pictures and mementos. Mère had sent out a Conventum call, and the mail was pouring in. This reunion of "old girls" would be the most important yet and many were attending. I'd set up tables for sorting. Sœur Liese flitted in and out of the room, carrying boxes of old ribbons, Excellence Pins, holy cards. Now and then, she'd throw an envelope of photos into the work.

"Hey, we lucked," said Cats, her face scarlet, hair stuck with pine needles.

I approached the table. "Charlotte, why is your hair full of dirt?"

"She stands on her head," said Suze.

"Why?"

"It clears my brain," said Cats.

Janey sorted photos and I looked over her shoulder. "This is a better job than learning to serve tea," she said. I smiled.

"Yup, we're cheap labor." Cats grinned.

There were photos of boarders in muted, filmy textures. They all looked impressive in the black dress with its high collar. They made me wish I'd been sent here instead of the high school at home.

Janey picked up the photographs marked 1935 of girls throwing our bean bags; a group by the swing tree; a play in the auditorium; girls in wool coats, galoshes and thick scarves at the bottom of the hill in snow to their knees. Where were these young girls thirty years later, now women?

Cats held a class photo to the light. The graduates stood in two rows, banked on either side by nuns, faces framed in the oval white coif, wings afly.

"Look at us," I said, "like a species of bird!"

"I love the habit," Emilie whispered.

"All of them together, floating and praying," said Jeanne D'Arc.

"It calms me down," said Janey.

I was about to ask them to say more when Emilie turned over a picture of girls standing together by the lower fence, arms draped around each other; one's hair was tied at the nape of the neck in a white bow. Another girl's dark cloud of hair took my breath. It was tamed with difficulty, escaping the tie and forming a rippling halo around her thin face. Her eyes were exactly like mine. And that was my hair too.

"Bien." Liese came up to the table.

I jumped. "You scared me, Sœur!"

"Great group of girls. Our Adèle. Bless her soul." She crossed herself and her lined face spoke reams. "I'm sorry, MaSœur."

"Why bless her soul?" Janey asked.

"It's my mother," I whispered in disbelief.

The girls looked from me to the picture.

Liese took a man's handkerchief out of her pocket and wiped her brow. "Adèle died young, in childbirth." She touched my arm. "Oh, oh but of course. My poor dear."

I could not utter a sound.

Neither Papa nor my siblings had ever told me my mother had come here. They'd shown me few photos. Papa's grief and anger at God had closed him in even further. How were they silent even when I entered this convent? My mother had been a boarder here. The connection would have meant so much; to know about her.

At recreation, I stayed close to the girls. My mother had run here in this orchard. Played basketball by that fence. I rolled up my sleeves and tossed the ball to Janey; a few girls circled in a relaxed game of catch.

Now I had an image of my young mother. I caught the flying ball. Right here at this Academie. I looked a lot like her. The trees and bushes were vivid now, there was new life in the apple tree branches, white and pink buds about to burst open.

I smashed the ball against a tree. Suddenly I wanted the plain life of a nun without drama, one who wakes and clothes herself, the smooth feel of the habit on her body. She kneels in Chapel before the Blessed Sacrament, responsible for her thoughts. No one could steal those thoughts—alone with God. But I was not my own anymore. Now I was responsible for the girls, for mothering them. Mother of mercy.

I watched the blur of open coats, serge uniforms, imagining my mother among them, stealing a hat, dodging a ball, their needs and budding bodies; my God, they still needed their mothers, yes, as I had so needed mine, *gementes et flentes in hac lacrimarum valle.*

The bell rang and they ran toward the courtyard.

This was too painful. *This valley of tears.*

My nine siblings had memories of my mother's smell, her arms, her voice. I had been a little girl playing near the fire in the kitchen, intuiting everyone's grief. And now I was seeing my mother everywhere—on the hills, in the course, in the chapel, in the dorm.

At bedtime, an envelope on my bed in Mère's hand. My fingers shook as I opened it and sat down on the edge.

My dear Sister Philippe, I'm writing this to you after much prayer and reflection. You are asking for advice concerning your vows. You remind me of just one person and this person is in the Gospels. The rich, young man asked Our Lord what he must do to be saved. And after receiving the answer from the greatest Teacher, he turned away sad.

My child, I believe you know the answers. Might you be bringing in the pretext of your former love to prevent you from the total oblation? Remember it is an invitation. You need not accept, nor should you toy with it. Be clear cut and definite.

The Church sees to it that the decision to remain in religion is our own. If outside pressure is noticed a sister is asked to leave. The "I do" of the married state has to be just as free. Both states require great sacrifice and will have times of doubt and darkness.

Either you want this life and are ready to make the sacrifices, or you must go and serve Him in another way. This is not pressure but rather an occasion for you to grow in holiness, take your life into your hands, and present Him with something whole and holy. We can be carried away and then deplore the loss of time. We accept the ready-made, but recoil from the shaping up.

You are now in the process of determining your life, through prayer, intellect, and yes, feelings. I can suggest a plan, but only you can do the discernment!

Honestly, what life can guarantee freedom from earthly trials and longings? I have had my own share of dark days! Sometimes we learn that loneliness is an invitation to intimacy with God.

MaChère, you are in my daily prayers. If writing me back helps the tension, please do. And you can always send another S.O.S. I will do what I can.

Devotedly in Him, Mère

I lay back on my bed. Impressive, glorious Mère. She inspired me with compassion and clarity. In a heartbeat, I heard him whispering to me, in my ear, my throat.

How was it that his whispers, his touch never went away?

Was it Skip? Or was it God?

Chapter 19

Late February 1965—Janey

The following Saturday morning, we walked in our long line of twos to the Roller Palace.

It was to be a quick break until noon and then we'd have our first play practice. Jeanne D'Arc danced around in the line, telling us she'd had a mystical experience in prayer.

Cats rolled her eyes.

We passed the clothesline with the nuns' whites whipped up in the wind. Emilie had pleaded cramps, but they made her go anyway. She walked behind us.

I'd caught Cats exchanging notes with Denise on Friday. Something was up for this trip.

Cats and I hadn't had a private minute. I threw back my bangs; Jeanne D'Arc, her gummy smile and red hair. But her eyes were large and hazel and against my wish, I often noticed them.

Philippe walked in her regal way, eyes on the road. She and Sœur Pacifique brought up the rear. Then they split up and joined different pairs of girls.

"Cold?" a soft grain to the voice. Philippe joined us on the path that sloped ahead, the lake now out of sight. Pacifique came running. "Emilie must be taken back," she said, "she's doubled over with cramps. I'll send a replacement." I asked if I could go back with her. Philippe said no.

Inside the Roller Palace door, the room gaped. Sœur Philippe stood in the solitude, directing the girls, finding skates. She'd told me that God was opposite to the expected. She'd taught us that he was "*all things counter*" as Hopkins had written.

She'd told me that at first, God's love could be like a death. To your desires I guessed, to your freedom to be what you wanted to be...it was all so confusing. And what about her man?

At once we were gliding onto the floor. "Will you still love me tomorrow?" The bad Catholic had recent hits! The moldy air stirred. The space grew frenzied, I shuffled and rocked.

Our black uniforms stuck to our ribs, ribbons flying up over our shoulders. Philippe gave a hand to Jeanne D'Arc who'd refused to skate, but then glided shakily onto the floor.

Now we picked up speed.

Philippe stood against the booth. I watched her as I came around the corner. All she wanted was God, it was such an ideal. She was the most authentic person I'd ever known. There she was covered and hidden, silent as the hills in the midst of all the blaring. Wouldn't God want his beloved bursting with life? Fathering forth like the magnificent Hopkins?

The old man lit a new cigarette, bluish smoke wafted by my nostrils.

Virginie found the rubber ball; Suze's hair was matted. Cats' cheeks, pink; the twins were high on the speed, their eyes sparkling. We tore around the rink.

Suddenly in the frenzy, Jeanne D'Arc's skates slipped out from under her, and she fell backwards. I heard her head thud when she hit the floor. Her hair splayed. I felt a little thrill, then guilt.

Philippe skated over; the floor screeched with her brake. She knelt beside Jeanne and called to the old man to bring a cold cloth.

Jeanne was deathly white. So was Philippe. Two white faces. I had to find pity and concern, that dimwitted Jeanne. She might be putting this on.

But ever so gently, Philippe lifted Jeanne's head, tapped her cheeks, felt for blood, her fingers came away smudged. She washed her face carefully. "Can you hear me, Jeanne?"

She cradled her gently in her arms, head on her lap, stroking her forehead. "You're frightened, that's all," she comforted.

I backed away, watching her slim fingers, her striding before the class, collecting herself at the window, throwing herself down the icy hill.

I saw the wonderful strong body asserting itself despite its binding, the black habit bowed in prayer, the handsome bearing more than anything reminiscent of a noble young prince, shrouded by the sorcerer and made to obey him forever.

And there on the floor with a girl in her arms, she looked for all the world like a mother.

Philippe and Jeanne were picked up in the priests' car. She was fine but played up the suffering. Holding her head, she needed a hand as she climbed into the backseat. We started walking back but not without stuffing our bras with popcorn. Suze and I looked everywhere for Cats.

Finally, we saw her bringing up the rear and she made a thumbs-down motion, grimacing.

Her plan had been dashed again. When she caught up to us, she whispered, "Denises' boyfriend was bringing Kentucky fried chicken, darn it Jeanne."

Play practice was not canceled. Philippe had given us free rein in the writing. We had a draft ready and Sister Joey was our director. She'd had theater experience on the outside and directed everything at the convent. This Senior farewell for Conventum would be a dramatic series of skits, poems and songs. The set Cats was designing required large paper machè caves studded with jewels. So far, nothing about God in the script, HA! The caves represented the individual, the jewels, her heart and mind. The journey out was to life and career—the return was to the depths and riches of personal meaning. Our theme was "Individuality." The idea was murky, but we loved it. Girls would act in skits and songs representing our future occupations.

Emilie had joined us but sat apart. Was it the flu? She belonged in bed, but the infirmary was not a place you wanted to be. Cats drew me aside. "They came with chicken and cigs. They were on time too. Stupid Jeanne had to go down like a diseased oak. Our whole break was cut short by that clown."

We ran through the script for the first time. Then Joey said: "You are Seniors. It's time you enjoyed our costume closet." We'd heard about this closet where the girls entering the convent would leave their street clothes. She led us there with a lilt in her step.

"Bien." She opened the door. "All the way back to 1904!" It was a cramped room with two free-standing rods choked with dresses. The shelves held boxes of hats and shoes. There were maroons and greens, net, velvet, and smells of old wool.

There were two trunks against the back wall.

"Bon," Joey handed Suze an old Abbot's robe for her part to play "Wisdom." Cats would be a successful businesswoman. She pushed through some suits and found a jacket with shoulder pads from the 1940s. I was supposed to be a singer, famous I hoped. I picked a yellow sateen dress, slippery to the feel, pulled off my uniform and slipped it on. Discarded by a young girl who had lived her life in a habit, never again to feel this silky sleekness of a dress against her thighs.

"Emilie," said Joey. "You'll need this!" She threw her a red lace dress. Em caught it mid-air. We all stared. What in heaven's name were they doing with a dress like that? Em was playing an actress, one of the suspect professions, but really?

"I will tell you the story of the dress," smiled Joey. So that was it, an excuse to tell a story.

"A woman of ill repute called 'the sinner' came knocking on the convent door in the middle of the night. 'Save me,' she'd sobbed to the Portress.

"Heaven rejoices over the repentance of even one little sinner!"

Em held the dress up to herself and shook her head. But Joey was having some fun. She beckoned Suze and me to help, then turned to welcome Jeanne D'Arc, who'd arrived from the infirmary glowing with health.

Suze pulled the uniform up over Em's head while I held back her hair and we both saw it at once—a tummy bump. *Holy Mary Mother of God, have mercy.* Suze's eyes widened. I glanced at Joey and pulled the red dress over Em's head. Suze enfolded her, whispering, "You missed?"

"I miss sometimes, don't you?"

"How many?"

"I don't know." She looked terribly young suddenly, frightened.

"*Tiens,*" Joey tucked at Em's sleeve with bony fingers. "*Bon, sait bien.*" The red lace dress was actually beautiful, not decadent on Em. Then Joey went to sit in a chair against the back of the closet and called us to her.

Suze sat against the corner, curly hair behind her ears, black-rimmed glasses on the tip of her nose. Em lay on her stomach in the red lace, her long hair parted and hanging over each shoulder, as lovely as a work of art that Germaine might have painted.

Joey pulled out her ring of keys and unlocked a trunk. She lifted out a long box, the kind for roses. She pulled at the cover, intake of breath. Inside in tissue long hair, brown with gold highlights. It had to have hung below a woman's bottom. She lifted it, shook it out. "This is what I left here when I entered," she smiled. "My novice mistress allowed us to keep it for our plays."

Joey's long hair was frizzed its whole length, fastened at the top with a rubber band. It fell in ripples over her lap. "Jeanne," she said. "We shall pin this over your red head, and you shall be transformed into Saint Catherine!" Joey crinkled her eyes.

"That's not all she'll be transformed into," whispered Cats.

We brushed the hair with the tips of our fingers. It gave a heavy illusion but was as light as a cloud.

Then stroking the hair, Joey told us the story of the great Saint Rose of Lima. How she was described in 1617 as having been "comely" and having long golden hair. "Even as a little child, *mes filles,* she feared that her beauty would be an occasion of sin to others and of pride to herself. So she would rub her little face with Indian pepper, causing blotches and disfigurement. So when the priest said that a woman's hair could draw men away from God?

Oui, she took the scissors and cut it all off!"

Joey held up the golden cloud.

"So, she was free of it then," Em said.

"Ah non," said Joey. "Her mother made her grow it back. And she was obedient to her parents, so she did. And she wore a kerchief until it all came back in."

"So, someone had some sense," said Cats.

"Ah, but do you know what she did? She hid a branch with sharp thorns underneath the kerchief because her mother had frustrated her mortification."

"Uh gee." I felt ill—about this poor saint, about Em, everything. What would we do?

Em, meanwhile, lay there listening. Suze had moved close to her and combed her long hair with the tips of her fingers.

After supper, in our relax room as large as a gymnasium, we sang a song by a new English band. Lionel had tried to stop us sometimes, but we'd sing in fierce whispers down by the fence. "I wanna hold your hand," keeping an eye out for Philippe. Justine and Lorraine from New York were teaching us a new dance. They'd been arrested back home for petty theft and sent to the convent to "straighten out." Jeanne D'Arc was moving like a crazed chicken, jerking her arms and shoulders, a miraculous healing.

Sitting at formica tables, girls knitted wispy yarn. Others draped over the hard wooden chairs as if these were couches, eyes closed in reverie, singing along.

When Philippe walked in, we stopped, a habit from Lionel days. She didn't seem upset but Suze, Cats and I went to sit at a table near the window. Jeanne came too. "Can't we do anything to help Em?" she asked. "I think she has the flu. I've been hearing her sobbing at night."

"She has a cold," said Suze.

Jeanne glowered. "Shouldn't we tell Philippe?"

"NO!" Suze left the table abruptly.

I picked up *Wuthering Heights* disguised as *The Life of Bernadette of Soubirous.* Inside the cover, I'd hidden Michael's poem. As I opened the book, the onion skin paper floated to the floor.

Philippe came out of nowhere, leaned down, and snatched it up.

"Sister, that's not a letter," I faced her. "It's something someone copied for me."

Her eyes mischievous, she opened the paper slowly. He'd addressed the poem *My Sweet Kid* and signed it in his slanted hand, *Love, Michael.* Her smile faded. Slowly and systematically, she ripped it across in halves, then into quarters.

I smarted with each rip. "You know the rule," she said.

My friends were speechless. Other girls surrounded us and watched.

Michael's poem disappeared into smaller and smaller pieces.

Philippe walked away, holding the pieces in her fist.

Chapter 20

Philippe

For hours, rip, whisper of paper, Janey's gasp. Hail Mary full of grace, *rip*. After the lights went out, when I was sure the girls had settled down, sitting on my bed, *crack*. Watching at the open window, I couldn't get a full enough breath. There was a sliver of moon behind the Roller Palace. Oh, Janey. The poem wasn't doing any harm.

Back at my chamber, I saw a shadow, slender, motionless. I reached my door, and it stepped out of the dark. "I can't sleep," like an accusation.

"Please. Go to your cell, Janey."

"You would have loved the poem," her voice shaking. "*Love's a treasure like your heart, so precious, pure and fine—looking for the special one that two hearts then may bind.*"

"See, you have it memorized."

"But his handwriting," she blurted.

"Yes. I know."

We listened to the quiet.

I sipped a breath, "*Then I felt like some watcher of the skies, when a new planet swims into his ken.*"

"Who's that?" It was too dark for her to see my wet cheeks.

"Keats," I said, "now *that's* a love sonnet. You can memorize that one too."

Janey's anger floated between us.

155

"It's against the law to open letters and rip up private proper-ty," she said.

"I understand the rule, Janey."

"I see that you do."

"It has to do with distraction."

"From God?"

"And studies. Some things are held down like this," I held my hand low, "and others flower out like this," I gave a flourish into the air.

"And I'm doing this." She flailed her arms everywhere.

I laughed.

"I think I might love Michael, you know."

"You're awfully young to know."

"And you love a God and gave him your whole life at the same age."

Suddenly I saw the picture of my mother, her burning eyes, and her young friends. Her choice of Papa, all those births that ended with me. "In any case, it's God's will—"

"That you rip up my poem?"

"That I be your course mistress."

"Don't tell me that. God made you a teacher."

"I am, whether I teach or not."

For a second, we stood in silence. Janey, usually in motion, now still.

"I'm sorry about your friend's poem," I said.

I knew Philippe was sorry. And I knew she had a temper.

"Janey, what is it you want to ask me all the time? Let's have it."

"I want God to be real," she said. "Not words, not rules. RE-AL."

"I promise you, our God is real."

"Then how does God call a person? If the call is in your mind, how do you know you're not making it up?" I breathed in, but she went on: "Is Christ really a lover? I want to know if you can live. I want to know if—"

"He's also calling you?" I looked around. I must insist she go to bed. But her questions were so like my own. I lowered my voice even more. "When I was young, I wanted to be a priest. I grieved because I would never touch the bread and wine, or be allowed to celebrate Mass. My mother died when I was born, and she had prayed for a priest from her many sons."

"Did she get one?"

"Only a nun."

"I loved the Mass too," she said. "The music, the scents, the mystery—"

"It's beauty you love, Janey."

"Does that mean I'm not called? People have been mixing beauty with God forever."

In the porous dark, I smiled at this plucky girl.

We heard the swish of slippers. "You'd better go," I whispered.

"No, finish, please," she pleaded.

"Well, I studied literature and decided to teach. My family couldn't afford college for the girls. But thanks be to God, the order is sending me."

"That's not Christ calling you!" she said. "It's supposed to be a love affair with a marriage ceremony and all that goes with it."

"It is! Christ is real, Janey. And elusive. I think that's just the way it is for human beings."

"But how do you do it? He says: love me first. And you do. But you can never totally have him."

"Obedience," I said.

"Oh NO! To Mère? To the distant priest?"

"To love. Do you think it's any different in marriage? You take one small step while you are promising extremes, forever, under all circumstances. Have you ever listened to those vows? Janey, I want this life, I do." I said, emphatically. "I gave myself to Christ, wholly and forever. I believe in what he stands for, who he was on earth. I believe we are meant to serve and love others through him. He says I must die so that I can be reborn in Him."

"But then you'll be a different person."

"No, I'll be the person He created me to be."

"I want that too!" she said, "Can't I love God in the world?"

"Yes!" I was shaking. "But you still have to die to self. Every seed must go into the ground. Only then can it bear fruit."

Our breathing rasped in the dark.

Turning quickly, I entered my chamber and came out with a piece of paper. "I keep this with me," I said. "Psalm 139. We stud-ied it as literature in high school. It was the first stirring of my call." I handed it to her and clicked the door shut behind me.

I was deliberate getting ready for bed, changing out of the coif and into the night bonnet.

I passed a hand through my hair, an inch all over. I would shave it off again on Saturday, better than a prickly mess. I reached for my night clothes, drew my hand back.

When I slipped naked between the sheets and lay back on the pillow, a longing for Skip surged through me from the top of my head to the tips of my toes—I rolled over to shut it out and fell asleep.

In the morning, a fog of pain in my head kept me still. I lay there nauseated at the thought of moving even an inch. Stretching my coif against my forehead was out of the question. When I tried to sit up, a vise squeezed it tight, a sharp pain pierced my left eye. Foolishly pulling on my night clothes, I ran to the toilet, knelt down and heaved. There was nothing in my stomach. I shook, hugging the toilet. I tried to stand up and retched. This was not like any other headache. I was alone. Upstairs in the cloister, my sisters would have helped me.

I don't know how long I stayed wrapped around the toilet bowl. Mercifully, the girls were still asleep. I took up my basin and dry heaving, dragged myself upstairs to Jacinta's cell.

Gasping, I asked her to take the girls. She looked alarmed but went quickly.

When I got back to my bed and leaned against the pillows, I eyed the film of ice on top of my pitcher. Poking it, I lifted a shard and placed it over my left eye. Relief washed into the pain.

I hadn't known what to do, the pain had known. I stayed motionless on the bed, fumbling with my fingers for pieces of ice from the frozen wash water.

I would have to tell someone, but who? I wanted to tell Claire. I lay motionless, it helped, but no sleep, I would never sleep again. Skip's tenderness wafted before my closed eyes.

The ice had melted into my ears and hair, wetting the pillow. I dipped my face cloth into the freezing water and placed it on my forehead. I heard the girls swishing back and forth now, filing out for Matins, the quiet falling over the dorm. Finally, after a time, I lifted the facecloth to wet it again, squinted hard in the light. I drank in the darkness and cold until finally, I felt ease instead of the python squeezing my head.

When I opened my eyes again, it was dark. And then, as I lay still, I felt my breathing go to the center of my being. The pain was gone, I was resting. I felt surrounded by well-being, completely healed, a deep, thorough release, a soul quieting.

All will be well. God transcended the pain; his Holy Being, the air I breathed, and the space I moved in. I would not try to decipher his will but rather give myself to it.

I thought of the hand-written psalm I'd given to Janey; I knew phrases of it by heart.

You have searched me out and known me,
You know my sitting down and my rising up;
You understand my thoughts from afar.
For You formed my inward parts;
You covered me in my mother's womb.
Where can I flee from Your presence?

Chapter 21

Palm Sunday—Janey

Palm Sunday Mass. We held the pointy palm branches, received Him on our tongue as incense wafted through the sanctuary, sang hosannas to the King of Kings. Afterward, we enjoyed a special breakfast. Easter was the next weekend and Conventum, the Saturday after that. I'd placed Philippe's psalm in my pocket with her poem. We didn't read Old Testament and I'd never seen that psalm. I would thank her when I could, she was a treasure-house of living words.

In the afternoon, we sat around the course with its big bay windows, working on preparations. Girls were at tables folding napkins, creating place cards. At around four in the afternoon, three nuns appeared in the course. "Girls, fast and sacrifices all through Holy Week," said Sister Joey, "but today, with our Hosannas, we'll take a break from Lent!"

Joey, Pacifique, and Gabrielle, their habit skirts rustling, clicked their clappers and launched into a French song; we gathered around them.

Philippe came out of her office. When she saw the nuns, her face broke into a smile, and she went to them. "*Salut!*" They brushed fingers like young girls.

"*Viens, viens, mes filles,*" Joey sang. "*J'entends le mou lin tique tique taque.*" She clicked the steady beat. The old Canadian songs were full of rhythm. Her mouth formed perfect O's. The bottom half of her habit swayed, keeping time. Her moist eyes danced.

Pacifique, a tiny tanned-faced nun, sang the harmony, Philippe clapped. "*Tique tique taque.*" What would they think of next?

Joey, our great storehouse of Catholic fairy tales with her cloud of rippling hair forever golden and young, while the rest of her grew gray. We adored her and sang our hearts out.

"*Il y'a un rat, Il y'a un rat, j'entends le chat miaule.*"

Philippe sang in her rich alto, the overhead lights making shadows behind her on the wall. I watched her in misery, still hurt despite her brief apology. I had so much to say. I threw my head back, pouring myself into songs.

That night, the dorm rustling ceased, girls' sleep-breathing all around me. I got out of bed and tiptoed toward Philippe's door, hoping for another chance, then took the narrow paths between cell curtains to the back of the dorm where the windows stood open. To my surprise, Cats was there, her hair glistening in the moonlight. She never let anything get in the way of her sleep.

We looked out the window together, spring air warming us, making us catch our breath.

There was comfort in the silent dark and we peered into it, the silver reflections of moonlight, the beckoning Roller Palace across the lake. Suddenly, there was a low whistle coming from behind the pines. Cats gave a delicious sigh and whistled softly.

I turned to her in surprise.

"I would've come got you, I promise," she grinned.

Two shadows were making their way across the grass. Then two more. We hung there and watched them stream across the grounds. I pressed my eyes to be sure I wasn't seeing things.

They came to just below our window five floors down. The dayhops, Denise and Denise and their boyfriends, Luigi and Dean—a shine of moonlight off their hair. It was hard to believe how stealthy they were being, their mouths usually never stopped.

"Hey you, sweet old Cats," whispered one of them. "C'man c'man. Hey, Janey, you there?"

Cats reached into her pocket and pulled out the end of a rope, lowering it slowly out the window, down into the shadows. A soft laugh floated up. One of the Denises got kissed. "Ooooh," Cats leaned against me.

"Go get Suze and Em," she whispered.

"Are you crazy?"

"Go. Wasn't going to miss our chicken. Tired of all this waiting for chicken."

The rope tugged twice. "Sweet-art," the voice said from below. Cats pulled the rope hand over hand. Up and up it came making soft thumps now and then against the convent brick.

He'd tied two Kentucky fried chicken drumsticks to the rope.

"Ohhh, still warm." She sank her teeth into the soft breaded covering, fumbling with the knot, bits of chicken coating dripping over the windowsill. She tore the meat off the bone like a little bear.

"Janey, chomp," swallowing, and handing one to me.

I was beside myself with the smell. If nothing else, the smell would wake everybody up.

I wasn't sure I even needed to taste. It might be a disappointment to taste. But oh, the taste, hadn't realized how hungry I was until my chest ached with it, the more bites I took of the flesh, the breading...

"Napkins," Cats whispered down through the shadows. She picked up pieces of chicken coating, licked her fingers, smiled her fox smile. It was impossible to argue, hard not to love her.

The rope tugged twice again. Up came two more legs.

"Go." Cats pushed me with her hip.

I wiped my fingers on a napkin and slipped off my slippers; then tiptoed to Jeanne D'Arc's cell. She was the reason we'd missed our chicken in the first place, but I woke her up anyway. Then I pulled on Suze's toes, shook Em, even woke Celine and the twins, carried away with good fortune. They followed me without question.

"Ah come on, "said Cats, "should've known not to send the Queen of Angels," as eight girls crowded together at the window, "gees—why don't we feed the whole world?"

By now, four ropes had been lowered and everyone had a drumstick. We chewed, whispered, arms around each other all squeezed along the huge windowsill. For a while, Suze sat up on it, her back to the night, shivering and chomping; and the chicken kept coming up through the dark, "just like the feeding of the five thousand," I said, munching.

Arm around Em, I blew kisses to Luigi and Dean and the shadow Denises who kept quiet except for giggles, along with the picked clean bones thumping back down on the strings. The night held the mirror lake in the distance, the blue-black Roller Palace, the warm chicken flesh between our tongues and teeth, the salty breading, the heavy fry oil, the fullness like no other, and the blessed chicken legs just kept coming up the ropes.

Chapter 22

Palm Sunday—Philippe

About to sleep. My head was better. Shakes, vomit. Please God, no more. Mother West Wind came to me, and I heard Brer Rabbit pleading— "no, no, not the briar patch." My will kept me going here. The headaches had to go. Suddenly I heard loud whispering.

I opened my door—oh those girls, I must catch them! I moved between the cells toward the sound—and what was that smell? The luscious scent of meat during Lent!

I hid behind a curtain. They were at the windows pulling something up on ropes, arms around each other, and chewing on something, bones?—my Lord, it's ingenious! Chicken legs. I watched, hungry, astonished, salivating.

Oh my dears! You even have napkins.

Cats wiped fry oil from her lips.

I tiptoed back to my chamber and let them be happy.

The next day, mid-morning, the girls in class, I was on my knees beside my bed, intense, arms outstretched, head empty of everything but pleading. If I served him with my whole heart, did it matter where?

God was silent.

I knew silence. When I was a child, Papa would come home from his construction work, hands cracked and blistered; he'd sit in the rocker with one or two of us in his lap. He'd do this every night. We knew he loved us; he'd smile often and stroke our heads but seldom spoke.

Dodie said that his words left him when our Maman died.

A mentor from my reading, Father Bede Griffiths, appeared in the dark. In his memoir, he said he knelt in his closet and vowed to God; he would not emerge until he got an answer. If I had a closet, I'd go in and shut the door. Now I closed my eyes like a secret door, my eyelashes brushing my under-eyes.

God, do you want me here or not?

Saint Theresa of Avila's Interior Castle came to me, the seven stages. The great saint was educated, brilliant—I trusted her. But she was a sixteenth-century cloistered nun, describing her certainty of Jesus when she mortified her body.

Mortification. I felt the word on my tongue. The ancient word.

She wore instruments of penance. The church sanctioned it. Wasn't it the most you could offer to Christ? But then I thought of my mother offering her body for me to be born. Dying for my new life.

And then there was Skip—beautiful in himself, strong, intelligent. His supple, muscular body—loving someone you could hold and touch and my body and its wants—but I gave him up, three years ago.

It's my body betraying me, not my heart. I must push back.

This dark penitential Monday of Holy Week, we prayed the Stations of the Cross, nuns and girls. Jesus falls. I stared at his crown of thorns and the red blood. He bled for us. I think there must be a way for us to bleed for him.

Tuesday morning when the girls were in class, I knew what I must do. The nuns' private library was warm and smelled of old books. My eyes ran along the book jackets. I pulled out a Carmelite manual and read through the table of contents: penitential instruments: hairshirt, scourge, chains. "To take up the sufferings of Christ." Chains covered with nails. The picture was gruesome. Worn for a brief period; permission must be obtained.

This is how I will bend my body to God's will. Worn on the thigh. The date, 1962, not that long ago! A Scripture reference, "I am pulverized to be reborn in you."

Father Girard was everyone's spiritual director, the only one we've had since Novitiate. He was a young man, an ascetic with sunken cheeks, and a slender but athletic body. He carried his breviary everywhere and studied most of the time in his rectory. Our cook made him trout with tomato, lemon chicken, pudding with whipped cream. Needless to say, we never saw food like that but all during Novitiate, we hung on his every word. I was embarrassed to remember. We were hungry for color, and he was the only man we had. He was gentle and quiet except when he stepped into the pulpit, casting glances over us with a sour expression, pounding and shouting about Satan and temptation, chastity, and obedience.

Easier than I dreamed; I'd never made a special appointment. I explained what I wanted to do through the grate. Father told me I was not alone. It wasn't something you shared with a living soul, deeply personal, private. He didn't require more detail—nothing about why I wanted to do it, only that I was having a crisis of call.

In ancient times, he said, mortification was part of every con-templative's spiritual life—monks and cloistered nuns alike. Many still believed it necessary for spiritual health. We discussed the dif-ferent choices. He would order the chains and deliver them to me with discretion. This was between me and my God, under strict order to use no longer than three days.

I planned all that night. As I decided my furtive steps, Skip was nowhere. He could not stand side by side in my thoughts with what I was about to do. There was relief in that. I would fast as well; it would be past Easter by the time the package came, so I'd have to take care. How will I hide it? If I'd been teaching, I might have fal-tered. But this strained motherhood of girls gave me some free-dom. And hadn't there been hints in convent life all along—the smothering habit, the shaving of hair—preparing me all the time for more? Can the ancients have been wrong?

Our community took up the activities of Holy Week. Holy Thursday when Jesus washes the feet and gives the bread and wine to his friends, "This is my body. My peace I give to you. Do this in memory of me." I could barely move out of the pew for Commun-ion.

My sisters knew how to celebrate, but this year the Day of Res-urrection was damped down, saving our flowers and linens for Conventum, next weekend. God would not be offended. During Mass, beautiful in its simplicity, we sang the Easter alleluia an-thems.

On Easter Monday, we turned to Conventum, and the play. After supper, Father called for me and gave me a brown paper package. My own Holy Week began.

I entered my sleep chamber with it hidden under some books. After the girls' lights out, I closed my door and sat on the edge of my bed. Carefully, I untied the brown string; my fingers shook as I pulled the fluttering paper open. The directions lay on top of thick tissue. I set them aside, pulled apart the yellowed tissue; lying there were two chains of steel three-quarters of an inch thick, studded with small nails, leather straps at either end that tightened in a buckle. My stomach turned. Slicing shards, sharp as icicles that hung from the convent eaves, shining silver in the faint light; they'd penetrate a quarter of an inch into my skin. The chains must be measured and closed tightly, and I removed two links from each as directed.

I removed my layers of habit one by one and stood in underwear and chemise. I'd gathered cotton and alcohol from the infirmary to wash the sharp points and links. My heart slipped. Readying the instrument, I stood on my towel and pressed each link into my thigh. Blood spilled out, red and running down my leg, a whoosh of breath, I slipped to the floor onto my hands and knees. The nails had come out; I held my bleeding thigh and re-entered them, cringed as I buckled the chain tight. Nausea crept into my throat.

I pierced the second thigh and stood up.

I was doing something real. This was my body; I alone controlled it. I was wrong and right at the same time.

And then something licked at me like a flame.

I was afraid. I wanted to take the chains off and get relief.

But no, suddenly I wanted to hurt myself more, pierce more and would I even be able to stop?

I closed the paper package. But something completely unexpected happened. Calm suffused my body. My breaths slowed; they plunged deep.

I lay back on the bed and pulled the covers over me.

I felt release.

Chapter 23

Janey

Holy Week was as mournful as promised with fasting, Stations of the Cross, and black cloths covering the statues. We kept the silence imposed by Mère, who seemed to be watching and showing up everywhere. Em dragged herself through services and carried her brand of silence. She wouldn't talk to us. We discussed endlessly how to help her. She must keep her audition; she could hide a lot in the uniform and graduate with us, but throwing up was tougher to hide. She was in a cloud of denial.

Cats wrote notes to the Denises thanking them for the chicken and planning her date for the prom. All forty of us kept the "night watch" with Jesus' body on Good Friday. They had a special statue for this, "Jesus is laid in the tomb." I kept my private, wordless watch over everything.

Easter came and went with far less of the usual fanfare. On Easter Tuesday, with four days to go to Conventum weekend, Cats' glamorous mother, Coco Devine, came to the convent to help us finish our sets for the play. Cats was in the best mood; she loved designing and planning. It was against the rules for her mother to visit during the week, and I was dusting near the main vestibule when I heard, "Say there, Sister, so what do you know?" I peeked around just in time to catch Coco breezing past the Portress who stammered, "I'm afraid I can't admit you, Mrs. Devine."

"No?" She walked down the hall. "But I'm to work with the Seniors today, didn't they tell you?" She walked on at a clip. The old nun waddled behind. "But, but," she wheezed, "it's your slacks, Mrs. Devine, we have a rule—"

"Of course you do, deah—"

The Portress caught up with her. Mrs. Devine turned around. She was a small, dazzling woman and a Protestant to boot! Slim in her wheat-colored slacks, pumpkin-colored collar turned up under a tweed jacket. "Now, Sister," she said. She had a forthright low voice, and an emphatic way of saying "deah." "I'm to be up and down a ladder all afternoon," and then she stepped around the old nun and continued down the hall.

"Janey, girl," Mrs. Devine said and grabbed my hand, "you're pale. What've they done to you?"

"I'm so glad you got in!"

"Oh, don't bother, they're just a bunch of ladies."

I laughed. We deposited her bags on a theater seat in the auditorium and went back outside. The girls had seen her pick-up truck and were converging from different wings into the courtyard.

"Here you are," said Mrs. Devine, reaching for Cats, who patted her arms in a quick collision. She unloaded a ladder and Jeanne D'Arc grabbed the other end. Virginie lifted pieces of scaffolding from the truck; Suze, a box of tools; Em, a box of glue and glitter. Em pushed her hair off her shoulder. Could we be wrong? We skipped our periods all the time at the convent, especially me, I hadn't had one in almost a year.

"Mom, this is great!" Cats said, unwrapping some crinkled gray fabric. She hugged her mother hard then. "I have a great idea for the cave." She smiled, satisfied, showing her gorgeous straight teeth. Cats had gotten braces at fourteen, a luxury most of us had not had.

When we reached the auditorium stage with all the materials, Mrs. Devine set up the scaffold; she had steel blue eyes, silky chestnut lashes, a tiny straight nose, a heart-shaped face.

She raised furry Shetland ponies on their farm, showing them and selling them. I loved Cats' farm, smelling of hay and honeysuckle. Her father was Catholic and here was no high school in Bolton.

Cats rummaged through her mother's bags for illegal snacks. Oranges, pears, a little bag of hazelnuts, M&Ms. "Mmmmm." She dumped them onto a bit of paper on the stage floor and started lining them up by colors.

"Hide them," said Suze.

"Fiddlesticks! Your whole life is Lent," laughed Mrs. Devine, her voice warm and deep for such a slender, wiry woman. "Eat, eat, girls."

She showed us how to hammer the rock paper to the scaffolding. I watched the energy that drove her, the raspberry blush at her cheek and honey hair, the wheaty clothes. I placed Philippe beside her in my mind—Philippe, black-clad, unadorned and promised, but also beautiful. And then both of them beside my own mother with her warm, round face and brown eyes, the floury apron over her house dress, the kitchen smells.

"Girls, where'd you settle on for the prom?" asked Mrs. Devine. We were holding a corner of the cave while she and Cats stapled. Cats whistled a tune.

"The dayhops chose the Holiday Inn," said Jeanne D'Arc.

"Oh dear." Mrs. Devine wrinkled her nose.

"That's not the worst of it," said Cats. "We're supposed to bring our dates here for a receiving line."

"You're joking." Raised eyebrows.

"Limits my date pool considerably."

"And it was huge before?" said Suze.

I surveyed the auditorium with its upholstered seats, baroque ceilings and heavy ornate draperies, the painted cherubs and the eye of God with its rays of yellow sun. No, I wasn't going to the prom.

"How are we even supposed to *find* dates stuck in here?" asked Jeanne D'Arc. "Janey, at least you have a boyfriend."

"Randy Hinkleberry wants to take you," Mrs. Devine told Cats. "And he has a friend!"

"Mom, you can't be serious," said Cats. "He has big ears."

We slathered the jewel shapes we'd cut out with glue and glitter and crawled inside the cave to paste them all over its walls.

"Caves of the person," sang Suze, "Now, off into the world," she ran out of the cave shouting, "What I do is me, for that I came!" and jumped off the stage onto the floor.

"INDIVIDUALITY OR DEATH!"

We laughed but it wasn't funny. Our theme was above all else, "individuality." It was a great compliment here to be called an "individual."

Now, we had one—Mrs. Devine. She'd worn a hat last time I was at the farm—a large brimmed one-of-a-kind hat, with pencil-thin green feathers, perched to one side and her matching coat and dress in mulberry and lime; the scarves she tied around herself. How did you learn to dress like that, to be yourself?

Em pushed me from behind. Mère Supérieure was coming up the aisle from the back of the auditorium. We stashed the snacks. She was carrying two teacups.

Mrs. Devine stood up straight in her forbidden slacks. Mère reached her on the stage.

Without a word, she handed her a cup of tea, all smiles.

Then they walked together to the front row of seats as though this had been prearranged, near the carved moldings and stage lights. Mère sat ramrod straight in the seat, turning her hand now and then in conversation, her little finger cocked from her teacup. They kept their voices low, as though intimate. Mrs. Devine's legs were crossed rakishly in the wheat slacks.

Finally, Mère stood up and clapped her hands. "A run-through, girls!" she called, beaming. "Let us see what you have."

I needed my script for a John Donne passage. I asked if I could run and get it in the dorm.

Mère was positively cheerful and nodded. We never went back to the dorm during the day. It was heartily frowned on to even think about your bed in the daytime. Off I went.

I took the stairs two at a time and rushed in. Sister Philippe stood high on a ladder in front of the first row of cells. It was huge, maybe eight, ten feet tall?

"Sister Philippe!"

She'd taken the light fixture apart with a rubberized screwdriver and yanked on a wire. My God, she could be electrocuted.

"Almost finished. Hold the ladder, Janey." She pulled and huffed. "What are you doing here?"

I told her I forgot my script. I felt an unexpected ease between us.

"Well," she said, "they teach us useful things in the novitiate," turning the screwdriver against the ceiling, "carpentry, plumbing," she wiped her brow with her other hand.

The ladder shook, I clasped it. She whistled a tune.

"Sister, I've been thinking about being reborn in Christ, you know, what you said."

"And I remembered another poem for you. What would we do without our poets?"

Suddenly, the screwdriver whizzed past my head, grazed my shoulder, and clattered to the floor.

"I'm so sorry," Philippe called down. "Were you clunked?"

"I'm fine," I said, handing the tool up.

She climbed one step higher. A lump in my throat. There were holes in her shoe soles. My eyes followed the threadbare black stockings. "*A Nun Takes the Veil. I have desired to go where springs not fail.*" The wire eluded her in the ceiling hole. She poked into the wires. "This is a live one," she laughed.

I dug my loafers into the floor and placed my hip against the ladder.

"Janey, grab that light over there."

I hated to let go. I quickly got the flashlight.

"To fields where flies no sharp and sided hail—"

I shined the light on the ceiling. Philippe tipped forward, stepped up.

"*And I have asked to be where no storms come—*" She swayed, her leg swung out, skirts opened wide.

"Oh," I gasped.

Nails pierced the skin of her thigh.

Her shoe found the step.

Nails attached to chains, cinched tight.

Had I seen it?

She was on her way down, black shoes coming toward me.

"Sister, I have to get back." I let go and ran to my cell.

Dried crusts of blood, fresh blood, chains...

"Wait, Janey," she called.

But I clutched my script and was out the door, whispering the ancient word, feeling it on my tongue, *mortification*...could it be?

That evening, scullery duty. Suze and I rinsed the dirty dishes in huge steel sinks; they clinked together, the water whooshed— brown gravy, mystery meat, down the gurgling drain. We loaded plates into the industrial washer, singing *By the waters of Babylon*. The cutlery added percussion, the scullery nun, Jean D'Orleans, sang and dried. I kept seeing the chains of blood.

Suze said I looked like a ghost.

Why was Philippe hurting her skin? I thought of how Michael gently opened our coats, his shirt, my blouse, and pulled me to him whispering, "I want skin."

That night in my bed, I tried to understand, taking shallow breaths like a runner.

We are cleansed by His blood.
He shed His blood for us.
He saved us by His blood.
We drink His blood.
   NO.

I needed to tell someone. I could sense the words on my tongue, the relief of getting help, but who? Surely not Mère? Cats? Suze? Philippe was private.

We'd learned about mortification from the lives of the saints, cloistered ones, ancient ones.

Maybe she was a saint.

She was my teacher, my mentor, we loved the same God.

I was going to find out. I needed to understand.

After a day of anxious thinking, after supper, I asked permission to pray in the chapel.

The altar was lit by candles, Mary with her long hair and the background of dark blue sky and silver stars. Queen of our Hearts. I knelt in a pew.

The natural dusky light poured through the old stained glass. Shadows flickered. A click went off in my mind, like a slideshow— smooth white skin, sharp embedded nails. Once in the summer, I decided not to eat, prayed a lot and felt tremendous power. Then I broke down and devoured Maman's meat pie, thinking, why would I starve in the summer when we had convent food all year?

I understood the saints a little.

Intimacy with God. Was it possible? *"Let me be to thee as a circling bird..."* Hopkins' image of a flying creature who never quits, or lands, just hovers.

Like Philippe, I wanted beauty and truth, color, word.

The tabernacle sat in gold silk; its door closed. Silent.

Philippe was asking to be crucified *with him*. Pierced *with him*. In 1965.

Where did she even get the things?

I would find out in the forbidden nuns' library. I'd have to sneak down in the night. In the dark. I cringed, long halls, alone.

No, it had to be now. I stood up. I walked out the chapel door and along the hall.

To have time in there, I would need to be dressed as a nun.

I could steal a habit!

I turned around and went the other way. I'd never been inside the nuns' laundry; luckily it would be empty at this hour.

But it wasn't. When I cracked the door, an odor of alcohol and starch hit my nostrils.

Across the room were rounded backs of laundry nuns, ironing. The room was half the size of our course, with cement ceilings, and naked fluorescent tubes giving off stark, ugly light and humming on an irritating A pitch. How could they stand that hum? Why weren't they resting? I couldn't steal a habit with them here.

Well, I would have to. Philippe wouldn't miss me yet.

Black habits, cleaned and pressed, hung on a clothesline. I had to cross the room. Steam rose in a mist from a row of steel tubs. The stocky nuns pushed into their pressings, silent except for the rhythmic thud of the irons. And the hum on A. Nuns cleaned the wool habits by hand using naptha, something I'd never seen. Other ropes slung from pole to pole with white undergarments, night cloaks, wimples, veils; frontispieces and, for humility, white coifs that tightened around the face.

I wet my dry lips and eased off my red loafers, tiptoed forward in stockings. Along the wall of tubs, habits soaked; the smell was metallic, like hot tar. I kept my eyes on the nuns' backs and tiptoed past individual piles of whites topped with brassieres neatly folded on a long table. I picked one up, then reached the habits hanging just above me. Pinned to each was a black veil, frontispiece, cincture, coif. I reached up, pulled a set down. The hanger clanged into the steel.

I ducked.

Footsteps pattered toward the tub, hard, hollow.

The silence was the worst. I pictured the round nun, the beady eyes. Michael wouldn't believe this. No wonder he wanted to rescue me.

I would be punished, again—but this time repeat Senior year in the public high.

Then the steps receded. The squeak of the ironing board resumed.

A row of pins on the habit shoulder looked like railroad tracks. I slipped the hanger off and gently laid it down, peeked over the tub. The nuns thudded their irons.

I tiptoed to the door hugging folds of cloth, slipped into my red loafers and out.

Now I was late, but Cats would tell Philippe I was praying.

In the bathroom stall, still trembling, I examined everything. Sweet cloth, pressed smooth, inner and outer layers, light, dark. I buried my face.

Pulling off my uniform, I stood shivering in my underwear, small breasts hardened, protesting the cold. I held the huge brassiere by its strap. A fortress! I stashed my uniform and lifted a white undergarment, jumping from foot to foot, how long till someone missed me? The white skirt was yards wide, buttons down the front. But no, I needed only black to be hidden. I held up each white piece—slip, chemise and placed them with the fortress bra. But huge bloomers? I laughed and whipped those on. I wound the wimple around my head. There was no mirror. Wrapping, grabbing pins out of my mouth, fastening in back.

My scalp itched, the wimple hid my forehead, ears, contours of cheeks and chin. The black serge habit slipped over my wimpled head, against it my body felt new. The black frontispiece tied in back and fell to the waist, a crucifix usually over it. As I wrapped the cincture around my waist, I remembered the words of Jesus to the Apostles, 'Now you will be led where you do not wish to go.' The black veil pinned into place reached to the back of my knees. And I remembered the novices lying on their faces before the altar.

I stood in the bathroom stall and breathed in the smells: bleach, starch, naptha, sweat.

I was disappearing.

Hidden, whole, holy. I sank into Philippe.

So, this was a nun. I had put her on so easily. And if I kept her on, no one would ever wonder at me again. They'd say, "I know who she is."

I leaned against the door, feeling the unbending metal. I wouldn't have to search anymore or find a way to live what I wanted so much to believe. Or defend it. Or deny it.

Warmth and softness, edges gone.

Body, bread, poems, surrender.

I was inside.

I shook myself and gathered the pile of clothes, whites for purity. Was this God's call? Was I hearing God?

I opened the door of the lav and walked in small steps down the hall, keeping "custody of the eyes," but wait—there I was reflected in the window—Ha! Look at that tiny, lost nun!

But go, move. If Mère caught me at this—

Shaken, I shoved a hand into the habit's deep pocket. Something was there. I rounded the corner, pulled it out. A stick of gum, silver wrapper. They had their own Denises!

Passing the Blessed Virgin with folded notes in her fingers, I felt the whoosh before sin, jockeyed my uniform and the whites, reached up and took the notes.

I unwrapped the silver paper, popped the gum in my mouth. Ugh, the taste. Metallic.

In the library, stacks of old books lined up beside each other; there must be one that would describe what I'd seen. But maybe I hadn't seen anything. My chin locked into the coif, no way to see from side to side and my skin itched. How did they live like this? Holding the bundle, my eyes ran along the books, physically beautiful and worn. The metal book stacks stood four or five in a row in the middle of the room. I went down into the farthest one.

The category? *Mortification.*

I scanned titles, running my finger over the jackets: Sainte Thé-rèse, Saint Francois.

The word, Penitential. I placed the bundle on the floor and pulled the book, a Carmelite manual.

Illustrated. Table of contents. *Mortification, submission.* I licked my finger and tripped the thin paper. In the meager light, I stared until my eyes smarted. *Hair Waist, hair shirt.* A picture of a shirt covered with rough hairs.

"For the body which is the Church." My body twisted inside the layers.

STEEL CHAINS—oh. There it is.

The nails are worn inside. What about tetanus? My chest ached.

It was an instrument to be used for brief periods of time; $16.95. Wait, you paid for the things?

Someone was coming. My hands flew to the veil and the book dropped to the floor. I shoved strands of my hair into the coif, Ha! They all do that. I would never pass.

I bolted through the stacks, out the door, red shoes flying, around the corner, into the hall, picking up the layers of skirt to my thighs and throwing my legs out as fast as I could run.

Relief as I reached the bathroom, no, *get out of here.*

I burst out faster, shoved my pile against the flapping cincture, holding it in, grabbed the veil in my other hand. One set of stairs was close.

As I tore down them, I heard a muffled, "MaSœur," but did not look back—ran right out the door into the courtyard, all the way down the hill under the grape arbor and down to the lower fence.

I whipped off the layers, the veil, wimple, frontispiece, habit, coif, the cold wind helping, bringing me back to myself.

Chapter 24

Philippe

In the course, recreation over, girls lined up. Where was Janey? Up in the dorm, they stood at the sinks with pitchers and Cats frowned at me.

"Did she say anything?" I tried to stay calm.

"No, Sister, nothing." This was strange, given how close they were.

I felt a stab of hunger, or was I going to be sick? The girls washed and I went to find Jacinta. She was at her desk in the cloister. "Janey's missing. Would you cover for me?"

"Of course," She followed me immediately.

"Any ideas?"

As we walked together, I wiped sweat from my upper lip, twisted to avoid the pain in my thighs. Jacinta's warm, freckled face made me want to spill everything.

I hurried down the stairs. The ladder, the straining to reach the fixture, Janey below...I flung open the chapel door. The wind was strong outside the rattling windows, the old wood creaked. The red light on the altar glowed with God's presence, the golden sanctuary lights, always on. The chapel was empty.

Down the hall, a line of light bled from under the library door. I opened it slowly, then fully and searched up and down the aisles. A book on the floor. I pushed out to the courtyard. Had she walked right off the grounds? Under the apple trees and down the hill. There, something moved behind the branches.

I peered to see, in the rising moonlight, a nun. Tearing off a veil...

And then in a glimpse of light among the leaves, I saw Janey's face in the coif. *I was seeing things.*

The nun was ripping off her cincture as though on fire, frontispiece up over her head, no longer holy, falling into dead leaves.

She unbuttoned the stiff collar, detached the wimple. My heart howled in pain watching the layers tear off her—I flinched with each piece.

The pieces of my life. And my private prayer and discipline. What kind of game was this? I wanted to scream.

She was down to the bloomers. I crept closer, staying hidden. They fell to the pine needle carpet. Her own chemise too. And then she couldn't stop – everything else. She stood there naked and trembling, finally still. The moon cast a bluish light on her skin. I held my breath.

Oh, my dear Janey.

Of course she'd seen the chains. She had to know things for herself. She must be so confused. What did my mortification have to do with God?

There in the light, skinny and vulnerable, the sight of her filled me with tenderness.

We were given one body for our journey—one skin that held together all the passion, and intelligence, and searching.

Janey was a brave traveler.

And I was seeing myself.

Chapter 25

Janey

As I wriggled back into my uniform, Casper appeared out of the darkness, meowing. I picked up the pieces of habit and something fell. The folded notes.

I made my way along the apple trees up the hill, hugging the black and white clothing, bloomers, coif, veil and bra. Casper and I climbed up the back stairs where I tried the door; locked. Now what? Luckily Mère was still away.

I placed the pile on the porch step, sat down and rummaged for the notes. Cats had stolen a note once—she said it was a formal prayer, unsigned and boring. They needn't sign them because God knew. Didn't need to write them either! Casper rubbed my arm with his nose.

I unfolded the small one and even in moonlight, could see it was Emilie. *"Please God, please, please, tell me what to do."*

I sighed. What kind of a friend had I been lately, and now stealing habits and running around?

It was wrong to read notes meant for God.

Still, I opened another. *"Lord, this is a special intention,"* red pen, tiny letters like bird tracks. *"Dear blessed mother, for a girl's struggle to know God. Send your wisdom and your light. Give me words for her."*

I closed my eyes. I thought Philippe was too cool to leave notes. This was all wrong. I must return them to the fingers—and the habit to the laundry. But instead of moving, I opened the larger note. The door opened. I hid the paper.

"Come in here," said Philippe, a tensile worry in her voice. "What have you been doing?"

"Finding God." I shivered.

"You've figured out who He is?"

"Well, I—"

"Come in," she said.

We waited.

She stood, erect, probably hurting all the time.

Then, she walked out toward me and the pile of clothes. Wonder of wonders, she leaned over and picked up Casper, stroking him in the dark. He mashed her with his paws, purring, nestling against her habit. She couldn't have hugged me more if she'd surrounded me with her arms.

I presented her with the clothes.

She placed the cat on the step and took the bundle. "Janey?!" she pleaded.

"I know. I was sinning. It was stupid. I'm…"

"Oh my dear. Did anyone see you?"

I shook my head.

"Janey, I'm so sorry, but my mortification is private."

Misery rose in me.

"It's not something we can discuss."

"Are there saints that still do it?"

"That's discussing," she said. "And I'm not a saint."

"Was it taught in the Novitiate?"

She went still. "Penance is a part of our rule, not that specific penance."

"Then why?" like a cry. It was too dark, but I felt her worry. "I can unsee it," I said quickly.

"I'm afraid you cannot. And it's not your fault. But we must get you in, quietly, Janey."

She turned and climbed the stairs.

In the dorm, I pulled the covers over me; the warmer I felt, the more I shook. I should have walked right off the grounds and taken a bus home, forgotten all about Hopkins and chains, but that was not what I wanted. Would I ever be able to fix it?

I must have fallen asleep.

Floating in a dream, clothed in a warm habit—*lily colored clothes spouse not labored-at nor spun*—I wound the coif, draped the veil, sat up, wide awake.

Really, I'm hearing a call! I let out all my breath. I should lie here and think about that.

But there was another note...

A pang in my chest. The entire sin catastrophe.

I got out of bed, felt in my uniform pocket, found my flashlight, and burrowed under the covers. My fingers shook as I unfolded the paper. Again, the writing was hers. It was ripped from a journal.

August 2nd, 1964.

"Lord, in your light, I want to reflect on the field—Sister Roland, Sister Marc and me. We pitched hay in the sun...

I let the paper drop. Hot all over, I got out of bed and tiptoed to the bathroom stall. I opened the toilet lid and tried to throw the notes in, to leave Philippe to her God.

But I could not.

Instead, I shined the light and sat down on the lid.

When the noon bell rang, we knelt and sang matins. We walked to the shaded wood, open, hungry... I became detached from myself, yet full of a kind of joy I hope to find again. That is the breach of my vow, I think. I would do it again. There were sounds of reality that should have pulled me back—twittering birds, water, I was aware and not aware.

I lay back on the pine needles...it was so hot.

I took off my habit and every bit of clothing and boots. It was me who led the others. Then I entered the pool and my hot skin sang.

I forgot everything except your goodness. I did not feel shame, only grace; we laughed like girls, splashed, dove. Pure water, diamonds of light, nourished skin.

It was only after we came out naked and dripping and tried to hurry into our habits that I felt the wrong of it...

The next morning at breakfast, my eyes watered with sleep. I fought off images of Philippe out of her habit, swimming in a river. She had not given me a glance all morning.

Crusty warm rolls for breakfast but I wasn't hungry. The empty bread plate made Cats grimace and I gave her my second roll. A new platter arrived, and the girls flew at it. Philippe frowned. The loudspeaker in the refectory shot static, we all turned in its direction. A throat cleared into the silence.

"Sœur Philippe and Janey Chadderton, *requête à l'office.*"

I stared at Philippe.

She shook her head, no.

We walked together in silence to the office.

Mère sat at her long, buffed desk with the spotless blotter. There were two hard-backed wooden chairs for us.

She took a nervous, shallow breath. "MaChère Janelle, it has come to my attention that you have been speaking after lights out with Sœur Philippe."

I glanced up sharply. Mère had spies.

"Perhaps you convinced Sister that your need could not wait until morning? Have you not been apprised of the rule, Janelle?"

"*Oui MaMère.*"

"We do not countenance 'particular friendships.' Between a student and her teacher? I tremble at your pride, Janelle."

"MaMère, with respect, what rule?"

"God has given you many invitations to come to Him, yet—"

"I am coming! I'm on the way."

Mère swallowed a smile.

"Now, now, you refuse to take Perpetual vows with the other Sodalists." There was a painting of Saint Sebastian on the wall behind her, arrows piercing his skin.

"MaMère, what rule did I break?" Thinking of all the rules she didn't know I'd broken.

"You are an occasion of sin to Sister Philippe."

"Sin?"

"Words, Janey, the sin is words—words and the intellect. Together, you are being drawn away from God."

"But don't you see? Sister Philippe teaches me about God."

"*Tais toi*," she demanded my silence.

She kept her eyes on me, avoided Philippe. In a pained voice, she continued, "Janelle, Sœur Philippe is your course mistress and that is all. You will never speak alone with her again. You are to obey this, or you will be expelled. And more's the pity, you are to be accepted at a good college. If you defy the rules again, you will never be reinstated. These are the rules that I am still expected to uphold."

I felt dizzy. This dressing down in front of Philippe was punishment for us both. And Mère didn't even know the half!

She stood up. "I prayed for direction in this, Janey. I was more than convinced that you should be sent home. But I have thought better of it. You have a headstrong nature; you do not place yourself under our tutelage. Your arrogance causes our Lord great anguish. Do you know what the early Mother Church did with heretics, Janelle?"

"MaMère. I am not a heretic."

Her face brightened. "Thanks be to God."

She lifted her hand and I stood.

"We cannot force you to take your Sodalist vow, Janelle, but you will still crown the Virgin on May Day. It is your duty as Prefect, and we hold duty at Academie in the highest regard."

Philippe stood up too, but Mère lowered her hand, and she sat back down.

I clicked the door behind me.

The sin was new to me, "particular friendship." It all felt so deeply sorrowful. Sr Philippe *was* my friend, I realized, not merely my course mistress.

On Friday night, April 14th, we sat around the course, huge as a gymnasium, its big bay windows dark with night, putting the finishing touches on tomorrow's Conventum. Girls were sitting at the tables, folding napkins, creating place cards. Philippe stood silently by, the overhead lights making shadows behind her on the wall. No more words.

Would she ever forgive me?

Joey came into the course carrying a large box. "*Mes gentilles filles*, this night, we happily prepare for the great event—seventy-five years of our beloved Académie." She dug into the box. "*Pour les boucles*," she exclaimed, "for curling, how do you say?"

"Rollers," gestured Philippe.

"Oui," said Joey, "curl your hair!" We couldn't believe it. Lionel had never allowed curling hair. Rollers interrupted sleep. God made you the way you are, she would say, humility, simplicity. Over the years, Cats and I had longed to curl our hair. I looked around for her and headed for the lav. "Are you in here?"

"No."

I got down on my stomach and looked under the stall. She'd kicked off her shoes, toes curled together, sitting on the john lid, reading the newspaper.

"You're not going to believe it."

"Yeah. I figured you'd finally all flipped."

"We're curling our hair."

"You're kidding."

"Remember when we went to the speech contest looking like something out of Jane Eyre?"

The newspaper crinkled. "Consider the lilies," in her best Lionel voice, "they neither toil nor spin."

The newspaper headline said: President Johnson fires aide.

"Where'd you get it?" I asked.

"Denise, who else?"

"Any news?"

"You think I sneak in here for the news?" She laughed out loud.

"Well?"

"Ann Landers. There's this woman who's best friends with her husband's brother—"

"Come on," I went out the door.

Girls were handing out glasses of water, Suze held a box of bobby pins. Oh, Michael!

Pacifique had combs. Philippe stood by with cans of hairspray. They had bought the new aerosol product. "This is like the end of prohibition," shouted Jeanne.

Jacinta took up the rollers and started on Paulette's thick mop. Pacifique combed Jeanne D'Arc's wiry red hair and Gabrielle rolled Suze's. Cats tried to roll mine—straight and fine; our eyes stung from the spray. Philippe stayed close by, arms folded. I wondered what she was thinking. I was locked in a bubble of silence, going inside the habit, coming out of the habit.

What did it mean that I kept thinking about the habit?

Joey called everyone to gather close. "*Une histoire!*" She paused for effect.

Cats threw the roller into my lap and said: "I give up."

"Here, I'll give it a try," said Philippe. I did a double take. But, matter of fact, she took up the rollers.

I sat down, unsure.

Joey began: "Once, long ago, an arrogant young girl would not accept the doctrine of the Real Presence. She fought with her betters, insisting that the Host could not turn into Jesus's Body and Blood, that it was scientifically impossible."

Philippe tugged on a section of my hair and rolled it.

"They punished the girl. Her heart would not be moved. She wished to prove that physical bread could not change into Jesus' flesh. One dark night," called Joey, "the girl stole into the church. She carried a sharp knife. She opened the Tabernacle door where the consecrated Host was stored, took a host, lay it on the altar and sliced it in two."

"Oh," and "No," the girls murmured.

"As immediately as it was cut, blood oozed from the two halves."

Philippe lifted another section of my hair. Miserable, I sat there.

"The blood began to gather in a pool. It spilled over the altar onto the floor and down," Joey thrust her hands down, "each of the three stone steps. The girl ran to the broom closet for a mop." Joey gestured and mopped. "The more she mopped, the faster the blood flowed."

Joey had us riveted. Philippe calmly jabbed a pin into my roller. I wanted to scream at her, "I'm sorry. Say something. Anything."

Yet, I knew she was saying something. Simple, reassuring.

When we got to the dorm and my friends were settled in bed, I found the stolen notes and went into the lav, stony, empty, and silent. I hid in the stall, sat on the john lid, and stared at the folded papers.

"Janey, are you in here? Are you sick?" Philippe was doing her rounds. And she was talking to me. I should have thought of getting sick before!

"I'm sick of words," I said, "I hate them."

"You were in love with them, last I heard."

I sensed a smile.

"I always want them to mean more than they do." I said.

"What is it you need, Janey, do you have a headache?"

I pushed open the stall door, startling her so that her eyes flared. "I need to tell you something," I said.

"No," she motioned with her hand, held one finger to her lips, opened the door and walked out.

The bare light bulb hung suspended from the ceiling.

A few minutes later, she came back with aspirin and a glass. "You don't need me, or words, as much as you think," she handed me the glass.

"You're the one who makes God real. And now you'll never talk to me again."

"Words are not everything," said Philippe.

"But you taught me that they were."

"Yes, they distill truth for just an instant sometimes—but truth is more than words, Janey. God is too. And love continues even into silence."

I thrust the papers at her. "Here." My voice broke. "I did something terrible."

She offered me the aspirin in her palm.

"I said I committed a sin."

"Stop talking —"

"Here," I crammed the folded notes into her hand.

Her mouth opened.

"They were meant for God," I said. "And neither you nor He can ever forgive me."

She backed away. Her brown eyes darkened, the lines around them tensed. She unfolded the paper slowly. "Why?" her voice low, "Oh, I wish you had not done this!"

"I didn't mean for it to be you."

"Oh, anyone's secret prayer would have done?" She was raising her voice, something I'd never heard her do.

"I, I was dressed in the habit and walked by and—"

"Got more than you bargained for? I understood why you might steal a habit."

"It was the first time—the habit, the notes, all of it. I'm so sorry!"

"Janey. What are you doing? You're breaking me apart to get to God?"

"I didn't mean to," I said. "I wanted to know why the saints hurt themselves, why you—"

Her eyes flickered. She looked away. "It's private. Personal. Do you understand the concept?" Her face was so white the crease lines around her mouth looked blue. In a nervous gesture, she cracked the door and checked the dorm. "Stay here," she said, cold.

I wiped my eyes and slid to the floor against the wall.

I'd never undo this. She'd protected me, chosen me.

When she came back, she turned off the bathroom light. I stayed on the floor, she, by the door.

"So now you know some things," she whispered in the dark. "Wasn't that just the sin of Eve, to know what was NOT hers to know? And I asked for words for you. I should have listened when God silenced me."

"No," I groaned, "It wasn't God who silenced you!"

"For heaven's sake, Janey."

"I did something unforgivable, but Mère does not always speak—"

"You really like being God, don't you?" her fury mounting. "So exactly what did you learn dressed in MY LIFE?"

Gripped, hot-faced, I pushed away the pool—"That I believe in your Vows! You are God's true servant," I choked. I stood up and walked to where she stood.

"Really?" her tone was rough.

"But you're not like any other nun."

"I try to answer to God."

"But why in a convent when you could serve Him anywhere?"

"For love, Janey," with fervor, "for me, love is here."

"I overheard you with a man." I flinched at her sharp intake of breath. But I had to confess it all, right here, right now. "In the grotto," I whispered. "That was by accident too, I—"

The slap cracked across my face.

My hand flew to my cheek.

"Go find your God," she said. "Leave me out of it."

She pushed through the door.

Chapter 26

Philippe

I leaned back against my chamber wall. My fingers, my palm stung. *God, forgive me.*

I pulled off my veil and wimple and flung them across the room; ripped my habit up over my head and threw it too, and the whites. I could feel Janey's cheek under my quick hand.

The chain squeezed my thigh; vomit rose to my throat, the wounds, pink and swollen. I loosened the buckle; it took a second to release. Dry blood had crusted, and it hurt to pull the nails out. No words and no prayer.

I was losing control. And failing. I would not finish this penance.

But was it a contest? Did Jesus care? He never talked about mortification, never once. He only said he took our pain and death onto himself so we could be free of it. What an extraordinary thing to say!

I shook in the cold, looked down at my limbs. There was no mirror. The bones of my hips protruded. I felt my jutting clavicles, my wounded thighs, the ring of pink skin with mean red holes. I went to the sink for fresh wash water, dipped a cloth into the cold basin.

"Our bodies are of no importance now," Eugenie, our Novice mistress, would say.

We knew the body was of no importance by how they fed us. We lacked good nutrition, exercise, unless there were grapes to be harvested, or manure to spread over the gardens, hay to pitch at the Motherhouse farm. The delicious bread we baked was sold, the grapes went to a monastery where the monks made jams and wine.

But was I not partially my body? My mother's body had nurtured mine!

Jesus had given us his Body! We professed the resurrection of our own bodies at the Second coming, in the creed at every Mass! Now that was almost impossible to believe, but we must do so.

Slowly, I found my night clothes and pulled the gown over my head, shaking with goose bumps. I collected the crumpled habit and folded everything methodically. Sitting on the edge of my bed, I touched my thigh through the fabric of my nightgown. It was hard to believe how much it hurt, from thigh to ankle.

And I couldn't sense God with me at all.

I opened the door and tiptoed to the open window. The sky was dark with rain and fog, the Roller Palace, a shadow. Cold air hit my face.

Oh my Lord, Janey, that child. I had to forgive her.

What had she made of all this? I pressed my fingers against my eyes. I looked at my hand that had slapped her and shook my head in disbelief.

Satan must be thrilled to see me right now. Satan—some of the nuns joked about him, reducing him to a mischievous elf. "The devil is giving me distractions. He hates it when I pray."

But Satan was not trivial.

Dear Jesus, I prayed, the chain had seemed the answer, but I was wrong. St. Paul had said, "to make up in my own flesh the sufferings of Jesus."

I mean, Saint Francis did it, and Clare, but perhaps they were on an earthly path too and coming to know you as they could. Just like me.

I went back to my chamber, got into bed, sweating even though my room was frigid. Suddenly I longed for Mère, to tell her everything. I admired her, truly. She held the bar high for us yet loved us. What stopped me? Did I need to keep her good opinion? But that was ambition, not humility—no, Mère surely had had some doubts and perhaps failed like me. Would she forgive me?

Suddenly, my breathing grew steady, and I felt an aura of serenity. I threw off the covers and knelt beside the bed. I thought about Papa, silent loving father, taking care of us through toil, his big hand on a shoulder, his firm hugs.

The chains were packaged securely on the chair, I would bring them back to Father. I would confess my sins to him and woman to woman, to Mère. I needed all the mercy I could get. A warm, protective shadow wrapped itself around my heartache; I heard a voice telling me I'd get there; that my self needed to move over, my ego. It would hurt, but then I'd be open to goodness, to the God already inside me.

I did feel it.

I climbed into bed and fell into a deep healing sleep.

When I awoke in the morning, I realized I'd slept. Staring at the crack in the ceiling, I was flooded with colors and details; my nerves were live electric wires, my mind, wrapped in images of the dream that had just fled.

I'm alone in a huge house, running along a corridor, opening door after door. There's danger, panic. I don't know what I'm looking for. But I must hurry. Light bleeds out from under one door, I open it.

An old man stands there, lit from behind. He has white hair, mustache and beard. He's the prophet, the great one.

I kneel before him in relief and ask him to forgive me. To bless me.

"No," he says, taking my hands and lifting me up. He has electric blue eyes.

He bows his old white head.

"It is you who must bless me."

Chapter 27

Seventy-fifth Conventum, 1965—Janey

Conventum day dawned sunny and warm. Cats stuck her head into my cell, her hand went to my cheek. "What happened?" she whispered. I ducked. "Tell you later."

We lined up, our hair tied every which way in white or blue ribbons for Mary, satin or taffeta, some yellowed with age. Were these the ones the old girls wore in the pictures? Philippe's mother had worn a large white bow on the back of her head. She'd had burning eyes. We'd donned Sunday uniforms, Excellence and Honor pins in rows at our shoulders, Sodality medals around our necks on blue ribbons. When Philippe's eyes met mine, her color deepened.

All morning, we worked on separate assignments, buffed the stone floors, carried trays of maple candies and sugar cookies, petit fours and galette. Cats and her group set the tables with the buffed silver. Suze filled the sugar bowls and creamers, shook out the white linens, embroidered by nuns and girls.

Seventy-five years of this convent school in America; two hundred since the Canadian order was founded. The French-Canadian nuns had thought themselves "missionaries on American soil" bringing their peculiar Quebecois rituals and way of life, ministering to the French who'd come here to work in the mills.

In the kitchen, soups bubbled; oranges and lemons squeezed and grated for zest. Jeanne D'Arc and I carried big branches of forsythia, magnolias, apple blossoms; the nuns had been forcing them in the parlors. The cherry trees had blossomed. We dumped them into the sinks in the kitchen where the altar nuns were arranging them, some carrying them upstairs to line the edges of the pews, crown the statues, wreath the doorways. Em carried boxwood and daffodils in china vases to the refectory tables, where their tiny dewey drops dampened the fresh linens, glistened in the sun pouring through the bank of windows. She wiped her brow and leaned against the table. I went to stand beside her for a second. "Are you all right?"

"They know how to throw a party," she said, smirking. "No place for poverty today."

"Em, come on, talk to me. You've got to tell someone."

"Are you crazy? Tell them what? I don't know what you're talking about."

Now I was truly worried.

"Look, I tried to get out of here," she said, "It didn't work. I must hang on. I'm not even sure what's wrong with me." She touched my slapped cheek.

"Slipped in my cell," I said.

"Hmm."

I put my arms around her. "I'm so worried," I whispered. "What about your period?"

She waved me off.

"Have you talked to Larry?"

"He's acting like a jerk. We can't get married now."

"Oh No! Why?" Sœur Robert came by and summoned us to choir.

All boarders had a final rehearsal for the Mass. I felt choked with worry. Em had a solo, a Communion meditation, and Sœur Robert poked her middle several times trying to get her voice to stop quivering. Her eyes gleamed with tears. I had no idea how it worked, if she was fragile, if it would hurt her to be poked; and was she expecting? Finally, her voice came out clear. What a haunting, soaring sound; we loved her, we all felt her tears.

At eleven, we ran the play for the last time. Jeanne D'Arc would soon become Saint Catherine in Joey's long hair, she reminded us every chance she got. We were cautious with Cats' scenery; it must last through the play. She was holding her breath.

At one o'clock, the "old girls" arrived. We pulled on white gloves to greet them; I was thankful to become invisible. My job was to collect the wraps, and pin name tags to shoulders. I had the chance to drink in the perfumes and the elegance, unobserved. A woman dressed in an orange linen suit came to the table, murmured, and touched my yellowed hair ribbon. The "old girls" were dressed in linen and silk, pastel colors, and matching hats. Their lips were a deep red, or softly pink, eyelashes and brows darkened, cheeks rouged; impressing each other. And flaunting the nuns! Some had charm bracelets, some, huge diamonds. One had a ruby choker; and they looked one another over as they shouted their hellos. Surely, they'd dressed this morning anticipating this.

Girls did get out of here!

They came to just inside the greeting vestibule, accompanied by their husbands and beaux, to be sure everyone saw them. The men, of course, would not be staying. The women arranged themselves in packs, screeched seeing one another, their manicured hands studded with rings. "Ribbons!" they exclaimed seeing us. "That one was mine!"

Conventum would begin with a blessing in chapel. Then, a presentation, the play and a musicale. The guests would visit together all over the grounds until high Mass, and the special blessing, including "In Memoriam." It would end with a special collation, a huge feast in the refectory.

Jeanne D'Arc and I sat at the name-tag table. She smiled at an ancient lady in blue lace, a long-ago graduate who was every bit as wrinkled as our old nuns. The lady stood erect, her blue hat perched at the top of her head, veil to the eyebrows. She had not married, she told us. She was Chairwoman of the Humane Society for the entire Eastern seaboard. How had she gotten from here to there? I handed her the correct name tag.

The nuns stood in a receiving line all the way down the hall and into chapel where everyone would gather for opening prayer. Philippe was close to the vestibule door. She shook the hands offered, lavishing the women with her habit of "focus." No matter how little she knew them, she spoke to each person intently. I found myself watching her and looked away. I wouldn't know how to meet her eyes.

Meanwhile, as each gentleman held the door for his lady, I made a game of comparing him to Michael. Shorter, slimmer, ruddier, finer hair, darker hair, clear eyes, hooded gaze. A red-haired woman, who said she was Gloria Fréchette, came to us for her name tag. Her man had come all the way inside with her. "See you at seven, Andrè darling," she said, and turned to regard him. He stood, legs apart, hands behind his back, a small frown at his brow. Gloria Fréchette wore her Sodality medal around her neck among her pearls. "I'm sorry," I shrugged, sifting through the cards alphabetically. She had polished maroon fingernails. "I most certainly have a name tag in that box," she said, "I spent four years here."

"Hey," Andrè teased, "maybe you dreamed it."

That voice. Slightly hoarse. I flashed to the grotto, the shrubs.

"Come on, if they don't find it, we'll go to lunch," he said with deep merriment, then he saw Philippe in the line. Subtly, he moved behind Gloria. He was lanky, browned in a craggy way, as though he worked outside, face creased easily into smiles, curly hair, cropped short.

I hadn't seen him that day, the branches too thick, but I'd know the voice anywhere. I sat, mouth open, pen poised in the air. Jeanne D'Arc found the nametag. "I'm sorry," she said to Miss Fréchette, and I mumbled, "Sorry," staring past Gloria to where the man had stepped back. She tapped her toe impatiently. But now, Philippe had seen him too and her face broke into a smile so brilliant and total, it had to be involuntary. The two locked eyes.

He went quickly to the door.

I looked around protectively. But Philippe didn't need protecting. The red-haired Gloria had approached her in the receiving line. "I came in with my fiancè," Gloria told her. Philippe looked down at her slender, naked finger. Her eyes were full of warmth, they held Gloria's for an instant, then proceeded to swallow her whole—aqua linen dress, heels dyed to match, and the cloud of red hair.

When we were all together in the Chapel, poised at the start of the festivities, and the Blessing had been intoned, Joey came forward. She stood just below the step at the nave, as no woman, not even a nun, was ever allowed into the sanctuary.

She bowed her head, then looked up at us, pleasure plain in the lined face, and said: "*Mes gentilles Sœurs, Mesdames, écolieres.* We will begin this Conventum of our order, as is fitting and right to do, with *une histoire!*"

The "old girls" murmured. They wouldn't applaud in chapel, but they wanted to. It was clear that they were thrilled to be back, and that Joey's stories were a part of what they'd left.

"In the early years of our Order," Joey intoned in a voluminous French, "in the late 1700's, our beloved foundress, Mère Marie Anne, lived and prayed in an abandoned timber storage barn in Québec with the five very first sisters. The building had been given to the fledgling order by their Bishop to found a school, with the directive that they educate the boys of the town. Mère Marie Anne had educated herself through many tricks and trials. Women of that time were not schooled, some a bit, some not at all. She asked the Bishop if she and her nuns might also teach a few of the little girls. But he forbade it under pain of sin. No, he said, education is for BOYS.

"Marie Anne and her nuns," intoned Joey, "taught the young ruffians of the towns and fields by day. But then at nightfall, in secret, they would slip out into the streets, hiding in their deep pockets candles, paper, pencils, books. They would ring a tinkling bell.

"And the little girls would throw down their crewel, sewing and cleaning rags, come out of their houses and follow the nuns. Hidden in the alleyway, they'd teach the little girls to read.

"And so, my dear colleagues, students, old and young, we gather here today to celebrate our foundress' triumph over darkness, a triumph which has benefited us and all women!"

Suze and I exchanged a look. This was a story we had somehow missed, the foundress breaking the rules for the sake of girls. It was impressive, this story of rebellion.

I looked at the backs of the "old girls," their dresses and hats striking; they were attractive, self-possessed. Could it be that something good had come out of this place? I was swept into Philippe's colorful classroom.

And for all this nature is never spent, there lives the dearest freshness deep down things.

Philippe, the Foundress, Mère—brilliant and forward-thinking originals. There was a God, and I would find the truth. There were women who devoted their whole lives to teaching, leaders like Mère developing women for the future. There was Joey and her stories.

"Stories," Maman would scoff.

"Our nun says that a lily sprang up from the spot where Saint Gemma's blood fell."

"A story," she'd say.

Or, "The nun says that Saint Clare's body was found perfect years after her death."

"Janey, that's a story."

"Maman, the nun said Jesus rose from the dead and broke out of the tomb even though the rock was impossible to move."

"That one is fact," Maman would insist.

"How do you know?" I'd ask.

"By faith," she'd answer.

Faith, the great, mysterious Catholic answer.

It was teatime. The play had come off well. Sister Joey's elocution lessons.

I poured tea to each guest's right. The old girls' bouffant hairdos leaned together as they gossiped. I backed up; wiped the teapot, listening.

"Gloria doesn't know."

"She'll faint when she finds out."

"Why? Andrè Lemieux is hers now! He's moving on."

"But word is, he carries a torch for the nun."

Mère came by and frowned. I went into the kitchen. In a corner, Philippe was deep in conversation with Jeanne D'Arc, who held her pitcher on her hip. I went back to the table, lingering despite myself. So, Skip had come here with Gloria, knowing full well that he would see Philippe. He wanted her to know that he was moving on. That hurt.

"I don't know, they enter for all kinds of reasons." The woman primped. I bent to pour.

"Giselle who went in from our class, you'd have bet money on her. There were five." The woman said this with pride. She turned to me. "How many plan to enter from your class, dear?"

I caught my breath in mid-pour. "Uh, not too many, we haven't heard of any yet."

"Hmm, it's getting a little late, don't you think?"

In the chapel, we sang the Palestrina motet in our green, suspended oneness of sound; every woman knew it from memory. The perfume mingled with apple blossom and beeswax, and the candles burned, haloed with swirling light.

I gazed at the monstrance on the altar, imagining Philippe and her fierce vows. Of course, her man wanted her back. But "I've vowed to be a nun," she'd told me that night. "Do you think marriage vows are any less a risk, any easier to keep?"

A slamming of car doors, thin light voices through the dusk: "call me," and "adieu," and "you must write," like litanies. The "old girls" departed, leaving a trace of flowery scent in the crisp air of the courtyard. The sun would soon set, but we'd been granted recreation. A sophomore, Elise, came running toward us. "Mère needs you, Charlotte. Right now."

"Hurry up and come back," I said. We started a game of hide and seek for old times' sake, raced and hid.

"Ollee, ollee, in free—" shrieked Suze. We ran toward the tag tree, laughing, red-faced, Jeanne D'Arc, still "out." We plopped under the big apple tree. *"Where is love?"* we lifted our chins and sang to the trees. *"Does it fall from skies above?"*

Cats bounded out the courtyard door. "Janey! Suze!" She came toward us, down the hill, waving long envelopes. "Our college letters. We're out of here! We're in!"

"You read them?" I called.

"The whole convent read them," she shouted.

My envelope from Emmanuel College was fat. Everybody knew a fat envelope meant you were in. We are pleased to inform you...and not only was I accepted, but they were also giving me a scholarship! Cats had gotten into Mount Vernon in New York. Suze read hers out loud, accepted to Catholic University on scholarship, the corners of her eyes shining. And Em was into Manhattanville, to the music program.

We threw our arms around each other.

Jeanne D'Arc ran toward us. "I have an announcement," in a bold voice. "You're the first to know," she giggled into her hands. We quieted and turned to her.

"I'm entering."

"Entering what?" asked Cats in her driest voice.

"The convent," she said, a little less secure. "After much prayer and agony of soul, I—"

"We get the picture," said Em.

I stared at Jeanne D'Arc's carrot hair.

"When did this all happen?" asked Em. "You never mentioned it before."

"I didn't have a Call before."

I fell back on my heels. Really? Her? I saw her shaky on skates, hanging medals on trees. I faced her. "Jeanne, how did you hear your call? How do you know?"

"Sister Philippe knows. She's my sponsor, my big sister, she's already sewing my habit."

I was stung.

Jeanne D'Arc. Really, God?

I hugged her, like a collision. Then walked away.

"Janey, wait for me," Suze called.

I wandered down the orchard run and paused under the tree where Sœur Jean had broken her leg. Suze caught up to me. We looked out at the lake together; the Roller Palace sitting on its hill.

"Janey," said Suze. "Most of us don't know what we're going to become."

"I know."

"I have something to tell you, I've been trying for a while."

"Not you too?"

She raised her dark eyebrows, a frisson of thrill in her almond eyes. "I heard Easter morning."

Everything in me went quiet.

Suze waited. She was, if anything, the most patient of us.

"Janey?" she said softly.

I threw my arms around her. "You, I can imagine in the coif! Have you told your priest-boyfriend?" She leaned her curly head on my shoulder. Was I hurt? Jealous?

No, I was overjoyed for her.

"What about college?" I asked.

"Mère will arrange it. I'll join the Novitiate in June, and study after my training. Maybe not Catholic U, but it doesn't matter."

I saw Philippe streaming up the aisle with the purple copies of Hopkins' poems.

"Sister Jacinta will take me on," said Suze. Her tanned face shone in the low light, her chiseled features. Our Lady of Sorrows would be proud to have her! She was as sharp as anyone I'd ever known.

"Janey, go easy on Jeanne," said Suze. "She's loyal and faithful. She'll be a good nun."

I stared at the fence below where I'd stripped out of the habit looking for answers. Philippe had just seen her lover, a real flesh and blood man. She must be saturated with sorrow. Yet she wanted the life of a nun.

My God, all my dearest humans were taking vows! What was wrong with me? Didn't I hear a call too?

I touched Suze's shoulder and hurried up the hill.

Philippe stood alone in the courtyard; my turmoil swirled. There was so much to ask, to say.

Holding the bell, she placed a finger to her lips and walked away.

I sank to a halt.

When she was far enough, she turned around. Her gaze belied her refusal to meet me. In her softened eyes and open lips was all the warmth and affection I craved. And heartbreak.

She lifted the bell.

In the dorm that night, after lights, I slipped out of bed to my window. The dark sky was powdered with stars, the Roller Palace glowed with falls of light pouring from the windows. Had the "old girls" come to this window to stare at its blazing invitation, had they loved skating there too?

I checked in with my soul. I would search for God wherever I ended up. But Suze had blown me away. She would offer her keen intelligence. She would enter religion. How had I not seen it?

As for me, I tried to see myself coming back to the one-hundredth Conventum. Who would I be? Would I have found a way to any kind of vow? Yes, where is love?

Chapter 28

May 5—Philippe

There he'd stood with his fiancèe, of all things, his high color, the way he looked at me, even with all my covering. We'd never had enough hours—with my studies, his basketball, our jobs after school—we'd rush the words and kiss at the same time—the mill yard not far from my house; the tree we leaned against, the empty storage shed.

I'd felt known no matter our age, five when we met, middle school and our warm entanglements, and later the touching as we kissed—all the way to the line we'd drawn.

Gloria Fréchêtte? Really, Skip? She's wrapped up in her appearance, might even be vacuous.

I knelt beside my bed. Oh Lord, what will I do? Back then, "being his" wasn't something I knew. It was just our space together, the shadow, the light. We'd had a perfect hiding place behind the mill and there, I'd let the craving of my body be a good thing. It was why I'd been made a woman and he, a man. My skin, my limbs were all his during those hours of happiness.

Had I made myself forget? Because when I saw him standing behind his girlfriend, his touch was mine alone, sweeping over me.

Mère had postponed the Virgin crowning and Sodalists' Perpetual Vows. The new date, May 15th, gave the Seniors a chance to see the error of their ways. Three had joined Janey in refusing—

Cats, Denise and Virginie. But Janey wasn't alone in questioning the old ways.

Change was sweeping through our country as well as the church. We still reeled from President Kennedy's death; the new pope, John the 23rd, was bringing "fresh air" to the Mass and deeper, more refined understandings of Catholic doctrine. The charter of our Order was directly tied to the Vatican. We were on some kind of edge.

Mère called me to the office.

"Can you do nothing with Janey?"

"MaMère, you silenced us."

She scrunched up her face. "So I did."

"I understand Janey."

"Now wait just a minute—"

There was a knock, another sister needed Mère.

"You will convince our girls to take vows," she said. "Janey must not be allowed to lead them astray. She has a filament of steel running through her."

Well, that was true. But with her hollow cheeks and skinny body, she didn't look it. She was more like a spindly fawn, not yet grown into herself.

The girls were preparing for exams. They were also planning the prom. In the midst of them, I was seeing Skip everywhere, the way his shoulders had squared since I left for the convent, how he no longer looked like a boy. I read King David's psalms in the library. I'd be saturated with Christ's light and rise from my knees filled with assurance. I'd hear a new voice, graceful and calm— "*As the deer longs for the waterbrooks, so longeth my soul after thee, oh God."*

I contacted Père Girard and requested a special confession; I asked if it might be better in his office because I had so much to say. He sent word through Mère that he would see me in the confessional. I hurried to him, trembling as though freezing, hugging the brown package, eager to be rid of it. In the dark chapel, I handed it to Père through the purple velvet curtain. I knelt on my side and spoke through the screen.

"Father forgive me for I have sinned. I wish to confess a sin committed a year ago; and one two weeks ago, and one last night."

"Please, let us start with one."

"I have been experiencing grave doubts."

"It is not a sin to have doubts."

I told him what happened on that hot day at the Motherhouse. How in that heat, we had stripped down and slipped under the water.

"You removed your sacred habits?" His chair creaked.

"Yes. But I don't think it was a sin."

"Then why confess it?" He grunted. "How could you give scandal to the weaker sisters?"

"I'm not sure I did, Père."

"All you did was swim?"

"Yes." The feel of pure water over my hot skin would be with me forever. "We were happy," I said. "We cooled off."

"What do you want then?" His soft whisper.

I fell quiet.

"Are you filled with contrition?"

"Perhaps, for whatever temptation I put the others in."

I *was* wanting forgiveness.

He sighed. "You're not sure? Are you still a child?"

Slammed.

He cleared his throat. "I absolve you in the name of the Father, the Son and the Holy Ghost." He moved his hand in blessing. "Say twelve Our Fathers. Now, go and sin no more."

I thought for a second of stopping, but there was Skip. I'd broken the Sacred Rule meeting him but technically, it wasn't my fault, and this non-confession was going badly. "Mon Père, I took the discipline. I wore the chains for twenty-four hours, then I had to get relief."

"My daughter, that is not a sin either! This is a confession of non-sins." He chuckled.

"I know, but I have more to say."

He clicked the screen with his fingernail.

"I lost belief in the efficacy of the chains."

"But you had me order them!"

"Yes. The fault is mine. I thought I should." He stayed silent, I rushed on. "I wanted to perform extreme penance. I studied saints' mortification through the centuries."

"But you've confessed no sins, so far. I'm confused." Père was breathing hard on the other side.

"I've been in severe conflict. The chains released a great deal of stress for me. But that is not the point. I've come to understand that God created the body as he created everything, tenderly and with joy. Jesus became human with a real body, with real sufferings. He rose from the dead and promised me Resurrection, not because of anything I did, but because he loves me. Hurting my body for his sake does not make sense."

"Are you, a woman, preaching to me?"

"No, Father. I'm using my mind. I believe that some of our practices are misguided."

He waited. Then, "You must discuss your views with your Superior. Your belief in the efficacy of mortification is a matter for your practice. Say five Hail Marys," he said abruptly.

He didn't know what to do with me. Well, neither did I!

The day before the Crowning, I walked into Mère's office, nervous, wondering where we stood. Would Père have spoken with her about me, not to mention my confession, but to express worry?

But her attitude toward me had changed, like the sun that shines after a rain. She delighted in who I was becoming this year, she said. "You have depth, Sœur, talent. We need you. You must have your work to be balanced and so we will return you to your studies. You will take your final vows."

I stared at my hands, feeling the fullness of her wisdom. "I have to talk to you."

"Yes, what of this man?"

Deep breath.

I chose careful words. "I will always love him, I think —"

"Of course you will. Love is eternal." Her sharp eyes.

I bowed my head. "With God's grace, Mère. I want to do His will. I'm sorry, I must tell you everything before I take my final vows."

"And I must tell you many things as well. But go on—"

"I wish to receive personal absolution from you."

Mère lowered her head into her hands. When she looked up, her lovely eyes were filled with empathy. Then she smiled at me, as one woman to another.

"We will find a time with space and peace."

"May I go?"

She nodded. "Yes, but go in peace, my child."

That night I dreamed my sister Dodie and I were in a dark wood full of silvery moonlight.

It was a small clearing surrounded by stationary pines like attentive acolytes. We had an important job. To bury Papa.

We dug the hole, each with our own shovel. It took a long time. He lay on the ground nearby, our beloved father who'd given us everything, his face smooth, his body at peace.

Already in the hole was a dusty box, old and disintegrating— Maman's. The sight of these things caught me up, but not with fear. And I was aware that I should be full of grief but was not.

A sudden radiance appeared, neither of water nor of moonlight, but luminous on the surrounding mosses and fresh dug earth, the clearing, the darkness.

This light filled me with comfort.

We dug. We rolled him into the hole. We filled.

We buried him.

Whether it was Mère's kindness or the dreams, I understood that I must safely bury my girlhood, and young love, and all the past. Live forward into love, Maggie.

My Novice Mistress Eugenie's words came to me: "Sœurs, if we are to hold to our vows, we must obey a concrete request."

Christ had surely requested me. Even during all my weakness and doubts, sin, and mistakes, I heard Him calling me to be a good nun. He wanted my total and complete dedication, my love. He wanted me.

The next morning when I began to dress, I kissed my habit, pulled it over my head murmuring the prayers, feeling it drape over my body.

I will have that honest talk with Mère.

I will be true.

But to which love?

Chapter 29

Janey

All afternoon, we had a good time of what Coco called "beauti-fying ourselves." Michael arrived at six in his Dad's newly waxed Buick and after the sweaty ordeal of picture-taking, Cats and I squished into the front seat with him. Cats' date, Randy Hinkleber-ry, Jeanne and her date, Ronald, piled into the back. Michael squeezed my hand; I felt shy in my blue gauzy dress.

Coco and Carl waved to us from the front porch. The big barn door behind stood open with the hay bales and decorations, ready and waiting for our after-prom party.

We drove the narrow, hilly roads and leaned into each other around the curves. Jeanne D'Arc and future priest Ronald kept in-terrupting each other about God's call. Michael drove faster with each interrupt—his jaw tensing. Pretty soon, we saw blue lights flashing behind us and a police car waved us down. It felt like a bad dream until Michael only got a warning, but the police car followed us until we turned up the convent drive; the convent, finally good for something!

Our car crawled toward the gigantic statue of the Virgin.

"Thunder thighs!" Michael sang out.

"Stop that," said Jeanne D'Arc.

"And why do we have to come here?" asked Randy.

"Because, that's why," said Jeanne D'Arc.

"I can't believe they let you have a prom," said Randy.

We were late when the car rolled to a stop at the front steps.

"They have to loosen up or soon they won't exist," said Cats. "But they insisted on meeting the dates."

"And what if they don't LIKE the dates?" asked Michael in a dry voice.

As we walked up the steps, my new white satin shoes peeked out from under my gown. Maman had not allowed me to dye them blue to match my dress; they had to last through graduation.

Jeanne D'Arc rang the bell and we waited, six irritated prom-goers. The Portress answered with her full wrinkly smile. As we walked in, I saw the gleam of the floors, the indoor grotto lit by a lamp at Jesus' feet, His bleeding Sacred Heart, all through Michael's eyes. The nun receiving line had gone to prayers, but Portress summoned some of them back by ringing the bell.

Three nuns walked down the hall, eyes "in custody," arms under the frontispiece—Joey, Philippe. My face fell when the third was Mère.

There was something about the way boys acted around nuns, a bristling recognition of power. They were thrown off their tracks and shook hands respectfully.

"Late, aren't you?" Philippe asked, raising an eyebrow. She shot a look at me.

I looked away.

"Sam, my dog, jumped on my date's trousers," said Cats.

Randy nodded and brushed his trousers.

"And my mother had to work on the spots because he couldn't go to the prom like that."

Philippe perused Randy to about his waist. "Hmmm," she said. Then she took in Michael with his wide shoulders and open expression.

Jeanne D'Arc introduced Ronald, proudly telling the nuns about his vocation, matching hers. Our late arrival forgotten, Mère and Joey chatted us up like old friends. We were trapped listening to Jeanne D'Arc in her green gown, carroty hair French twisted, and the pouf-haired Ronald.

When there was a pause Philippe asked, "Michael, what are you studying at university?"

"English literature, Sister," grateful for the question. "I'm a Freshman," his voice, deep, yet boyish.

"What made you choose English?"

"I am interested in Shakespeare," he said. "I would like to get my Ph.D." He treated Philippe with watchful deference, as though she might strike like a rattlesnake.

She gave him a satisfied nod. "And you, Randy?"

"Business administration, Sister."

"And I play football," said Michael quickly.

"What position?"

Michael blinked. They proceeded to talk football, a game Philippe knew—warm and vibrant, appraising my tall date. I'd never seen Philippe look up at anyone.

Michael was magnificent. Then I felt a familiar ache. I wanted to be like Philippe in this world. Why was there only one word for *love*? Why did we get only one life with such divergent paths?

We stepped out onto the front porch; Portress closed the door. We stood a minute, six regal young people in white dinner jackets, black pants, pastel gowns and spiky heels, about to descend the stone steps toward the waxed and waiting Buick.

And then, as though by imperative, Michael slipped his hand into his vest pocket. Slowly and deliberately, he pulled out a cigarette, its slim whiteness catching the fading light. And quietly, on the steps of the convent front entrance, he flicked a match. Jeanne D'Arc protested, but I placed a hand on her arm. We heard the delicious hiss of Michael's inhale. There was a pause, then he released a long thin stream of bluish smoke.

We walked into the Holiday Inn. The lights were dim and apple blossoms decorated every table. A large, shimmering tree stood in the middle of the banquet hall. The last time Cats was home, she and Coco had built it and Coco had hauled it into the Holiday Inn last night and stuck it into an enormous plaster base. Silver paper blossoms captured the light.

Suze had her date, Thomas, in a vise grip. I introduced them to Michael. She wore her hair in the same wiry curls with her glasses in place. Thomas was a surprise, older, square-shouldered. She'd been seeing him whenever she went home, but he, too, was planning to take vows.

"Is Em here?" I asked. Suze shook her head.

The mirror ball turned above our heads showering confetti fireflies over the apple blossoms and dancers. Across the dance floor, Cats stood feet apart beside Randy, muscular, milky-eyed and quiet. His enormous hands and feet looked like they didn't be-long to him.

The Irish girls sat by the wall; their blind dates hung out over by the Coke table, heatedly discussing baseball.

Michael gathered me into a slow dance. I brushed against his chest, his eyes glistened, and I felt his fingers on the small of my back. From the time we'd driven up the drive to the convent, I'd felt unsettled. Maybe I was picking up a new distance in him—but geez, how could there be anything but distance?

He took my face in his hands and said, "Look at me."

His warm eyes and large head, all that black hair. "I've missed you, kid." He swung me around, I let myself dance and realized we had a whole evening.

Between songs, Cats came by and motioned to me.

"I'll be right back," I told him.

In the ladies' room, Cats' hair shone in the mirror. She applied lipstick, her pointed nails the same color.

"Cats, someday you're going to be gorgeous."

"I'm gorgeous now!" She laughed at my attempt to work with my hair.

"Leave it, your hair is not the point. With you, it's your eyes."

"What's happening with Randy?" I asked.

"He's not worth my wit." Cats grinned. "How about Michael?"

"We're a little funny." I bit my lip.

Cats whistled through her teeth, "Well, you didn't get home all semester."

"I know. I'm so confused."

"So, what else is new?"

Michael held me on the balcony. From the time he'd lit up that cigarette on the convent steps, he'd exuded a kind of ease, but we still weren't saying much. I thought of cold nights in the dorm; I couldn't get out of there fast enough now. Nothing was settled, but so what? I thought about Em's love for Larry and her struggle to be with him. What would happen to us?

I brought up the summer ahead. I'd be working for my Uncle at the jewelry plant.

Michael would be lifeguarding. He rummaged in his pocket. "I have a little gift for you." With a wide smile he gave me a folded piece of paper.

My heart soared. A note! A poem! I carefully unfolded it. "I — LOVE –YOU" spelled out in bobby pins and patiently fastened with scotch tape.

I placed the bobby pin love note carefully in my small purse, threw my arms around him, burrowed into his shoulder.

After a while, he brought up Philippe. "She's a knock-out, what's she doing in there?"

"Good question," I said.

"She's intelligent. Seems kind of normal, hey, she even knows football."

"But she loves God and she's called to be a nun."

He shook his head, "What a loss."

"I saw her with her lover in the grotto."

"Are you kidding me? Isn't that like a federal offense?"

"Yup."

"I feel for the guy, poor bastard."

It was time to crown the Prom Queen. Michael and I walked into the ballroom.

A day girl, Annette, stood on the raised platform under Cats' blossom tree. She wore a lavender dress, spaghetti straps, blond ringlets and had plenty of cleavage.

"She's a mistake," whispered Cats. "The band leader was told to get "the blond", and he got the wrong blond."

"It doesn't matter," I said. "It should have been Em anyway."

"See that guy over there?" said Cats, indicating the musician. "He wants to BUY our apple blossom tree for the next dance!"

"Cats, that's great. Your Mom won't have to get it out of here."

"And finally, I've made something that's not just for GAWD," said Cats.

The prom was over so quickly. Cats and I had just climbed on-to her four-poster bed. The after-prom party had been such a ter-rific ending, everyone had gone home. We'd arranged for Michael to sleep in the guest bedroom. Cats' antique canopy bed was so high our feet didn't touch the floor.

I slipped off with a thump and Cats called after me, "Go get him."

He'd jumbled his words, "wait a little while, then meet me out-side."

I tiptoed down the stairs. All those nights I'd sneak to the win-dow and think about him. I tied my sneakers and stepped out into the dark paddock. Coco birthed and groomed her ponies here, wrapped their legs, brushed their backs. She adored them, fussed over them—bay and blue, white and dappled. The down of their coats and long silk manes were more precious to her than anything in the house. And there was one that I loved best—the nervous buff-colored mare with round eyes, thick plush softness covering her body.

I waited in the cool dark, all my pores opening to the night. The very act of meeting him out here was enough to make me faint. I felt light, terrified, soaring, free. Suddenly I heard footsteps and made my way toward him. "Nuns, eat your heart out," I told myself. I could feel the air on my bare legs, my breasts free against the cotton of my nightgown. There was no moon, no light but what the night sky gave. The stars were thick and studded. I kept them in sight until I found him, touched his flannel PJ's. We made our way across the paddock, slipping in the soft places, his body, close and warm.

Would he ever understand the strangeness of my life? But we were here now. We sank into the still span between the blue glass stars and the warm trampled earth under our shoes. Then the ponies nudged us, smelling, warm breath. Michael spoke to them softly, we felt their moist noses, furry heads. Our eyes adjusted to the dark; we touched them with our fingertips, even the one who wouldn't let me near her in the daytime.

Inside the enclosed stalls, a flashlight and heavy blanket hung over the side, dry new hay piled in a corner. Michael spread the blanket, then pulled me down beside him. I was the one who found his lips with mine, the illicit cigarette on his breath. He kissed me back, then "Wait," he said. But we couldn't stop. I felt a wave of shock that my body was saying yes everywhere. I wanted him more than anything, more than any words we might say. This is what they called the terrible sin?

He held me against him shivering in the spring night, I heard his heart beat faster. He pulled off my nightgown, then his pajamas. Tenderly, he traced each breast, "You are beautiful."

Stirred in the forbidden places, all my feelings had swiftly, irretrievably begun to throb there, bound up there? He took my hand and led it to his erection through the cloth of his boxers. "Oh Mike!"

I loved his quiet laugh then. The way we whimpered and hungered, the lower half of my body surging, coming to life. We breathed into one another, then his became intense and changed. He could so easily slip into me right now, enter me now. I wanted it more than I'd ever wanted anything but we both rolled away at the same time. We waited apart, trembling, gasping.

"I don't want it to happen like this for us," he whispered. "It's too important."

He was the one to say it.

"I keep worrying you might stay there, Janey, I'm scared."

"Become a nun?"

"I feel it sometimes, the hunger, the mystery."

His quickening heartbeat made me sad. Outside the stall door, I heard the ponies' hooves against the rich earth.

"How about making me one of your vows?" he asked suddenly.

I searched his dark eyes.

"I'm teasing, Janey. But I guess not really..."

I could see the whites of his eyes, the glistening in the corners. I knew he needed reassurance, but I didn't have it to give.

"Janey, this semester, you were like something I dreamed."

"I'm not a dream now," I said.

He held my face in his hands. "You're a boss girl."

Yet he was unsure. And like everything else I'd discovered this year, so was I.

Chapter 30

May Day Crowning—Janey

Sodality Perpetual Vows:

I vow to devote my life to the Virgin Mary, by attendance at daily Mass; daily Rosary; examination of Conscience, weekly Confession; yearly retreat; and continual Acts of Charity, fasts and sacrifices.

Manual of Sodalities, 1897

I stood in my cell, curtains around me. Seniors wore caps and gowns for the crowning, and I adjusted mine. Last night in Mère's office, I refused once again to take the Vows and Mère still insisted that I climb the ladder and crown the Virgin. Maybe she thought I would change my mind at the last minute? And the others would follow me. We would see the light under the public eye.

I stepped into my heels, tried them out, teetered a bit and remembered the nun-brides weaving down the aisle on clothing day. So many vows in this place.

Em handed me a note through my curtain. She had bluish circles under her eyes. She still refused to admit that she was expecting a baby. And what did we know? I'd been around plenty of women having babies in our town—they mostly looked okay, certainly not sick like this. I was scared, and Cats and I both felt the weight of it. It was unthinkable to take it upon ourselves to tell. I tore open the note; "I told you about the fight—Denise sneaked in a letter. He says he wants to marry me, but not now. I thought he loved me."

Oh no, poor Em. My heart really broke for her!

She poked her head into my cell. Her hair was tied back from her face, intensifying the gray blue eyes. The white mortar-board cap made her look severe, cheeks stretched over the bones. She signed with her fingers, let's talk. "Meet me in the artist's room right now," she whispered.

I finished dressing, lined up with the others, then slipped into the lav and then down the stairs to the cellar. If we hurried, we'd have time to catch up in chapel. Em had left the flashlight for me by the cellar door. I entered the room, bare now of color, canvases, mosaics.

"Why aren't you taking the vow?" Em asked.

I was stunned. I'd expected her to tell me about herself. I hadn't been down here since Philippe had shown us Germaine's art. "Do you come down here a lot?"

She nodded. "Do you think you're not worthy?" She put her arms around me. "I'm the one who's not worthy."

"It's not about worth," I answered. "If I know I won't keep the vow, it's wrong to take it."

"But the rituals will keep you safe."

"I don't want to be safe," I said.

"Janey."

"If it's right for you, Em, you should do it."

She looked away, eyes filling.

"Talk to me. Please."

Her eyelashes fluttered. "I need the vow, Janey. I want to be a good wife to him. But he doesn't love me." She closed her eyes against this. "He wouldn't take me to the prom, he said it was silly. His letter—"

"He asked you to marry him."

"Yes, at Christmas. Now that he's shipping out, he changed his mind." We heard sounds and looked at the ceiling—clappers and heels clicking.

"But he knows about the, the—"

She turned red. "I'm not sure of anything, Janey." I reached for her, but she was already out the door.

The May Day procession began at the base of the courtyard, near the tip of the grape arbor. Postulants, Novices in white veils and professed nuns gathered, Junior girls in uniforms, veils and white gloves, Seniors in white caps and robes, golden stoles and tassels for honors, pins on the shoulders. It was a brilliant day; the lake shone hot with diamonds through the chain links of the fence. Cars whizzed by at the base of the hill.

My partner was Cats; the line started up the hill, girls and nuns processing two by two.

"*Ave Ave Ave Maree- ee- ia.*" Up through the apple orchard, my heels sank into the soft, muddy grass—satin fabric, now smudged. "*Fructus ventris tui Jesu—*"

Then, "*Mother at thy feet is kneeling,*

One who loves you is your child."

I carried a floral crown on my arm, weak in one spot where the violets and forget-me-nots were separating. We marched up through the apple tree runs, processed around to the street in front of the convent and began the final trek. Neighbors came out on their front lawns and watched, some sat on lawn chairs and some even joined the procession. The order of ceremony would be my climb to crown the Virgin, a prayer, then Sodality Vows. After the Crowning, we'd have a special collation of cake with the frosting actually on it.

The stone Virgin stood on a granite block, at the top of the quarter mile drive lined with towering firs. Nearly twenty feet tall, The Lady wore an enormous flowing robe, her legs were like tree trunks, her arms outstretched to embrace the whole world. The ladder leaned precariously against her chest. A sick feeling came over me.

This was our last procession. They could be beautiful, these processions, like the angels in the dorm on Christmas Eve; the Ostensorium on Trinity Sunday; the Sacred Heart—around the circumference of the school for all the town to see. The chanting and songs in our reedy voices. I forced my mind to Michael, his strength and gentleness. He'd promised to come for graduation. He would see all this and no, there would be no more statues in my life. And no more processions. I would run to him, I would find out about love, our bodies together, that was my vow for today. My only vow.

As we came closer, the giant Virgin reached out to me with her Goliath arms. She was Queen of our Hearts, and I did love having her, a woman and mother, be so important. Em walked ahead of me in the line; she was pale, but still so beautiful. Our plan had always been to crown her our queen. Damn Larry, what was wrong with him?

We gathered in a circle around the granite Lady. The sun, bright and blinding, washed everything out, making the distance up the ladder seem very far, but naturally there were no sun glasses.

I stepped toward the statue feeling like a lunatic. I hoped that any minute, Mère would stop the ceremony and choose a worthier girl. I checked the weak place in the crown and hoped it would not fall off my arm.

Just get it over with, I told myself. I started up a few steps of the ladder. It leaned against the Virgin's body, clacked against the stone—girls came forward to anchor it. "*Sancta Maria*," soloed Suze in a pressed voice, "*Mater Dei, Ora pro nobis.*" I began the ascent, already sweating under my robe.

I'd watched the Sodality Prefect do this every year. We'd laughed over it in the course, a miracle each time that she didn't fall. A car drove past in the street far away at the base of the hill. A breeze lifted my bangs. Sweat dripped down my underarms.

I let myself look down for a second at Em and Virginie, holding the ladder's base. I inched up, oh no, my mortarboard bumped into the upper rung, my heels slid on the lower one. Really these nuns were nuts. My father could sue them if I fell but he would never sue anyone. Below, the ground swirled. Suddenly, I thought of Philippe on the ladder, the nails in her flesh, the blood. I swooned and gripped the rung.

"Janey," Mère called. I breathed, in, out, in, out.

When I recovered, I climbed as high as the Virgin's arms and wobbled again, staring at my white knuckles. Girls had been doing this for years and not one had ever fallen. Well, how did I know that?

I looked down at the circle of upturned faces, white veils, black uniforms, white caps, robes, red ribbons, black habits, white coifs, sun and shadow, stone.

I stepped up higher, looked up. The Virgin's granite head, angular stone features worn by time, eyes gray. One more step, my heel caught in the hem of my gown. I kicked my foot. I looked to the outstretched arm, her parted fingers held the yellowed note that Dad and I had seen. "They must fly an angel up there to get it," he'd laughed. I looked down, swooned—all eyes on me, their upturned faces like a sea of white o's.

I reached up and positioned the crown on the Virgin's Head. It slid over one stone eye.

Suddenly, the ladder scraped sideways—"Ahhhh," I screamed, one foot hooked on a rung, the other groping. "Oh my God!" I hugged the neck.

"Janey," Mère shouted, "Hold on!"

I have a choice? I clung. I tried to jockey the ladder with one shoe and hung, my arms ached, sharp pains. Dear Jesus, this is how I will die.

A man ran forward from the crowd and took hold of the ladder as high up as he could reach. He jerked it back against the statue. I looked down at his bald head. I will throw my arms around that man if I ever get down from here.

"*Oh merci, merci, Monsieur,*" said Mère. "*Nous vous bénissons.*"

My heels held the rungs, stomach in my mouth, drained of everything.

Em lay in a heap; she'd pushed the ladder askew going down.

"Be careful with her," I cried, "Sister Philippe!"

"Oh, for the love of God, Janey," shot Mère.

"Shit," I said.

"*MaChère!*"

Everyone sighed with relief as Jacinta and Liese slowly lifted Em to her feet. "Good then," he said, "Come on now, my girl, it's all right." But I still hugged the stone. They supported Em away.

"Take off your heels," Philippe called. She sounded very far away. My arms were stuck to the neck. My heels clattered to the ground, my heart falling too.

The neighbor climbed up to guide me, I breathed and inched down, now cold with fear and sweat under my robe, even in the heat.

At the bottom, Jacinta sat me on the ground, head between my legs. I threw up.

Mère gave a short, breathless speech. The Vows would be called off for today, she said.

This was the worst crowning they'd ever had in seventy-five years.

We filed into the course. "But what will we do about our vows?" said Jeanne D'Arc.

"You'll have your own," snapped Cats.

No one knew what we'd do next. I sneaked off to the infirmary. No celebration, that's for sure.

Passing Mère's office door, I heard her raised voice. "I was explicit in my direction, Sœur! We cannot have this arrogance!"

Philippe cleared her throat. "I can explain—"

"Explanations," interrupted Mère, "weaken the character... Oh Lord, I am exhausted."

I pushed on. Poor Mère. She'd had it with us.

At the infirmary, Em had already been discharged. She'd been given our standard tea-and-toast medical treatment. I could see the empty plate and pot. The Sister infirmarian smiled at me and attributed her fainting to the heat.

When I arrived in the course, Em was there, girls around her, but I motioned to her and Cats and we found an empty table.

"You're telling someone," said Cats. "Fainting is not normal."

"How do you know?" said Em.

"Emilie, you need help," I whispered.

"No. Look, I'm not sure," she whispered. "I need to graduate. I'm obviously hiding it, I'm almost there." She started to cry.

We shielded her from Joey and headed to the ladies' room.

"And the doctor?" Cats asked, closing the door. "Tomorrow?"

"Philippe is taking me. If this is a baby, that's it. I'll be expelled."

"And Larry?"

"He's an asshole."

"I want you to tell Philippe everything," I said. "This is a mess now; she'll know what to do."

"No."

"She's different, Em," said Cats.

"Don't be stupid." Emilie's eyes flashed. "Philippe is still a nun."

Chapter 31

Philippe

That night, kneeling beside my bed, I prayed for Emilie; I would take her to the order's doctor tomorrow. Something was very wrong, even if she was expecting. She shouldn't be ill like this for weeks. I opened my breviary to Lamentations.

"*The steadfast love of the LORD never ceases; his mercies never come to an end; they are new every morning.*"

In my prayer, I saw Janey climbing the ladder, swiping at her forehead. "Sister, we shouldn't do it," Cats had told me in the arbor. "It's super dangerous." Janey's heels sliding on the lower rungs—what were we thinking? And we'd upheld this foolish ritual every year?

Suddenly I, myself, was on a ladder in the dorm, Janey looking up—everything swirling beneath me. Janey and her aching questions—me and mine—what would happen to us? To all the girls?

I had come to love them.

I stood up and went to Emilie's cell, hoping to speak with her, to let her know that I would help her. But she was motionless on her back in a deep sleep.

Or so I thought.

In the morning, when the girls exposed the cell frames in their skeletal maze, Emilie's curtains stayed drawn. Suze started toward the cell, calling her name, but I headed her off.

"All of you, line up," I commanded.

"But Sister," Janey said. "Can I talk to you?"

"Please line up," I repeated.

I waited in front of Em's cell until they were all out of the dorm.

Parting the curtains with a sinking feeling, I took a step back. The sheets were tousled, the bed was empty.

I went swiftly down the stairs to chapel and found Mère, folded in prayer. She saw my face and followed me out, alarmed.

"Emilie is gone."

"What do you mean, gone?"

"She was not in her bed just now."

"Have you checked everywhere?"

"I came straight to you. I'm afraid we won't find her in the convent."

Mère's black eyes, her pupils dilating; two deep crevices between her eyebrows. I would expect anger, not anguish.

We reached her office; she lifted the phone. "Officer, yes," she said, "A girl five foot eight, long black hair, wearing?" She looked at me.

"Pajamas," I said. "a uniform?"

"She can't have got far," said Mère. "Yes, we will."

She called Père Roland. Mère and Jacinta would drive out with him to search. Poor Em, she must be terrified. Mère took a second to gather Jacinta and me in a circle of prayer. We held hands. "*Sin abounds,*" she quoted St. Paul, "*but grace abounds the more. Guide us, dear Lord, to our girl.*"

When I went to find the others, they were just filing out of chapel, stretching their necks, breaking the silence. Liese shooed them toward breakfast. Janey stepped out of line, "Oh Sister, where is she? Is she all right? We should have acted sooner—"

My heart heaved. "She's nowhere to be found—she's gone."

Janey's eyes widened. "But—"

"Sh," I said. "We don't want the others to know yet."

Chapter 32

Janey

Standing before us in the course, Mère seemed smaller some-how, diminished as she let us express our sorrow. Sister Philippe's forehead was moist and tight in the coif. Amazingly, Mère disclosed that Em was safe and had made it home. No details.

Later we learned from Denises—she walked the five miles to town, hid in the terminal bathroom until morning, borrowed a dime, called the family housekeeper, and talked the bus driver into taking her.

Mère would not disclose much, but her warmth and compassion gave us hope. Em would not return for graduation, but she'd been a hardworking, intelligent presence all four years; yes, this was a terrible mistake. But the Order was considering her diploma, in absentia.

"Why won't you let her come back?" asked Jeanne. "I'm sure she's sorry, she's been sick and scared."

"She flew the coop," said Mère. Then coughed into her hand.

Philippe did a double take.

"Will she, I mean, what will happen to her?" asked Cats. "She's in physical danger."

"Danger?" Mère gave a quizzical look.

We knew that her parents were away in separate European cities. No one knew how to ask about a baby. Mère and Philippe exchanged a glance.

"We must pray for her," said Mère, flustered. "And for you, Janey my dear," she said, shaking her head. "How do you feel about trying again and crowning our Lady properly this time?"

I rolled my eyes, was she serious? And in a heartbeat, I pictured myself hanging onto the immovable granite Virgin—had I really clung there for what felt like hours?

During Senior week, Em was a deep hole that we circled round and round. Philippe stayed close and all the while, I fretted, full of remorse for reading her private notes and all the other treacheries, and no way to speak. And then the Denises came through with more news.

Could we trust it? Did Mère know it? *Em's in the hospital with fever. Five months gone. Her mother finally flew home. Larry abandoned her.*

"The day we leave here," Cats assured us, "Coco is taking me to Em's. That kid needs us."

Five days before graduation, we attended Senior Decisions, comic relief in the midst of the rest. Emilie's situation was fully on Sister Theophile's mind. Our teacher of Home Ec., she called out from the study hall desk. "*Mes filles*, any boy, even a good Catholic one, will demand more of you than you want to give him!" She didn't use the word sex. With a downturned mouth, "*Mes filles*, he might do it to you by force, because," and here she paused and looked at us, "*les hommes sont des cochons!*" (she actually used the word pig) "They get swept up in their strong bodies." Her eyebrows met in exasperation. "What was God thinking," she lifted her palms, "to give them the stronger bodies?"

I thought of the way Michael responded to the least hesitation in me. He was like my beloved horse from childhood books—Black Beauty, who'd given up physical power for the love of a person.

Theophile then launched into Saint Maria Goretti, knifed to death at eleven by the son of her father's boss because he wanted her body, and she said no. It was better to die than allow him his grave sin and the church had canonized her for that. It was a bizarre story of attempted rape, murder, forgiveness and didn't seem relevant to our mess at all.

Cats gave a soft snicker and was asked to leave. Darn, we all should have thought of that! Em had made Senior decisions impossible this year.

And then another story. Saint Barbara. A brutal soldier tore her dress and forced her to the ground.

She screamed to God to deliver her and in one second, her face grew a coarse black beard. The soldier gave a howl and ran away. Barbara, turned into a man, was made forever safe.

Safe? No, God might save you by a creepy bizarre trick, or he might let you die and become a saint. Nothing was fair. And then there was beautiful, trusting Em. No one had saved her.

On the way to recreation, Cats caught up with me.

"Last was best!" I told her. "Barbara and the beard. God, did Theophile really think that would help matters?"

We met Jeanne D'Arc coming the other way. "Janey, I will intercede for you."

"Don't do me any favors," I groaned.

"Perpetuals is the least you could do for Him." She said *Him* as if He belonged to her.

"I will kill her," whispered Cats.

"I'll ask Him anything for you," she chirped. "Just USE ME, USE ME."

Chapter 33

Philippe

On Friday of Senior week, we walked down the path to the Roller Palace. Mère had made a last arrangement with the Bad Catholic. Spirits were high and the girls sang "White Coral Bells" in rounds all the way down the hill. When our eyes met, Janey looked away.

I walked with Sœur Pacifique. Suze and Virginie just ahead. A glimpse of white fur under a bush. Casper. I envied that cat, free in the world. We rounded a corner. Jeanne D'Arc skipped over the sidewalk lines, cars whizzing by in the street. I heard her say: "If Sister Philippe walks with me, I'm going to ask her stuff."

"What stuff?" Janey snapped.

Oh my dear, Jeanne, have some self-control.

Jeanne gave a little hop. "What she dreamed of becoming when she was our age."

"Don't you know? She's your big sister," said Janey.

"Dry up, Jeanne D'Arc," said Cats.

I looked out onto the open wooden rink. Our last outing, I wouldn't be strict with rules for the girls. They needed release from sorrow. Em's close friends still mourned—still wondered.

But it was all happening fast now. Jeanne D'Arc's skate-lace snapped. "Take mine," Janey said, "I'm not going to skate."

"Yes, you are," I went to find another. "You're all going to skate. It will do you good."

251

The music drove them forward, wheels on wood, thwacks and thrums over the dusty, wide space. The old geezer lit a new cigarette.

Oh, Skip…

The skaters shuffled and rocked, their blue uniforms pressed to their ribs, red ribbons flying up over their shoulders, catching on their Excellence pins in rows. The rink was immense, walls in need of paint, the booth coming apart, but nothing had blemished the smooth, golden wood of the floor. The wood of wheels on wood gave perfect percussion to the music, made the girls shimmer.

Girls skated hard here and Mère looked the other way. That was girls, of course, not us. Maybe we were supposed to feel our sacrifice by coming here and watching their release? I put on skates, tied the laces tight, I would skate a bit to be with them one last time. Like a frayed wire in my brain, I kept seeing Em step out into the night.

Girls formed a circle, calling to each other. Cats offered Janey gum. She smiled and popped it into her mouth. They were buzzing with plans.

The music rang out and girls sang, "Mashed potatoes—yeah yeah yeah," I threw my head back and laughed. The drums boomed. I helped Jeanne D'Arc to her feet; we skated past the blaring speakers, oh the glide felt good—past the cubicle with its empty drink fountains. The old man making his popcorn, puffing and popping away.

I glanced around for Janey. She thought I hadn't forgiven her. She'd graduate thinking that. I could whisper a quick word, but it would seem empty. The dash of the skaters—like electricity passing from one girl to another. Their skates pushed forward, their arms outstretched, weaving in and around each other.

Jeanne D'Arc skated to me, following the other skaters with her eyes. She stopped haltingly and I nudged her back out onto the floor where she promptly fell on her bottom. Cats skated by and hauled her up.

"I won't have to do these things anymore," Jeanne D'Arc called. "I'm entering!"

"Suze is entering too," Cats shouted, "and we never hear about it!"

The old man sifted through his stack of forty-fives, placing them on the player in clumps.

I found Janey leaning against the wall and motioned with my arm. She reached me in two glides. "Janey, get out there and skate." She bit her lip and made it bleed, went into the booth to get a tissue.

When she came out, she said: "Sœur, there's a funny smell in there."

"What kind of smell?"

"Coming from the popcorn machine."

"Never mind, go skate while you can."

I stood just outside the booth—and there we were, unbidden, Skip whipping around to skate backwards, holding me at the waist and shoulder, wind in the hair—our bodies sensing each other's every move.

Suze threw the ball. Cats came up from behind to catch it, flew into Janey who was pushed into me.

I caught her in my arms and held her tight.

We stared hard at each other; her eyes flickered—like the first time in the hall.

"Oh Sister, I am so sorry," she said. "I never meant to hurt you," she whispered, "I would never want anything to hurt you."

"Sh." I placed my finger on her lips. "I know."

Tears welled up in her eyes. We listened to the rolling wheels, the deafening noise. The old geezer boogied to the song.

"Please, can you forgive me?" her voice, breaking.

I grabbed her hand and pulled her into the crowd of skaters. There were only a few times in life when words would not do—this was one of them. We rounded the first corner, our skates steady, rhythmic. I laughed into the breeze, leading Janey into a turn, faster and faster, my habit clinging to my legs.

We sped on, skate over skate, hand in hand, leaning into the corner, more speed into the straight. A kind of hush fell.

Coming around I caught a glimpse—Mère at the door.

But I could not stop. Veil flying, cross up over one shoulder, hands and arms released.

Janey flew alongside, our bodies angling dangerously at the curve.

Then, into the throng of skating girls, I let go of Janey's hand, and set her free.

Chapter 34

Janey

That night after dinner we walked in the arbor, and I went alone to the lower fence. I needed to think, eased and grateful for the first time in days. *Philippe forgives me, my wondrous teacher forgives me. I do not deserve it.*

I stopped short in the path. Jesus' forgiveness. After all the studying, I'd now *experienced* it. I thought I could never be forgiven and then by grace, I was.

Jeanne D'Arc ran to me, nearly knocking me over. "Mère wants you—she's talking to a few of us alone, asking questions about Philippe—it's a trial."

I grabbed her arm. "What do you mean, trial?"

"She asked about Hopkins, she wanted to make sure he hadn't confused us. And about skating—and tobogganing, but I wasn't there."

"I was," I said.

"You were?" She looked so worried, I put my arms around her.

"Oh, Jeanne," I said, realizing that she *was* my friend, no matter how crazy she made me. We'd been through it all together.

"Go," she said gently.

My shoes clicked along the polished floor. I prepared my strength. I probably knew more about Philippe than Mère—the man who loved her, skinny-dipping, chains. But I'd stolen that knowledge. Again, I felt my treachery.

The one thing I knew for sure was how completely Philippe wanted to be a nun. But hadn't I unconsciously hoped she'd leave the convent and go free?

I opened the office door.

Mère at her desk. The room smelled of powder and serge.

"Sit, Janelle," she nodded to an empty chair. "Will you answer a few questions? Be concise. Nothing extraneous, please."

I clasped my hands.

"In recent months, have you probed Catholic doctrine on your own?"

I forced my eyes down.

"Tell the truth, Janelle."

"Is this about Sœur Philippe? Jeanne called it a trial."

"Jeanne is dramatic. I want to help her, Janelle—both of you, all of you. Did Sœur Philippe encourage you to probe the Sacred doctrines?"

"Of course. She taught us to probe everything, and that God is not limited by doctrines, or by anything created."

Mère's eyes flashed. Then she gave a soft laugh, impressed.

"MaMère, let me explain how she gets at the truth—"

"Did you speak with her after lights?"

I flinched. "Yes, but it's not what you think. Sister Philippe serves Christ in all things—"

"I am not interested in your opinion."

"She helped me to know Him. She gave me Scriptures and poetry."

"That will—"

"She lives what she believes, Mère," I stood up and faced her. "If I could grow to be even half of what she is."

"You have interrupted me, MaChère." A bell rang.

Mère slowly shook her head. "We've had a big mess these last few days. Emilie running away, you, refusing to take perpetual vows and then nearly falling off the ladder. Sœur Philippe is exhausted, as well she should be, as well we all are."

I saw myself clutching the Virgin's neck.

"One more thing, Janelle. Sœur Philippe loves Christ above all earthly things. As you know."

"Yes! Oh yes." I nodded. Thank God, the most important answer.

"When she told you this, what were her very words?"

I looked straight at Mère. "She doesn't have to use words."

Chapter 35

Philippe

When we returned from the Roller Palace, I asked Joey to take the girls and went to chapel. Again, I prayed on my knees.

"Dear Jesus, you were there with me as I skated. I know you will never leave me. Thank you for lifting me up, for giving me new life by your death and Resurrection, for loving me."

I fell silent. Comfort. Safety.

Then thoughts poured in. Janey knows that I've forgiven her, thank you God. Now I must talk to Mère. *Please, give me discernment, give me truth.*

Approaching Mère's office, I met Janey coming out. She blushed, nodded to me. I touched her shoulder.

I sat down in the empty chair once again. "I've come to explain myself."

"Yes, MaChère." Small lift of her hand.

"At our college, I lived in the world true to my vows and studying. But of course, in classroom discussions, I met women on different paths."

"That is exactly what we are up against."

"The women's choices are not my main confusion—you and I have spoken about Skip. Even he is not the whole story. I've been wrestling with my final vows to our God. Like Jacob and the angel, in the morning, the angel blessed me."

"My child, why did you take this on alone?"

"I thought I needed to. I thought my vow to serve Him was my own, that of an individual."

"We have never been individuals here. *No man is an island,* surely you know your Donne." She stared straight ahead.

"Mère, I sought mortification. I became convinced in prayer that it was the only way."

"Such as?"

"Chains studded with nails to the thigh."

"Oh no! Oh, dear God have mercy!" she drew back. "Where did you get such things? How did you arrive at the decision?

I shook my head and told her about Père.

"Where are the chains now? You should have come to me!"

My God, she's shocked.

"What was Père thinking? He, too, went rogue!" she squinted.

We sat in heavy silence.

Finally, Mère cleared her throat. "Through all these storms, what decision have you come to on your Vow?"

I threw back my head. "I will serve Christ all my life. I hope here, in this house!"

Her elegant shoulders straightened. "MaChère, we wish you to take your Final Vows. God needs you. You will be a great blessing to the Church, and yes, to me here as well."

She held my gaze.

"It is not our spiritual understanding that we can depend on, it is God, nothing less, it is God alone. The call is His, it's His work and He knows where to put us and how to use us. His ways are a mystery. Again, it is our obedience to God that brings us peace."

I could feel Mère's struggle, her hesitation.

"But now I must draw you into a confidence. I told you I had something to tell you as well. We've been in discernment as an order, and our conclusions will affect all our future."

Her eyes widened, the lines around them deepened.

"All nuns have received a mandate from Pope John's Vatican II encyclical called *Perfectae Caritatis*. We've been asked to study it and comply. It is radical, Sœur, we must renew our rule and tradition, we must modernize."

"Modernize? Out of the blue?" My mind tangled at the word.

"Superiors will suggest, then open individual decisions to the sisters."

"Individual decisions?" Wasn't that just what I had striven for? Yet, I was shrinking.

"I know this will come as a shock, but we are about to be given a choice—to remain in habit, modify our dress, abandon it all together."

I gasped. My morning habit fell over me in a whoosh, with its smells of naptha and bleach.

She ruffled her fingers. "You and your independent ways. You should do very well. We will vote on all the changes. To remain enclosed in convents or split up into small groups, living together in twos or threes. Each sister will discern for herself."

"But we've no training for that! We've been in strict obedience." I bounded out of my chair. "Make our own *life* choices?" A knife into my forehead, I leaned over.

What was I vowing to now?

Mère came around to my side of the desk.

She raised me up and put her arms around me. Her frontispiece brushed my face—scent of serge, incense. I breathed it in and sank into her inimitable strength. I never dreamed how it would feel to be safe in her embrace.

"Take it off?" I whispered, "Wear Street clothes? No more coif, veil?"

"It's all unknown. But we believe that the Councils of the Church are led by the Holy Spirit. So, while we do not know how it will all play out, we trust in our Faith. We may feel alone, but we are not alone in this discernment of habit."

"But I've been desperate to take mine off," I said softly, "and did take it off, and swam in pure water—MaMère, the habit is sacred! It holds great meaning, as does our enclosure and our vow to contemplative prayer."

Mère stepped away. But her arms stayed open. "MaChère, you've worked so hard to understand these stirrings in the Church," she said, "and in yourself. Even as you craved freedom, you obliged always to hierarchy."

I stayed still. She kept a hand on my shoulder. In the face of everything, her leadership was steadfast.

"Our own Superiors must determine our fate," she said, "not the Bishops."

"*Will* we abandon the habit?" *the feel of the whites against skin...*

"There's dialogue ahead—I cannot imagine it. But our future is wide open."

I couldn't believe what I was hearing. *Bridal gown off, blessed habit falling on, hair cut off, white veil...*

"Oh my dear, we're trying to determine what *comply to the mandate* means."

Everything in me slammed down.

She placed a hand on my cheek. "I promise you this—we can serve God through many offerings and ours here, though sacred, can be changed. Our habits, as you know, are disciplines, not doctrines."

I hurried over the stone floors, stepping quickly over the buffed shine. We were being asked to leave this shine—to leave here and live in twos?

I knew right then, without thinking it through, that I would not choose to partially clothe, or live a half-nun life. I headed to the Chapel to pray before the Blessed Sacrament.

Kneeling, I understood Janey's quest—pieces of habit flung onto the pine needles—coif, frontispiece, veil, wimple. Wood-smell, moonlight.

I had struggled for years to be on my face before God in the totality of the offering.

I would not, could not do it, as Skip would have said, in some half-ass way.

Chapter 36

Janey

That night, burrowed under the covers, my ease continued. *Philippe forgives me.*

Out of the quiet, "Hurry! Come on." "NO, what?" Girls, shouting in the dorm.

I bolted up, flew through my curtains, girls were sweeping them open as they ran by.

Cats called from the window, "It's burning down, it's on fire!!"

"The convent?" Jeanne called.

"We're not that lucky," chuckled Cats.

As we approached the twelve windows, we slowed down in awe.

The whole sky was a smoldering flaming orange, intensifying with every second. Across the lake, on the hill, columns of flame shot up and swirled around the Roller Palace, squares and triangles of flame. From all the way across, a sizzling, whooshing, thuds and crackling timbers. We covered our noses, the smell, a mix of burning plastic and old wood. A lot of coughing suddenly.

I went into a kind of stupor. How could it be?

It was just an old building, wasn't it?

No.

The violence—a conflagration of everything good.

More girls crowded the windows. The sky glowed with a smudged red-gold. Sirens screamed.

"What does it mean?" A stunned Jeanne D'Arc.

I looked at her eyes, like dark beads. I let out all my breath. We were watching it burn with no power to stop it—no power ever.

"There goes our joy," Suze said.

"Insurance money," said Cats.

Fire trucks scrambled toward the flames. I flashed back to the odd smell of the popcorn popper, sparks flickered up into the sky. It was hard to see anything for sure.

They were dousing it now, the force of the water, helpless against the inferno.

I turned around—Philippe behind us, transcendent in the glow, the corners of her eyes gleamed.

A bird-like twittering—I looked up.

Nuns in white night bonnets hung out the cloister windows, murmuring—their mouths and eyes twitching in the pink light.

I held my breath.

An eerie, orange glow stole over our orchard, grape arbor, meadow, wood, and lake.

The smell of smoke burning our eyes and throats.

A black frame emerged against the rolling flames.

Then it collapsed.

The next morning, we could not speak. Our great escape was, in an instant, gone. No one gathered us. Standing around in the orchard, we were silent without an edict, with one more day to go—practicing all the parts, our widened, leaping eyes in retelling the flames—the horror of loss. Em and the lack of news—we moved through smells of burnt wood, acrid melted plastic, checking every few minutes the smoldering palace, the metal pieces jutting up and glowing in the rubble.

The last night we would ever sleep in our cells, smoke permeating even the sheets, windows rattling. I got up and went to my window.

There was a desolate purple sky, a black glowing rubble, a gaping emptiness. I leaned forward and remembered the night of the chicken drumsticks. Best night in four years! Far off across the lake were fretted patches of dark sky, the wind whistling in the pines. I breathed the acrid, smoky smell.

A light caught my eye, an orange, garish blinker inching up the drive. I ran to the windows above the side door.

Two white headlights crept up the hill like floating eyes outside a face. They cast long beams on the drive and because of the blackness, it was impossible to see anything else. When it came closer, from four floors up, its yellow roof with blinking cab light came into view. It rolled to a stop at the door. Its motor purred. Its slick yellow side reflected the moonlight.

Two figures came out, both tall, one in street clothes and a coat too large; I could make out a kerchief. The other was in habit. I gripped the window ledge. They walked directly to the cab.

They embraced for what seemed like forever.

Philippe leaned into the cab, bowing gracefully at the waist. Mère raised her hand, hugged herself, bunching her frontispiece.

I was inside…

And I had put it on so easily, inner white, outer black, everyone would know who I was — into the habit, out of the habit…

The cab swallowed Philippe and disappeared into the night.

In my cell, I lay awake, eyes wide open.

My friend, my teacher... Heavy with sorrow, I tossed and rolled on my narrow bed—*my fault. My fault. My fault.*

Mère had thrown her out after all. And it was my fault.

But no.

Mère's benison of farewell. Their embrace said everything.

In the afternoon, Graduation finally here, families and friends arrived and gathered in the courtyard for the final procession. A burnt tinderbox smell pervaded everything—smoke like a fog. Mère stood at the head but her inimitable strength had not returned, or at least, it seemed so to me. She was wide eyed and wary. I was suddenly leveled by all that she had been to her nuns and to us.

Seventy-five years of ritual and rule in place, caps and gowns, *Pomp and Circumstance.* It was a blur. Our hugs felt stiff and wrong. I longed for Philippe...I mourned for Em. *Oh, where are you?*

Cats stood beside me and squeezed my hand, and I sensed that wherever we went in the future, she would stay beside me. Suze was behind. I searched the eager faces—Dad, Maman, Gloria, Memère, where was Michael? He had been so eager to finally see the convent—the insides over the wall.

This was the moment I'd been waiting for—to climb over that wall—to go free.

The persistent smell of smoke held everyone in a kind of trance. Across the lake, bits smoldered, a skeletal metal frame glowing, and silhouetted against the sky.

I saw us in the night kitchen stealing the honey—Philippe standing at the door, deciding to love us. Philippe flying beside me at the Roller Palace.

I pictured us at the grave for the dead nun and how Thiacre had placed our names in the casket for talking in class.

Today, our names, our nuns, the Academie, the girls, even Casper—all were going into the ground.

Everything that happened here was gone—an odor on the breeze.

Chapter 37

Philippe

Alone in the cab for two hours, I arrived at the place I once called home, my father's doorstep. Papa's shock was profound, he was tender and quiet. As night deepened, surrounded by siblings, I wept.

Finally, I lay back on the pillow in my old bed, tears spent, eyes shut. I drifted, floating back. I was prostrated on the floor, on my face, before the altar—smooth stone against my forehead, arms outstretched like a raven's wings. Again, I made my vow to God. My life and all my being.

Tomorrow, I must search everywhere and find the precious thing I almost lost.

Early in the morning, I walked to my childhood church to Father Pierre, my parish priest. He was not surprised to see me. His hair, now white, his shoulders stooped; he led me to the confessional; his attentive face, so familiar through the screen. I confessed that I failed in my vows. He said no. I did not fail. In his calm voice, "My daughter, God loves you still—inside the convent or out." When I lifted my head, his eyes were wet, and so were mine. And that was my confession.

Now I must find Skip and make my new vow of love. I held him and prayed for us. Was he at the university now? At home? I was careful with my thoughts of him, tenderness swelling with each step.

That first night, we will claim our love from all the way back to our youth.

And my totality, covering his, will be my final vow.

Epilogue

Janey

I buried Sorrows and its nuns. At graduation, I weighed 90 pounds; I was exhausted. My Uncle hired me for the summer at Monet Jewelry in Providence and I filled orders and got to know some colorful Italian full-timers, their profanities and humor, a great antidote. I needed it in more ways than one. I was pushing towards September and college.

Cats called me about Emilie. She'd come through and was at Florence Crittenden in Boston. She would be cared for through delivery, then give the baby up for adoption. I starred my calendar to visit her there.

In the spring after the prom, Michael had fallen for a girl at URI. He hadn't waited after all. Our first date after graduation, he told me about her. We parted.

I had no tears for that; I felt hardened and clear-headed. I just wanted to work and get on with college life. Maybe I'd made it all up that he liked me, just to get through. That made sense. Philippe was more complicated, but I was helpless, I couldn't drive, and what would I say if I called? Or wrote?

She went into the ground with the rest.

Emmanuel College was a new wind blowing and I was swept up. I loved Boston, all my classes, the bands, theater, and the mixers. Boston was a college town. Emmanuel was a Catholic college with Sisters of Notre Dame de Namur, but it might as well have been Berkeley, California, for all my freedom. If I saw a nun on campus, I went the other way. And by the time I graduated, shockingly, nuns' habits and enclosure in convents were unraveling. I could barely take in what my friends were telling me—Suze and Jeanne would never have a Clothing Ceremony; would live in apartments. Mère, in a simplified habit.

I was stirred by my dorm-mates' questions, the longings, and dreams of girls. My feelings were almost too much to hold, and I didn't know what to do. So, I learned to play the guitar and led the folk Mass on Sunday nights with a wonderful musician named Mary. I heard poems in the middle of the night, felt Philippe streaming up the aisle of our classroom—*Glory be to God for dappled things, for skies of couple-color.*

I started writing poems and shared them with my friends in the dorm. They needed them too—they would wait for the next one and pass it around.

How like a dove that soars to breathless heights I would become
Only to feel your hand in mine.

Right before graduation, I found a small press and sent in thirty-five poems. My subjects were anything but God. The collection was accepted, the editor sent encouragement. I'd written about love and nature. Then I had a friend at Brightways Books who asked me to give a poetry reading.

We were in a small cozy space at the back of the store, surrounded by bookshelves; chairs had been set up six across and eight deep. I stood at a podium with a small light. I wore black pants, a white silk blouse and black flats; I had a longish haircut, still straight and blond. There was coffee.

My friend Roger introduced me as a lyric, nature poet. We'd been in a writing group together at Boston College. I started with my poem "*Stones,*" then "*Turtle.*" People had been coming in quietly until, to my surprise, many seats were filled.

I loved readings and went to many, so I felt comfortable. Poems should be read aloud. They were like music to me with their own inherent rhythms.

I took a sip of coffee and read.

Amber
I have a small rock the color of rich honey
with flecks all through it
that mar its clarity.
Imperfections.
Enhancements.

Like our life
spilling, sticky
so sweet it stings,
sings,
then strong,
formed and
full of light.

I looked up from the page. My heart slipped.

A woman's familiar gaze caught me from the back row; she was upright and tall, dark hair swept back in a chignon, shining eyes like black river stones, full lips, unmistakable. She had natural beauty, no make-up, a touch of rose at her cheek. She wore a jean skirt with high brown leather boots, and a white embroidered sweater.

I felt a pang of unaccountable disappointment to see her without her coif, without the habit mystery. That was so unfair of me. I felt she would be less intriguing, less inspiring now. But this was all in a beat. Then our eyes met.

My cheeks burned. I sipped some water and continued to the end of the reading without looking out again. For all I knew, she had gone. People clapped, I heard murmuring; I was supposed to take questions but, flustered, sat down in the front row.

People came to talk to me. I was smiling, grateful. Then the group thinned out.

Still, I couldn't move.

She came and sat beside me. The high leather boots...

"Stunning work," she said. "Our honey. So sweet it stings!"

I swallowed a smile.

It was her low alto, the voice of Philippe in this elegant woman I didn't know.

"It's all right, Janey," she said. "It's impossible for me, too, when I see nuns in street clothes. Give me your phone number."

Her hand flashed—on her fourth finger, a wedding ring.

I was rife with joy for her.

Her dark eyes, the same, taking me in.

"Would you meet me for a glass of wine sometime?"

An Endnote

In 1965, there were 179,954 religious sisters living in convent communities in the U.S. By 2015, that number had dropped to 48,546, and most of those lived independently, or in Senior convent facilities. Those aging sisters had watched their numbers shrink since the days of Vatican II, Pope John the 23rd's encyclical that forced even the unwilling out of the habit and into the modern world. Those sisters who remained were forced to resize their once-sprawling convents. A lack of vocations through the 1980s and 90s brought about the sale of many Mother Houses that the sisters had occupied for decades. Sisters learned to drive cars, balance checkbooks, and live in apartments that were closer to the people they served.

In a 2014 survey of 1,049 sisters in the United States and Puerto Rico, *The New York Times* found that only 3% were 40 or younger; 37% were older than 70 and 12% were more than 80. The median age for nuns in the survey was 65. "American Catholics have no idea how very soon there will be no nuns," wrote Sister Patricia Wittberg, a church sociologist at Indiana University, after reviewing *The Times'* data. Sister Eleace King, a research associate at CARA, the Center for Applied Research in the Apostolate at Georgetown University, Washington, D.C., concurred. "It tells me that the majority of religious congregations of women in this country will not survive. Most are dying." The latest data comes at a time when the church has found a steady exodus of nuns, who in the first half of this century were a bulwark in the U.S. church.

Author Bio

Cynthia Linkas, née Chadwick, is the author of the collection of poetry, *Tumbled Time*. Her short story *Baggage* won the PEN Syndicated Fiction Award and was published nationally and read aloud on NPR's *The Sound of Writing*. An earlier version of *Vows* under the title *The Roller Palace* was one of five finalists for the Midlist Press Competition and shortlisted for a publication prize by Tupelo Press. Her short story *YiaYia Toma* was published in the literary magazine *Scop* in 2023.

A professional singer and lifelong music teacher, Linkas especially loves Renaissance choral music and performed for years with Convivium Musicum of Boston and the Christ Church Choir of Hamilton-Wenham. When at home with her husband, Tom, she enjoys walking her dogs, spending time with grandchildren, cooking Greek food, and gathering family and friends.

www.ingramcontent.com/pod-product-compliance
Lightning Source LLC
Chambersburg PA
CBHW011351010726
47494CB00008B/2266